Broken Together

Also by K.L. Gilchrist

Holding On

Thick Chicks

Engaged

Let Me Love You

A Christmas Kiss

SHORT FICTION

Hallway Lights

Daily Bread

Jack & Diane

The Ride

The Honeymoon Journal

Broken Together

A NOVEL

K.L. GILCHRIST

Revised Edition: 2026. This edition features a brand-new cover design, updated formatting, author's note about the new edition, and an exclusive Book Club Discussion Guide.

ISBN-13: 979-8-9927469-1-4

eBook ISBN-13: 979-8-9927469-2-1

Original Edition: 2017

The author confirms that *Broken Together* is a work of human imagination and lived experience. No generative artificial intelligence (AI) was used in the writing of this manuscript or the creation of the supplemental discussion guide. The cover art and interior design were produced by human creators.

SECOND EDITION

Cover design by Beetiful Book Covers.

Interior design by Infinite Solutions Group, LLC.

Library of Congress Control Number: 2026901391

A Note from the Author

When *Broken Together* first found its way into the world in 2017, I knew Tracey and Brian's journey was one of the most difficult stories I would ever tell. It is a story about the "messy middle"— the space between a devastating betrayal and the first light of grace.

Much has changed since then, both in the world and in my own life. Re-releasing this novel has given me the opportunity to look at this story through a new lens. While the heartbeat of the book remains the same, this edition represents a "coming home" to these characters with the benefit of time and perspective.

I chose to refresh this edition with new, human-crafted cover art to reflect the raw, handmade nature of healing. Healing isn't an automated process; it is intentional, sometimes painful, and ultimately beautiful.

To those who read this story years ago: thank you for keeping Tracey's journey alive. To those picking it up for the first time: I hope you find comfort in these pages, and a reminder that even when things are shattered, they can be made new.

With gratitude,
K.L. Gilchrist

For Chris.

And we know that in all things God works for the good of those who love him, who have been called according to his purpose.

CHAPTER
One

A BRICK.

A colossal, crimson brick traveling at supersonic speed and positioned right for Tracey Jones's head.

No warning. No time to duck. The brick came at her as her husband, Brian. Same shape and size and everything. With news that did not make her want to drop to her knees and pray for him.

Oh no. This news made her want to smack him.

Hard.

But she didn't do that. Nah. That wouldn't have been right.

She sat and listened to him. Why? Because it was almost half past ten when he opened the back door and trudged into the kitchen. Tracey had just cleared out space in the refrigerator so Brian could put the leftovers away after he ate dinner, but she stopped and stood up when the door opened. She looked over to him, flashing a big grin. The smile vanished from her face when he failed to look over to her at all.

"Hey!" She hoped her upbeat voice would prod him to greet her with a kiss.

"Hey."

Tracey followed Brian's eyes. They focused on the floor, then the wall, but never on her. His lips mashed together as he pulled off his weather-beaten leather brown jacket. Snow sprinkles slid off the shoulders and tumbled onto the cream-colored tile floor. He hung his coat up quickly on the hook by the kitchen door before walking over and sliding onto a stool at the kitchen island.

"Want something to drink?" Tracey asked.

"No, thanks."

"Dinner?"

"Not hungry right now."

Tracey raised an eyebrow. She closed the refrigerator door and walked over to him, watching as he leaned his weight on his forearms, still directing his eyes away from her face. No hello kiss. Still no eye contact. She slid onto the stool across from him and balled her fists in her lap.

"How are you tonight?" He asked.

"I'm fine. What's going on?" Tracey shifted her body weight on the stool.

Brian cleared his throat and stared down at the granite countertop. "I need talk to you. About the practice. And, ah, about one of our nurses. Lisette Santana."

"What about her?" Tracey said, crossing her arms.

"Well, I've gotten to know her since she came on board. We've become friends. We. She and I. We talk a lot during the day. She's a smart young lady. Interested in medicine."

Tracey raised an eyebrow. "Oh?"

He cleared his throat again. "Yes, well, this afternoon, Ruthie and Lisette had a fight. A loud one. I'm sure patients heard them. Very unprofessional. Anyway, Ruthie accused Lisette of having an inappropriate relationship with me and Dan had to come out of an exam room to quiet them and —"

Tracey had stopped listening right after she processed the words "inappropriate relationship." She didn't give a rip about a cat fight at the practice. *Inappropriate relationship?* Did Brian really zip past those words? She watched his lips move for a few more seconds, then interrupted him. "Was she right?"

"Huh?"

"Was Ruthie right? You. Lisette. Inappropriate relationship?"

Brian shook his head. "No way!" He rubbed his hands together. Moved his index finger back and forth over the thick diamond and gold band on his ring finger. "Ruthie was the inappropriate one. It's a good thing she's been with us since the beginning and she's an outstanding nurse. Dan talked with her and she apologized to Lisette for the incident."

"Then why did you wait until you came home to tell me?" Tracey asked.

Brian's face went blank.

She pressed him. "And what about Lisette? What are you two talking about every day if someone as reliable as Ruthie needed to accuse Lisette?"

He shrugged. "Listen, I talk to folks all day long. My partners. Pharmaceutical reps. Our patients. The nurses. All of them. Ruthie, Lisette, Janette, Donna. I talk to everyone."

"Let me put it a different way. Does this lady have feelings for you?"

Brian rubbed a hand over his chin and sighed. "She knows I'm a happily married man."

A chill ran down Tracey's back. The word "happily" seemed to tumble out of his mouth by accident. "Happily?" Her brow furrowed.

"Of course." His tone softened. "You and me. The kids. Our life is great. God blessed us and I wouldn't trade our relationship for anything. You know I'm not that guy."

The words sounded hollow as they penetrated Tracey's ears. *Not that guy?* Well. He wasn't. Tracey knew who she married. She didn't marry a cheater. Brian was a good man. Still. This bit of news bugged her. She chewed her bottom lip and tried to think of something to say to communicate her frustration. But when she opened her mouth to ask another question, Brian leaned in and gave her a kiss. The touch of his soft lips provided comfort. She sank into the warmth. And it eased the tension. A little.

He broke the kiss and stared in her eyes, stroking her cheek with his fingertips. "I shared it with you because the whole scene irritated me."

Tracey pushed his fingers away from her face. "Gee, thanks for sharing."

He ignored her sarcasm. "I'm gonna grab dinner now. Hang out here with me?"

"You said you weren't hungry."

He shrugged and offered a half-smile. "I smell rosemary chicken, and I know you made roasted red potatoes to go with it. That's too good to pass up."

Tracey's eyes trailed him as he stood up, shuffled over to the stove and filled his plate with food. She studied him as if he were a stranger, trying to see what someone else would observe if getting acquainted with him for the first time. She ran down the checklist. Colgate commercial straight white teeth. Handsome face. Terrific eyes. Not a wrinkle anywhere. Fit and trim. Chest and arm muscles you could see move beneath his shirt. Friendly demeanor. Good career. Intelligent.

Yep. Enough checks on the list for a nurse to be interested, even if he was older and married.

Brian's phone buzzed in his leather jacket. A muted sound. Tracey heard it from where she sat, which was close to the hook where he had hung his jacket moments earlier. She glanced over at him eating, then shifted her gaze back his jacket.

"What's the matter?" He asked.

She jerked a thumb toward his jacket. "Your phone."

He motioned to her. "Pass it to me."

Tracey stood up, dug into Brian's jacket pocket, pulled out the device, walked over and pushed it at him. He took one second to glance at it, then shoved it in his pants pocket and went back to chewing his chicken.

She stepped back, curious. "Not going to answer it?"

He shook his head and swallowed. "It's one of the guys. I can call him back."

"What guy?"

"Huh?"

"What. Guy. From. Where?"

"Men's Fellowship. He joined us the last few weeks. We've had a few conversations, and he said he's interested in starting a fitness program. I said I would give him some pointers."

"So he's a member of Rise?"

"No. City Church."

"This guy have a name?"

Brian let his fork clatter to his plate, wiped his mouth on a paper napkin and rose from his stool. "I know where you're going with this."

Her eyes narrowed as she leaned in closer to him. "All right. Let's go there. Who just called?"

Tracey watched her husband turn and pick up his dinner plate. In a swift movement he ate the remains of his food, then brushed past her and placed his plate and cutlery in the sink. Silent, he reached in his pocket, pulled out his phone and passed it to her.

She snatched it and pressed the icon that led to the archive of recent calls. "Who's Troy?"

"Young guy. Wants to start a fitness program. We talked about nutrition and supplements and—"

"I get it."

"That all you have to say?"

She pushed the phone back at him. "What do you want me to say?"

"An apology would be nice."

"Apology?"

"Yes."

Apologize? Please! Or, no. Wait. Maybe she should apologize for not believing that stupid story about nurse Ruthie talking crazy for no reason. Apologize? No way. Tracey shifted her weight from foot to foot. "You know what? I'm tired and I don't know what to say."

Brian reached out and snaked his arms around Tracey's waist. Her arms lay stiff at her sides. After a few seconds of an awkward hug, she wriggled out of his grasp.

"Don't pull away from me," he said.

She pushed back further. "You told me what you told me which is not cool and right about now I need you to get out of my face. For real."

He stepped away, glanced down at her and opened his lips, but no sound came out. A moment passed before he turned to the sink. He washed and rinsed his plate and cutlery and put them in the dish rack before stalking out of the kitchen.

Tracey made a beeline for the family room. She plopped down in the leather recliner and grabbed her worn Bible off the wooden side table. She read Psalm 91 twice and Psalm 121 three times, and then sat still for fifteen minutes. Quiet. Anger subsiding. When she calmed down enough to stop bouncing her knees up and down, she prayed.

Lord, I'm not sure what to make of the story my husband told me tonight. It doesn't seem right. Please open my eyes to the truth about this matter. You are my strength and my refuge, and I thank you, Lord. Amen.

She'd put the situation in God's hands. Nothing else to do but go to bed.

As soon as she stepped in the bedroom, Tracey heard water running in their bathroom. Brian taking his nightly shower. She yawned, pulled off her robe and let it drop to the floor, crawled into her side of the bed, and stretched out. One second away from relaxation, her ears perked up. Brian's phone buzzed again. She popped open one eye. The buzzing stopped. The phone lay on his nightstand. She rolled over, snatched it, and read the caller ID. *Troy.* Why would he call again? Tracey switched over to look at Brian's list of text messages. Empty. She looked at his voice mail list. Also empty. Should she call this person back? Her fingers itched to press for call back, but her brain shouted, *leave it alone*. She held the device another minute before following her brain. She put the phone back on the nightstand and settled back under the sheets. But now relaxation escaped her. She'd never, ever snooped on Brian's calls. Never had a need to. Until now.

Tracey forced her eyes shut. Go to sleep. Forget about it and go to sleep.

Five minutes passed, and Tracey couldn't drift off. "Brian," she called out.

"I'll be out in a minute." He called back. "You going to sleep now?"

"Yes."

"Good night."

That was his way of telling her he didn't want to talk anymore. So whatever he thought or prayed about in the shower, he wasn't about to share any of it.

The sound of rushing water kept going. She guessed he'd hang out with the soap and the bath puffs until he figured she'd drifted off to sleep. Fine. She rolled over on her belly. He could stay in there until he shriveled up.

Two minutes later Brian came out of the bathroom smelling like ocean breeze shower gel and shea butter lotion. He didn't utter a word as he slid into bed, clicked the light off, and pulled the covers up over his shoulders. Tracey turned again so her back touched his. His skin felt moist and warm.

All right. No sticking her head in the sand.

Tomorrow. First thing in the morning.

Find out what Ruthie knows.

CHAPTER
Two

A CLEVER FAKE.

That's what Tracey was when she met Brian nine years ago. On the outside she wore three Fs like a costume: fine, friendly, and focused. Inside? Lonely, broke, and sad. Every Sunday she gripped her six-year-old son Tyler's hand tight as they walked into Rise Church. No one there had ever seen Tyler's father, but they sure knew Tracey and they knew she looked good. She kept a tight rein on their budget so she could shop the consignment stores, putting quality clothes on their backs and trendy shoes on their feet. And every Sunday there she was in the church pew. Perfect hair. Flawless makeup. A smile plastered across her face as she sang each worship song played.

Most people assumed she had it together. But she was flustered and had tears in her eyes the day Tyler pulled on her skirt and whined for her to buy him a candy bar from the vending machine after church service. She'd stood staring at the pens and lint at the bottom of her purse when a muscular guy with a lopsided smile and warm brown eyes walked right past her, dropped coins in the machine, bought a granola bar and handed it right to Tyler, telling him candy would rot his teeth and winking at Tracey. She said thank you. When she saw the man the following Sunday, he introduced himself and asked for her phone number. They talked that week. He asked for a date. Then another. A few months later he asked her to be his wife. She said yes.

Now Tracey wasn't broke or insecure, and hadn't faked happiness for years.

And she'd battle hell before she took a trip back to Club Loneliness.

Believe that.

When the alarm sounded at 5:45 a.m., Tracey swung her legs off the bed and squinted in the darkness for her fluffy red house shoes. She stumbled into the bathroom, rubbing her eyes. She gripped the edges of the bathroom sink as she peered at herself in the mirror. The rough night she'd spent tossing and turning showed on her face. Now why hadn't she called that Troy person back? Afraid of what she might've heard?

Tracey washed her face and brushed her teeth before looking in the mirror again. Wake up, Tracey. You better wake up right now.

She shuffled back into the bedroom. Brian had rolled over in bed, facing the opposite wall. She stared at his naked back. He used to start each day with prayer, but it had been a few weeks since she'd seen him kneeling by the foot of the bed. He didn't join her for devotions and coffee in the morning anymore either. These days he stayed in the bed until she came to get him. Tracey didn't know when he had his private time with the Lord. Maybe he took a break and read and prayed during his day? She sighed as she touched his shoulder. His skin felt warm and smooth.

"Time to wake up," she said.

"I'm awake." He yawned and placed a hand over hers. "We good?"

Tracey pulled her hand back. She didn't answer.

Brian showered, threw on a blue pinstripe button-down shirt and khaki pants, and by seven-thirty he was on his way to work. Neither of them brought up the previous night's discussion.

By eight Tracey herded Tyler and Brianna out the door to drive them to school. She kept a tight grasp on Brianna as they headed to the driveway. Above their heads icicles hung from the roof threatening to crash to the ground at any moment. Tyler had shoveled and salted the driveway earlier, but below Tracey's feet were large cracks with tiny pieces of asphalt chipped off, peppering the snowdrifts on the sides. She noticed the chips spreading, making their home exterior look more and more imperfect.

BACK IN THE house with everyone else gone, Tracey itched to talk with Ruthie. But running over to the practice while Brian handled patients, playing the role of the jealous wife? Acting crazy in front of his partners? Not cool. She'd have to make a phone call.

She grabbed the portable phone from the side table in the living room then pressed the autodial number for Germantown Family Medical Associates. It rang once. The system picked up.

Thank you for calling Germantown Family Medical Associates. We take great pride in offering our patients the highest level of efficient and quality care. Your call is very important to us. If this is a hospital calling, please press zero now. If you are calling in reference to a prescription refill, please press one now. If you are calling for an appointment, please press two now. If this is a medical emergency, please hang up and dial 911. All other calls please hold for personal assistance.

Tracey held. When someone picked up, she recognized the voice of one of the other nurses, Donna, on the line.

"Yes. Ruth Evers please." Cool and casual, Tracey. Keep it cool and casual.

"Ruth is unavailable at the moment. May I have her return your call?" Donna said.

"Hi Donna. Tracey Jones calling. Can you take a message to have her call me as soon as possible?"

"Oh, hello Mrs. Jones. I'll give her the message."

"Thank you. Have a good morning."

Tracey hung up and slid the phone back onto the side table. It was good neither Lisette nor Janette answered the call. God must be in a blessing mood.

What to do now? Tracey had returned home after kid drop off just to talk to Ruthie. Since that wasn't going to happen right away, Tracey snatched up her keys and purse. She'd use her nervous energy to go to the store.

SHOPPING DIDN'T WORK out so well. Tracey hadn't made a list. She ended up roaming the grocery store aisles. Every fifteen minutes, to break the monotony, she called someone. First, she called her best friend, Monica Bonner. But Monica was rushing to a meeting and couldn't chat over twenty-seconds. Then she dialed Charla, her sister-in-law, but that diva was ignoring her calls, busy with a hair appointment, or gossiping to two or three other people because she never answered her phone. Tracey didn't want to shop. She wanted to talk.

And that was how she ended up sitting at the kitchen table of her mother, Alice Watson. Tracey wound up telling her the whole story from the night before. Alice frowned when Tracey got to the part about calling Ruthie.

"He's a man," Her mother's voice droned. "Trust me, he's just letting a young chick flatter him for a hot minute." A solid woman with a handsome face, Alice never minced words. Understanding and affection were not her strong points.

"So I'm supposed to go with what he told me?"

Alice walked out of her pantry and over to the sink where she washed and peeled white potatoes and yellow onions to place in the crock pot for dinner. Then she moved to the counter where she took a drag off the cigarette she'd left burning in a tin ashtray, stubbed out the butt, and pushed her glasses higher on her nose. "He's not going anywhere."

"I never said he was."

"Yes you did. When you came in here looking like your dog died."

Tracey chewed her bottom lip. "Ma, I'm not worried about him leaving me."

Alice stopped peeling and slicing potatoes and looked over at her. "Then why'd you come see me? You enjoy watching me put food in my crock pot?"

Tracey recognized that look. In Alice's world, Brian either had the son-in-law role in her life or he did not have it. Anything else fit in the category of pure drama.

"So what if he lied?" Alice said.

"What?"

"Let's say he lied. You ready to go plant a foot in his behind?"

"Ma please."

"Ma please, nothing." Alice opened the refrigerator and pulled out a thawed rump roast. "If you go digging around for garbage, you'll find it."

"You're saying leave it alone?"

"I'm saying, do what you have to do. But be ready for what you find."

Tracey swallowed hard and stared back at Alice, who had left the crock pot and started shutting the kitchen down so she could leave for work. When Alice exited the kitchen, Tracey followed, though she fought the urge to go back and check the pantry for half-empty bottles of Bacardi Rum to make sure Alice hadn't fallen off the wagon.

"I only stopped by to check on you," Tracey mumbled. "I figured I'd say something about me and Brian while I had your ear."

"Well, you said something. And I'm letting you know it's nothing. Brian is a sweetheart, better than most, I'd say. But he's still a man. He's over forty, and he's feeling it. He still home every night?" Her mother asked.

"Unless there's an emergency, yes."

"At church each week?"

"Like clockwork."

"Y'all still going to that Christian strife group?"

"It's called life group Ma, and yes, we go once a month."

"Um-hm." Alice dropped items for her day into her burgundy leather shoulder bag: a crumpled pack of Virginia Slims, a lighter, a red-handled hairbrush, a tube of hand lotion, and spearmint gum. "He been charging or spending a lot?"

"I pay our bills. I balance the checking account every week. Our money is fine."

"Then drive me to work, will you? Quit this foolishness and forget talking to Ruthie." Alice turned around, leaned toward the staircase, and hollered. "Jamal! Get up!"

A door creaked open. Then came feet walking the wooden floor above. Then another door squeaked, followed by a toilet flush.

"Plug this pot in and turn it on medium before you leave today!" Alice yelled up the stairs.

Tracey's baby brother would shuffle around upstairs for a few minutes until he heard the front door slam; then he'd dive back in bed. He'd phoned Tracey the week before, needing money to fix the transmission in his battered Honda Civic. Since he hadn't called back to pester her, Tracey guessed he either found another method to get the cash from someone else or he decided he didn't need to drive his car right away.

On their way out the front door, Tracey spied an envelope in a small wicker basket on the glass-topped end table. She grabbed it fast, speed reading the words: Final Notice. Electric bill. Tracey shoved it in her coat pocket. She'd open it later on and see how much her mother owed PECO.

In the car, Alice pulled out a cigarette and rummaged through her back for the lighter.

Tracey protested. "Ma, please don't smoke in here. The smell lingers and you know Brianna is allergic."

Her mother made a face as she returned the items to her purse.

They drove out to the Haven Senior Living Center where Alice worked as an LPN. At least a hundred times a year she told Tracey and Jamal that she was getting too old to do this work. Most days it involved moving and lifting heavy people. But every time Alice's kids tried to talk with her, she brushed them off and continued with life as usual. That was Alice. She said she planned to work until she died.

"Bring my granddaughter around sometime. It's been weeks since I've seen her or Tyler."

Tracey stopped the car in front of the entrance. "I promise I'll bring them over next week. I'd drive them over sooner, but Brianna has dance practice twice this week."

"When's the recital?"

"March."

Alice stepped out to the sidewalk. "Listen, call me later and let me know the date. Last time I almost missed it."

Tracey wanted to say there's not much to miss with a group of awkward five-year-olds in glittery leotards and bright stage make-up, grinning and missing their steps most of the time. "I'll bring you the flyer this Friday."

"Mm-hm." Alice changed the subject. "Kyle coming to see his son anytime soon?"

Ugh. Not now. Kyle Addison, Tyler's biological father, worked as a sports agent in New York City. Tyler stayed with him and his parents on Long Island every summer. Kyle only traveled for business and vacations. Alice knew that. And she never missed an opportunity to discuss it.

Tracey sighed. "Ty will stay with him in June—same as always."

"Mm-hm. Bye." Alice shut the door and headed into the senior center.

Tracey pulled the car out into traffic. Her phone buzzed. She grabbed it. "Hello."

"Tracey?"

"Yes."

"This is Ruthie. Is there something you need?"

Tracey ignored everything her mother just told her. "It's about Brian."

Long pause. Ruthie spoke again, her voice lower. "Can you meet me today?"

"We can't talk right now?"

Ruthie's words dripped out low and slow. "We should meet face to face."

Whoa. Wow.

"Can you come here today, during my lunch hour?" Ruthie asked.

"Yeah . . . uh . . . I'm free until three."

"Don't come in the office. Pick me up on the corner at one."

"This is about Brian and Lisette."

"I figured that," Ruthie said. "See you soon."

Tracey pulled over and parked. She sat motionless for a minute. Her phone buzzed again.

"Hello."

"Tracey, what's going on?"

Monica! Comfort washed over Tracey at the sound of her best friend's voice.

"Bestie," Tracey sighed. "You will not believe what's happening."

CHAPTER
Three

TRUE TO HER WORD, at one that afternoon, Tracey spied Ruthie waiting on the corner a block away from Germantown Family Medical Associates. Ruthie wore light green scrubs beneath a black leather jacket. Most days she styled her waist-length silver hair in a neat bun, but on this day it cascaded in soft waves down her back.

Ruthie opened the car door and slid into the passenger seat. Tracey leaned over for a quick cheek kiss and a hug.

"We'll go to the North Side Diner," Ruthie said. "You know the way."

Tracey nodded, her stomach muscles tightening. She gripped the steering wheel until her fingertips tingled. Ruthie could have instructed Tracey to drive to Constantinople and she would have said no problem and kept going.

"A CUP of clam chowder and hot tea with lemon, please," Ruthie told the brunette waitress.

"Just coffee for me. Thanks." Tracey pushed her menu to the center of the table. Her appetite was nonexistent, but sipping the hot drink would give her something else to concentrate on as they talked.

Two beats after the waitress walked away, Tracey glanced at Ruthie. She cleared her throat and rubbed her hands together. "I want to know if —"

"Brian is involved with Lisette?"

"You've seen things?"

Ruthie nodded. "I've noticed changes in Brian's routine for weeks now."

Tracey searched for the right words. "What have you seen?"

"Little things. Wherever he is in the practice, Lisette finds a reason to be there. There's not tons of space in the rooms and hallways up there, but I walk by his office and I see her sitting in there chatting with him at least three or four times a day."

Tracey took a minute to digest that piece of information. When the waitress returned to the table and put their orders in front of them, Tracey didn't budge.

"They talk." Tracey nodded. "What else?"

Ruthie pushed her long hair away from her shoulders and leaned closer. "Lisette volunteered to work the late shifts on Tuesday and Thursday."

"Okay."

"You know I don't do evenings, but I stayed late one Tuesday last month. I went to his office to ask a question and saw the door half-shut. I tapped on it. Then I pushed it open. Lisette was in there. Brian had his back to me, and I saw her arms wrapped around his waist."

"Whoa." Tracey slumped in her seat.

"A kiss? A hug? I'm not sure," Ruthie said, shrugging her shoulders.

Tracey's hands shook. She dropped them to her lap and laced her fingers together. But then her nose decided to run, and she pulled a tissue from her purse to wipe the wetness. Her drink remained untouched.

Ruthie shook her head. "This isn't like Brian." She looked

away. Her voice dripped with disappointment. "He's like family, you know. Like the son I never had. When we first met—when I worked at Einstein—he even dated my middle daughter for a while. Jennifer. The one who moved to Miami to sell real estate. I've known Brian since then and I never took him to be a cheater."

Tracey pulled out another tissue. Her nose was running like a faucet. And she wasn't the only one shook up. From the way Ruthie's voice wavered, it pained the woman to discuss this.

Ruthie continued. "I tried to talk to him. The day after I walked in on them in his office, I pulled him aside to ask him about it. He insisted I didn't see anything. Now I'm getting up there in age, but I don't have dementia. Don't let the gray hair fool you."

"So he kept denying it?" Tracey asked.

"No. He caught up with me later, mumbling and looking embarrassed. He said it was a mistake. That they'd gotten too close. Then he told me he'd appreciate it I'd keep the incident to myself."

"Besides the embrace . . . is there . . ."

Ruthie leaned over the table further, nearly spilling clam chowder down the front of her scrubs. "There's pictures."

"Of what?"

"I'm not sure. Lisette was talking to Janette, and I overheard her saying how much fun she had with Brian. Then she whipped out her phone. But when she looked up and saw me she shut up real fast, grabbed a stack of files and hustled out of there."

Tracey's cheeks grew hot. "So you didn't see the screen?"

"No. Sorry."

"Anything else?"

Ruthie scrunched up her face. "I think they're using nick-names for each other. The other day, I heard him say something that sounded like "Boy" or "Troy" and she answered to it. Twice."

Tracey grit her teeth. Brian's explanation of Troy? Big bold hairy *lie*.

Ruthie she sat back from the table. "Nothing else to tell you. That's it."

That's it? That spoke volumes. It blew Tracey's mind. Ruthie described a different man than the one Tracey married. The Brian Michael Jones she knew was a Bible reading, choir singing, holistic-health following, God-fearing Christian. Now this fool with the nicknames, taking selfies with smart phones, was hugged up in the office with a hot nurse? Who was *that* guy? Not her husband. No way.

"Are you all right, sweetheart?" Ruthie asked.

Tracey glanced at her hands resting on the gray and white patterned Formica table top. Why'd they look so strange? She blinked. It was hard to see the sparkling diamond and gold wedding ring on her finger because tears had blurred her vision. Stop it! An issue needed to be handled. Nothing more. Tracey loved Brian. And he loved her. One tear dropped out of each eye. She blotted both salty drops before they could race down her cheeks, crushing the tissue tight in her palm. No more of that.

"Divorced my husband twenty years ago," Ruthie said before pausing for a sip of tea. "My ex-husband Carl? Hard-working guy. An electrician. Worked for the city and took care of his spouse and children. But he grew up old school where if you were a family man, you had your respectable wife. And you could also have a woman. His wife raised his kids, cooked his meals and went to church. His woman laid with him on Saturday nights, drank with him, hung out with his buddies and stayed in the background. That life was fine for Carl, but it wasn't okay with me. We had three daughters when I discovered his lies and I filed for divorce."

Tears threatened again. Tracey blinked them back. If she dropped any more her face would be a mess of streaked foundation and liquid disappointment. "Brianna's in kindergarten.

Tyler has two years of high school left. We want to take the family to Hawaii this December."

Ruthie reached over and covered Tracey's hand with hers. Tracey kept talking, throwing out random statements about life in their household as if speaking about normal life would overcome the exposure of her husband.

Ruthie spoke the words Tracey couldn't seem to express. "Can't see yourself leaving him?"

"No." She sniffed. "My son doesn't live with his father. I do not want a repeat performance with my daughter."

"I see."

The diner seemed quieter than earlier, and Tracey noticed customers leaving the tables surrounding them.

"Ruthie, I looked him in the eyes and asked if he had a relationship going on with Lisette." Tracey sniffed.

"What did he say?"

"No."

Ruthie took a deep breath. "That could be a good thing."

"Really?"

"If he's denying it, it means he's ashamed and praying to God he doesn't get caught. He doesn't want to hurt you or the kids. It means he doesn't want you to leave him. Now, if he was a different man? He might have said he's entitled to his happiness. Or, he can do what he wants. Or, he could tell you he wants to start a new life."

"This is crazy." Tracey sighed. "But I appreciate you talking to me."

Ruthie turned her gaze to the window. "I wish I had more to say."

"Did you ever confront Carl's girlfriend?"

Ruthie grunted as she turned back to Tracey. "What for? Going after her wouldn't have done anything except ruin my dignity. If I'd chased her away, he would have found another one to take her place."

"Where's Carl now?"

Ruthie's lips upturned into a slight smile. "Retired. Married to wife number five. He never could keep it at home."

"You were right about him."

Ruthie nodded. She slid her arms into her leather jacket and glanced at her watch. "I have to get back now."

Tracey asked one last question. "Did you start that fight with Lisette?"

"No. I tried to talk to her about spending so much time in Brian's office, and she got loud on me. When she walked out into the hall, I followed her. She called me a nosy old woman and a few names I don't answer to, and then she screamed at me to mind my business. Brian told you?"

Tracey snorted. "Yeah."

Ruthie placed a ten on the table, stood up, and slid her purse on her shoulder. "So that's why you called?"

Tracey didn't answer. She placed money on the table, grabbed her purse and coat and followed Ruthie out of the diner.

When Tracey dropped Ruthie off, she kissed Tracey's cheek before she got out of the car. "Call me any time, you hear me. Talk to your husband again. Ask God to give you strength and help you. You can always ask God to take this cup away from you."

Tracey nodded, let go of Ruthie's hand and watched the older woman walk away. She glanced at the clock on the car stereo before she pulled into flowing traffic—2:00 p.m. More than an hour until time to pick up Brianna. Extra time in the car gave Tracey a chance to calm down.

Winter sunshine poured through the windows, warming her skin. She grabbed a CD from the overhead organizer and pushed it into the slot. Tamela Mann. *Best Days*. Tracey let "Take Me to The King" play over and over. The words calmed her soul, ministering to her as she drove . On the way hone, Tracey called Brian. The call went to his voice mail. Fine. She could take time to get her words together. She left a curt message for him to call her back and went in the house. Twenty minutes passed before her phone buzzed. She answered without looking at it.

"Hello."

"You talked to that nurse, didn't you?" Alice said.

Tracey rolled her eyes. "Ma…"

"Didn't you?"

"Yeah, and I still haven't heard from Brian yet."

Alice wouldn't let up. "What did she tell you?"

"Who?"

"Daughter, don't act like your brain malfunctioned."

Tracey sighed. "They've been working late in the practice together and there might've been a date or something because she has pictures of them with each other. Oh, and he has a nickname for her."

"Um-hm."

The house phone rang, saving Tracey from continuing talking to her mother, though it was good she called. Hearing from her mother reminded her she needed to take care of the late PECO bill. Brian hated it when she paid her mother's bills. He said it enabled Alice to be irresponsible with money.

"Ma, I gotta go." Tracey clicked off the cell phone, and then pushed the talk button on the cordless. "Yes."

"Hey, I'm calling you back." Brian said.

"You and me. We're getting together to talk tonight. It's important."

"I'll try to be out of here by six, but you know how it is."

"Yeah, but right now I don't care." She rolled her eyes. "If there's last minute change or a patient emergency, call me."

"Tyler? Brianna? Are they alright?"

"They're fine. Why?"

"You made it sound like someone was in trouble."

Boy, was that ever true. "We need to talk. Face to face. As soon as possible."

"What's the deal? I've got two patients in exam rooms right now and the rest of the day is full."

"Get here after your last patient leaves."

"I'll try."

CHAPTER
Four

SIX FORTY-FIVE.

No white Lexus turning into the driveway. No Brian. The time shouldn't bother her. Late nights and sixty-hour work weeks were the norm for him. But tonight?

Tracey pulled back the curtain and peeked out the kitchen window. Nothing but darkness and swirling snow.

"Mom! Hey! You need to come up here!" Tyler yelled from upstairs. "I think Brianna is flooding the bathroom. She's got water and baby dolls all over the place."

"Handle it please!" Tracey abandoned the window and sighed as she pulled a Pyrex dish of veggie lasagna out of the oven and placed it on top of the stove.

"Mom?" Tyler stood two paces behind her before she realized he'd walked into the kitchen. "Can I get something to eat now?"

"Yeah," she said. "Stop Brianna for me, please. Tell her I said come to dinner."

"All right."

Tracey watched Tyler stride back down the hallway. Seems like he'd gone from overactive grade schooler to moody teenager overnight. Two years of braces had closed the gap in his front teeth. He was turning out to be a handsome young man, though

Tracey could see she needed to buy him medicine for his acne. He must have been picking his face— several small dark scars pocked his cheeks.

"Don't wanna eat!"

Tracey heard Brianna before she saw her.

"Too bad." Tracey wiped a bead of sweat off her forehead, turned around and pointed the girl to her seat in the dining room, and served the kids their plates. She could smell basil and olive oil on her fingers as she massaged her temples. She walked into the kitchen and peeked out the window again. Dark driveway. Snow.

"Mom . . . I don't want it!" Brianna whined.

"You know the rules. Dinner or bed. Do you want to go to bed?"

"No."

"Then eat your food."

"Where's Daddy? I want Daddy."

Tracey ignored the comment. She stood with her back resting against the refrigerator and watched through the doorway as Tyler inhaled his meal and Brianna turned hers into a science experiment. When the phone rang, Tracey snatched it off the kitchen counter in a flash.

"Yes." Her voice loud and firm.

"Why'd you answer like that?" Jamal said.

"What do you want?"

"The same thing I called for last week and you didn't call me back. I need a loan. My transmission, remember."

"I was at the house earlier. Why didn't you ask me then?" She pressed the phone to her ear with her shoulder and scrubbed a stainless steel pan with Brillo. "How much?"

"Around twenty-five hundred."

Tracey stepped back from the sink to peer at the kids. She caught Brianna shoving bits of food into the white paper napkin crushed in her palm. Tracey cleared her throat and glared at her daughter. She stopped. Tracey turned back to the sink. "You can't save up the money?"

"That would take too long. I need my car. I promise I'll pay you back." Jamal said.

"We'd have to make a schedule . . ."

"And . . ."

"Look baby brother, I haven't talked to Brian or prayed or planned to give anyone money today, so let me get back to you."

"That's it?"

"Yes. I'll call you in the morning, so answer your cell okay?"

"Do I have a choice?"

"Yes, you do. You can call someone else."

"Call me tomorrow."

"All right."

Jamal was a trip. Last October when Jamal called to ask Tracey and Brian for seed money to start a personal training business, and Tracey asked him for his business plan, he mumbled about not having one. She'd told him to take a few entrepreneurial courses first. He never enrolled and never mentioned starting a business again.

Tracey glanced in the dining room. Brianna squirmed in her seat and stared at her plate, her tiny lips in a pout. She'd eaten half her food. The rest was a red, beige, and green squishy mess spread across the plate.

"You're done," she told Brianna. The girl scrambled from the table and skipped upstairs before Tracey could say another word.

Tyler finished his lasagna and served himself a second helping which he swallowed as fast as the first. He moved around Tracey, put his dishes in the sink, made himself a waffle bowl full of chocolate ice cream, and lumbered over to the family room. Loud cheering sounds from a football video game kept Tracey company as she loaded the dishwasher and cleaned the countertops. Then she swept and mopped the kitchen floor, settled on pretending she wasn't waiting on Brian.

BRIANNA FOUGHT GOING to bed even after Tracey gave her a bath and read her three bedtime stories.

"Can't I stay up to wait for Daddy?" She begged as Tracey pulled the Princess Jasmine comforter up to the girl's thin shoulders. "Please?"

"No." Tracey kissed her on the nose. "Now, let's pray."

They prayed. Tracey snapped on Brianna's nightlight and left the door cracked. She stepped into the hallway, and the silence surrounded her like a heavy blanket. Tyler was still downstairs playing PlayStation in the family room, which meant he was a permanent fixture on the couch until Tracey told him to give the games a rest.

After eight-thirty. Still no Brian. Not even a phone call from him. If Tracey's house didn't contain two kids she'd sprint out of the house to find him. No, wait. Dumb idea. What would she do when she found him?

She trudged back downstairs and stretched out on the living room sofa for a second before grabbing the phone off the side table. She pressed the speed dial number for Brian's cell. The call went straight to voice mail. Tracey hung up without leaving a message. She dialed the practice. No answer. Not that she'd expected one after eight in the evening. The calls went to the answering service.

She wrapped her arms around herself. The words of Philippians 4:6–7 ran through her mind at warp speed: *Do not be anxious about anything, but in every situation, by prayer and petition, with thanksgiving, present your requests to God. And the peace of God, which transcends all understanding, will guard your hearts and your minds in Christ Jesus.*

She repeated the verses. They brought comfort for the moment.

Thirty minutes later, her eyes popped open.

This was bananas. She needed to do something else.

INFORMATION. Hmm. Brian's phone bill was the obvious choice. Trouble was, his phone bills didn't come in the mail. He had opted for online statements.

The office desktop took way too long to boot up. She chewed her bottom lip as she stared at the screen, waiting for the colorful icons to appear. Antivirus reminders displayed. She clicked those away, then opened Outlook. Time for online sleuthing. While the information loaded, the Holy Spirit jerked away at her conscience, telling her to stop snooping behind Brian's back. She rubbed her forehead as if she could wipe away the nagging thoughts. No time for that. If she was wrong, she'd apologize.

Brian's email loaded. Tracey scanned the list so fast her vision blurred.

Nothing.

She scrolled through the list again, one email a time. Messages from his buddies. Email newsletter from InTouch. Email newsletter from Crosswalk. Spam offer for windows. Email requesting support for missionaries in South Africa. Message from Compassion International. Spam offer for aluminum siding. A few messages from his fraternity brothers. One from his cousin organizing their annual family reunion in Chicago.

Tracey slumped in the chair. All this anxiety for what? Some totally boring stuff. She sighed, then scrolled down more. Right there. At the bottom. An email message from his phone provider. She clicked on it. The bill was overdue. But there was a hyperlink offering a convenient way to pay the bill online. She clicked the link. It popped up a browser window for the website.

The site asked for a phone number and password. Tracey had no password. She saw an 800 number for customer support though. Calling might give her what she needed. She sat still and listened. No movement coming from the downstairs. Tyler would play his games until his eyeballs popped out and fell on the floor. Brianna? Asleep in her room. Tracey dashed to the master bedroom, swiped the cordless off the dresser, then jogged back to the office. She dialed and when the representative came on the line, Tracey turned on the charm.

"Welcome to BlueSky Mobile. How may I help you today?"

"Yes, hello. I need help to pay my bill." Tracey lied.

"Well, I can certainly help you today, ma'am. Would you like to pay now?"

"I wanted to review the bill statements first, then pay my bill." Which was kind of the truth.

"I can help you with that, ma'am. Were you able to log in to the online portal?"

"I wasn't able to get on. I pay by online banking, but I noticed this bill is overdue and I want to pay it right away. I forgot my online password information. Could you help me retrieve it?" Since she'd already lied, the right phrases enabling her to get information slipped off her tongue like melted ice cream.

"I can provide your password over the phone, but you will have to tell me the security answers."

"No problem." Adrenaline flowed through her blood vessels, quieting her conscience more each second.

"Your mobile phone number please?"

Tracey rattled off the numbers.

"Ma'am, this phone call may be monitored for quality assurance." The woman stated crisply. "May I have the last four digits of the social security number of this account?"

Wonderful! Something standard a wife knows. Tracey gave her the numbers and prepared herself for the next question.

"Great," the rep said. "And your mother's maiden name, please?"

Tracey almost uttered Alice's maiden name of Waters. Then she stopped herself. The woman needed Brian's mother's maiden name.

"Hitchcock," Tracey replied.

"One more," the lady said. "Your security question is . . . what was your first car model?"

Brian's first car? His first car. Got it! First car he bought during undergrad at Howard. He'd talked about it often when they started dating, the battered used car that took him back and forth for years before it conked out during his last year at UMDNJ. Tracey jogged her legs beneath the desk, blood pulsating in her ears. A few seconds from getting into Brian's account. "Volkswagen Jetta."

"Thank you." The lady paused, sounds of fingers clicking a keyboard, then came back. "You'll want to write this down."

Tracey's hands trembled as she snatched a blank sheet of paper from the printer and scrambled for a pencil. "Yes, go ahead please."

"Your password is 'drjones1234'."

Tracey let the pencil drop to the desktop. Drjones1234? That's it? She could have guessed that. "Thank you."

"You're welcome. Can I help you with something else this evening?"

"No thanks." She wished she could teleport through the phone line and give the young lady a hug, but she settled for sitting up in the chair and typing Brian's phone number and password into the portal. "You've been a great help."

"Thank you, ma'am. Have a great night."

Tracey hung up and scanned the phone call entries displayed on the screen. A great night? Maybe not.

But it sure would be a night to remember.

CHAPTER
Five

EYES AND MOUTH DRY, Tracey slumped in her chair. Her fingers trembled as she clicked off the computer. She'd scanned Brian's phone call list for over an hour. Now she sat dazed, silent and unmoving.

All right. Okay.

She took a deep breath. She'd seen it—two months full of calls and texts. So many entries from Brian to Lisette and vice-versa left Tracey officially in shock. Oh yes, she had remembered the number in the information for the "Troy" she saw listed on his phone the night before. There was no mistaking the calls she'd scanned were definitely back and forth between Brian and Lisette. The communication between them after midnight on some nights really gave Tracey a Floyd Mayweather-strength punch to the gut. Those must have happened while she slept, dead to the world, ignorant of her husband's actions.

A knock on the office door made her jump.

"Hey Mom, you okay?"

Tyler.

"Yeah . . . uh, yes. I'm okay." A big fat lie. But no way was she ready to start jabbering to her son about the discoveries she'd uncovered.

"I shut off the games and TV downstairs."

"Yeah, thanks."

Tyler pulled himself away from the PlayStation? What time was it? She glanced at the wall clock. Five minutes after ten.

Tracey put her hands on her knees and looked around. Too darn quiet in the house. Her body hummed with nervous energy. She needed something. A distraction.

Tracey lunged up, left the office, zipped around the upstairs and shuffled through the bathrooms collecting hampers of soiled clothing, towels, and bedding. She shut off her brain and dragged four heavy baskets down into the basement laundry room. She cruised on auto pilot as she moved into the cold, far corner of the basement. As she pulled the chain above her head, the harsh light of the naked bulb illuminated the gray concrete space. This would work. She had to concentrate on a job containing no emotion. No trust or questions. Dirty laundry didn't get angry, lie, or make excuses. It only lay in soft lumpy piles waiting to get clean.

She was pouring detergent into the washer when she heard the back door open.

Showtime.

"Tracey!"

She heard Brian call out from the kitchen. She tracked the sound of his footsteps over her head as he walked to the open basement door.

"You down there?" He called.

"I'm here!" she hollered, up to her elbows in hot water. She jerked her wet hands out of the washer and stopped fishing for the blue plastic cap she'd dropped the second the back door opened.

"Where've you been?" Tracey demanded when Brian appeared in the doorway.

He leaned against the door frame. His muddy, snow-smudged boots left brown wet marks on the concrete floor behind him. "The gym," he said.

"Uh-huh." She kept sorting laundry, forcefully throwing dark clothes into one pile, and bright colors into another.

"How are you?" Brian asked.

Tracey sighed. "I've been better."

He cleared his throat. "Today you said you wanted to talk? Something important?"

"Yep." She stepped back to the washer, found the cap, fished it out, and twisted it back on the big bottle of Tide. She shook the bottle. Nothing left in it. Anger urged her to hurl the empty plastic bottle right at Brian's head. She gripped it tight for a moment then dismissed the thought, tossing the bottle into the battered green recycling bin next to the dryer instead.

"You want to talk now?" He asked.

She wiped away smears of water and blue laundry soap from the top of the washer then threw a tattered yellow rag on top. She faced him. "I had asked you to be here as soon as you could."

He rubbed a hand over his face. "Well, I'm here now."

The sound of the wash cycle starting filled Tracey's ears. She wrapped her arms around her body and shivered. She could start with what she heard from Ruthie. The nickname. The embrace. Or she could mention all the phone calls. The texts. She opened her mouth. Nothing came out. Sound bites of what her mother had said earlier flooded Tracey's brain. She actually heard her mother's raspy, nicotine-coated voice: *You go around digging for garbage, you'll find some.*

Tracey's nerve loosened. She gazed at the thick solid muscles in Brian's arms and shoulders pressing against the fabric of his navy blue sweatshirt. Shoulders strong enough to carry an entire family. Firm shoulders that captured her heart the first time she'd hugged him. She wanted to wind her arms tight around him and beg him to tell her things were all right between the two of them.

And he probably would.

And that would be a lie.

"This friendship you have with Lisette. Um, you had more interaction with her than you told me about last night." Tracey said.

"What makes you think so?"

She stopped. She didn't feel comfortable saying she'd talked to Ruthie yet. That could mean trouble for Ruthie at the practice. So now Tracey was dancing with deception. Bad enough she'd been polling his employee for information, now she was tempted to lie about where she'd gotten it. She could try a different approach.

"Let me backtrack for a second," she smiled. "Did you have a good day?"

Brian returned a half-smile. "It was okay."

"Let me give you the rundown on my day." No smile. "I saw Ma for a minute then talked to Monica for a bit this afternoon. Then I guess you could say I spent my time out and about thinking about what you told me yesterday."

Brian's jaw went slack. "Uh-huh."

She kept rattling things off. "So I came home. Made dinner. Spent time with the kids. Put Brianna to bed. Called your office. Called your cell. Left messages. Rested for a minute. Got back up. Read through your cell phone records and saw two months-worth of calls between you and Lisette. Started doing laundry. Now here I am and I need more Tide."

Brian opened his eyes so wide it surprised Tracey that his eyeballs didn't pop out and fall on the floor. "Back up for a second."

"No." She kicked aside a pile of clothes to clear the pathway before she stalked over and stood in front of him. "Now where do you want to start?"

"First of all, it's freezing down here. We should have this discussion someplace else." The washer's rattling sound accentuated the troubled look on his face.

Tracey glanced around at the concrete walls of the unfinished cellar. Kind of a *Silence of the Lambs* effect. Cold enough to see her breath. She'd been so heated with anger when she first came down lugging the laundry she hadn't noticed how chilly the basement was.

"Well, since you don't want to start with the good stuff, let's go backwards. We can go to Walgreens. I told you, I need some Tide."

Brian's deep voice bounced off the walls. "Walgreens? Now?"

Tracey brushed past him and started climbing the stairs two at a time. "Yes. Let's go."

ON THEIR WAY to the store, Tracey sank deep into the passenger seat, keeping her eyes on Brian. He riveted his eyes on the road and stayed silent. He parked in front of Walgreens, and she jumped out, ran inside, bought two giant bottles of Tide because they were on sale at two for ten dollars, came back, climbed back in the car and sat the bag by her feet. The bottles banged against her legs.

As he pulled out of the parking lot, Tracey said, "You have a nickname for her? You call her Troy. This is the same Troy who called you the other night, right?"

Brian didn't answer. Eyes straight ahead. Driving.

"I've seen your phone call list. You've been dialing or texting her something like three times a day. Sometimes after midnight." Tracey's nose started to run. Darn it! She wiggled around in the seat and pulled a crumpled tissue out of the pocket of her puffer jacket.

"I can explain," he sighed. "First, the Troy thing, that's a joke, really."

"A joke?"

"I started joking around with her one day when she came into my office, telling her she looked like an actress I'd seen once whose first name was Troy. She thought it was funny, so I started calling her that from time to time."

"You thought it was better to lie to me about that?" Tracey said.

"You were already upset after I told you what happened in the office. I didn't want to make things worse."

"And all those phone calls?"

Brian looked like he was searching for words. He didn't come up with any.

She went on. "Hugged up with Lisette? In your office?"

Crickets.

"I heard there are pictures of you with her."

"Wait a second, you could only know that if . . ." He stopped, then said in a lower tone. "You talked to Ruthie."

Tracey held up a hand. "Yes, I talked to Ruthie, but you can't be angry with her. You had the opportunity to be truthful with me yourself last night. Right there in the kitchen. I'm a grown woman. You could have told me about the nickname, the pictures, everything. None of it has anything to do with Ruthie. All she did was confirm the truth when I asked."

He shook his head. "You're right. Okay. You're right."

"Thank you."

"But you need to know about the picture. There's nothing to it at all. Definitely nothing nasty. Lisette and her girlfriends were going out to listen to jazz one Friday night a few weeks ago. She stopped in my office and asked me if I wanted to stop by and listen to music with them. I decided to go over there after I left the practice."

"Really? Tracey said.

"One of the her friends happened to get a pic of us when we were sitting at the table and texted it to Lisette's phone."

Tracey bit her bottom lip and looked out the window. All the ice on the streets had melted, but dirty piles of snow lay in drifts on the sides of the road. So Brian had been out having a great time and being silly with Lisette. Tracey sniffed and wiped her runny nose again. When had he stopped having fun with her, and why hadn't he told her?

"Fault me for bad judgment. I got caught up. I shouldn't have gone." Brian's voice grew softer with each word.

"What do you two talk about?"

He shrugged. "I don't know. Life. American medicine. Children's health issues. She's planning on going back to school." Brian cleared his throat twice. "I like talking to her."

"You like talking to her." Tracey breathed. "You really like this woman, don't you?"

"I guess I do."

Tracey swallowed, then bit her bottom lip so hard she tasted blood. Her husband just told her he likes another woman. Things definitely were not fine.

"You guess you do? Brian. I'm your wife." She whispered. "This can't happen."

"I know." He turned the car onto their tree-lined street then repeated himself. "I know."

Now Tracey wished she'd stayed in the house. Too late. She gazed at the pulsating veins in his neck. "Call me stupid." She shook her head and tugged at the tips of her gray leather gloves. "All these years I thought I could trust you. For months you've been hiding things from me. Months! Where did all this come from?"

"I can't . . . I don't . . ." He parked next to the Volvo in the driveway, but kept the car engine running. "Look, believe me when I say I love you. I cannot live without you. You're an excellent wife and an excellent mother."

"Then I don't get it, Brian!"

Brian finally stopped staring through the windshield and turned to face her. "I'm not good at expressing myself for something like this, but I'll try. Lisette and I, we connected in a way I didn't expect. We had a lot of fun conversations and at first, we talked a lot about medicine and most of those texts you saw were just jokes going back and forth between us. But honestly I don't want this."

"I don't want this either," Tracey mumbled.

"It goes no further. I promise you that."

"How far did it go to begin with?"

"We were friends. We got a little too close."

"Is there anything else? Tell me now if there is."

"No, and our friendship is over. From now on she's only another person who works at the practice." She watched as he shifted his body weight and unzipped his jacket. "I'm deleting her contact information right now."

Brian held his hand up as if to signal her to what he was about to do then used his other hand to fish the phone out of his jacket pocket. He tapped the screen a few times then flipped the device around so Tracey could view the list of contacts on the screen. "Look here." He pressed scrolled through the list as he held the device beneath Tracey's nose. "No Troy. Not anymore." He tapped the red DELETE button.

Tracey hadn't expected it to be that easy. Where was the screaming and yelling? She'd expected him to become angry and defensive. Start covering things up. Maybe fuss at her for going behind his back to talk with Ruthie and find out about his connection with Lisette. Or even ask for a separation. None of that happened. Instead she saw him look over at her with remorse in his eyes, his phone resting loose in his palms.

Tracey guessed she'd won? "Am I supposed to go inside, rip all your clothes from our room and throw them out the window?"

"What?"

"Saw that in a music video once," she mumbled.

"That's why it's in a video. That's nuts." He reached out and took hold of her gloved hand and sandwiched it between both of his. "Today I had a one-track mind filled with work I have to check on and patients to see. Some of my older ladies haven't been to see me in months because the Medicare changes are driving them insane. Insurance paperwork is still driving us all nuts. At the end of the day, all I thought about was getting in a good sweat. I should have called you to let you know. I'm sorry."

Tracey sniffed. Her skin still burned with anger, but what would be the point of blowing up now?

He squeezed her hand. "For better or for worse. We're in this together and that's how we'll stay. I told you that when I asked you to marry me. I told you that on our wedding day. I do not change my mind."

"So then what happened? What, Brian!" Tracey grimaced and snatched her hand away.

"I got caught up and I'm sorry. Tracey, I swear, this is the last you'll hear about her, and I'll never talk to her again privately. I mean it."

She snorted, turning away and looking out into the darkness. But really, what could she gain by refusing to forgive him? More tension in the house they didn't need. If she didn't trust him they wouldn't have much of a marriage. She'd become the enemy in his eyes. He'd become the adversary in hers. They'd draw battle lines, both end up wounded, and the casualties would be their children.

Tracey reached for the car door handle.

Brian grabbed her arm and pulled her back. "Stay."

She needed to move away from the hurt of the day. Her head throbbed, and she was sweating from wearing her winter jacket and hat and sitting in a warm car. Her forehead itched. She dropped her hand from the door, pulled off her gloves and tugged the hat from her head. Worn out.

Tracey gazed out the window. "The cracks in this driveway are getting worse."

"I know."

"We need to get them fixed."

"We will."

She turned to him and raked her eyes up and down his body. Raised her eyebrows so he could get the message she was talking about more than pavement.

"No more promises. Take care of it," she said.

"Consider it done."

CHAPTER
Six

TRACEY WOKE the next morning with a dull headache, sore eyes, and aching muscles. As she rolled over in the bed she stretched her arm out and touched the sheets where Brian's body usually lay. She sat up and looked over at the bathroom door. It was wide open. The bathroom? Empty and dark. She glanced at the top of the dresser. Brian's silver watch was gone from his butler. He must have awakened, dressed quickly and headed out while exhaustion rendered her dead to the world.

Fine. Hubby could flee the house. It saved Tracey the trouble of trying to figure out how to relate to him with a blend of anger and hurt making her stomach churn. *Brian is attracted to his nurse.* Sure, he said it goes no further—whatever that means. Sure, he deleted the contact information from his phone. What about his heart? What about all the attention he gave Lisette this winter? The fun he had with her? How easy was it going to be to leave all that behind if he had no problem starting in the first place? Tracey's stomach turned even more and her head ached as she thought about it.

And what could she do, really? She had already gathered information and confronted her husband. Now what? Should she ask friends in the women's prayer circle to pray with her?

Call the life group members? Call Pastor Downes? And then what? Sit around while people shook their heads in pity towards her because her husband wasn't as interested in her as he was in the side chick at the practice?

Three soft knocks on the bedroom door broke the silence, followed by a tiny voice. "Mom, are you up? Can I be up now? I'm hungry."

Brianna. Oh Lord, the kids! Tracey had to be there for them. Feed them. Get them to their schools on time. She rubbed a hand over her face and swallowed hard. She reached for her robe on the bed post and pulled it on as she swung her legs over the side of the bed. "Come in sugar."

The door swung open and a petite brown blur rushed over to the bed and wrapped herself around her mother's legs.

"Hi Mommy!"

"Hi baby." Tracey ran her hands over Brianna's braids.

"Mommy, why didn't you come get me?"

Tracey turned around to look at the clock on her nightstand. After seven already. Good Lord! Brian could have at least woken her up before he left. And why didn't she hear Tyler moving around? Never mind. Time to get moving.

"Can I stay home with you today?" Brianna squeezed Tracey's legs.

Tracey peeled her off gently. "No, honey, this is a kinder-garten morning for you. Let's go."

Up and moving. Good. She scratched her scalp and grimaced, her hair so dry she might as well have pushed her fingers into a haystack. One more thing had to go to her task list for the day: stop by Weave Me and see her sister-in-law, Charla.

PINK HAIR. Well, not completely pink. Charla's hair tumbled down her back in a thick glossy black sheet with hot pink streaks scattered throughout the front.

"What did you do!" Tracey paced around Charla in a slow circle, gazing at her bold new hairstyle.

Charla wrapped her arms around Tracey in a long hug. When Charla let go and backed up, she winked and flashed her megawatt smile. "You know I like to change things up. I felt like 22-inch tracks this week." She reached over and touched Tracey's chestnut-colored locks. "Your hair feels dry again."

Tracey slid out of her brown leather jacket and hung it on one of the stainless steel hooks mounted on the front red wall of the salon. "That's why I'm here, sis."

Charla clucked her tongue as she sauntered back over to her work station where a pretty young lady sat in the salon chair. Charla sat down on a stool behind the girl and began working the final touches on the stunning flat-twist hairstyle.

Charla directed her words to Tracey. "I asked you a month ago to start coming in here regularly. You never listen." She shook her head, multi-hued hair falling about her small brown face.

"Come on now, my hair's not that bad," Tracey said, settling down on the plush red love seat.

"Yes, it is. Last month when I did your hair I saw the same dry hair I see you have now," Charla said. "Get in here more often."

"I will," Tracey said, as she glanced around the room. The white tile floors gleamed. The black sink bowls sparkled like always. Not a speck of dust appeared on the large artwork prints hanging on each tomato red wall. Ambient spa music played from hidden speakers and the whole room smelled like sandalwood. She closed her eyes and rested herself, soothed by the comfortable atmosphere. It wrapped around her like a comforting hug—a healing balm during a time of insecurity.

It took Charla less than fifteen minutes to finish her client's hairstyle, lead the lady up front to settle up payment, sweep around her chair and call Tracey over.

Tracey followed her sister-in-law to the row of shampoo

bowls. That's when she zoomed in to pay full attention to her outfit. Charla wore a hot-pink poncho with a tight micro mini skirt layered over black tights accented by high-heeled black boots.

After Charla draped her with a cape, Tracey sat down in front of the shampoo bowl. She raised an eyebrow. "Does Ricky know you're out in public wearing that skirt?"

"Girl please, that man *loves* this outfit," Charla said as she tapped Tracey to ease her head back into the bowl. She adjusted the water temperature and pointed the nozzle onto Tracey's head.

"And don't those heels hurt your feet from standing all day?" Tracey asked.

"Real divas aren't caught dead in flats, sweetie!" Charla laughed.

"Date night tonight?"

"That was last night. We tried the new Brazilian steakhouse in the city. You know the one where those cute waiters keep serving food to your table until you signal them to stop. The food . . . oh my goodness . . . food was incredible! I never tasted steak and chicken so flavorful. Even the side dishes were amazing! I can't wait to go again."

"You know what? Why don't we all go out together sometime soon? It's been awhile since we've done that."

"I know. Let's organize, I wouldn't want you all to miss this place. And if our schedules don't all work out, you and Brian can still do a date night there. The restaurant is open from noon to midnight all week."

Tracey envied Ricky and Charla. They managed to have regular date nights and they never missed a week, not even for bad weather. If it snowed or rained on a night when they scheduled a date, they would bundle up and walk to the Japanese restaurant around the corner from their home. Since they were childless and Ricky's job as a project manager allowed him time at home each evening and on weekends, they spent lots of private time together.

Tracey eased one eye open as Charla reached into the cabinet above her to grab a bottle of shampoo. "I wish I could look forward to something as nice as date nights. Brian and I . . . we haven't been consistent with it. We get out sometimes, but not as much as should."

Charla massaged shampoo into Tracey's hair. "Why aren't you getting out together?"

"We get busy. You know the kids take up a lot of my time. The more activities they're involved in, the more I have to do. And the practice keeps Brian busy." Tracey closed her eyes again and breathed in the sweet coconut fragrance in the shampoo. "But . . . we need some spice I think. We need *something*."

Neither of them said anything else after that. Charla finished the shampoo and prepped Tracey's hair with deep conditioner. She placed a plastic cap around her head and guided her up out of the chair and over to the row of dryers. Tracey put her purse on the empty seat next to her and sat down under the dryer Charla pointed out to her.

But instead of switching on the dryer, Charla stood in front of Tracey for a moment. She stared in her eyes. "How's your sex life?"

"Okay."

"You sure?"

"Positive." Tracey directed her eyes to the floor. *Sex life.* When was the last time . . . hmm . . . one? No. Two weeks ago. Pathetic. Were they that busy? But if Tracey had not been feeling romantic in the previous months, then she definitely didn't feel like doing it after she found out about Lisette.

Charla tapped her booted foot. Tracey stared back at her, but kept her lips shut. Charla sighed, then reached over and pulled the dryer hood down over Tracey's head. She turned on the dryer, pushed a few magazines into Tracey's hands, and scooted away.

Tracey glanced at the magazine covers, selected a few and slipped them onto the seat of the dryer beside her. She nodded off without answering the questions rattling around her head. Minutes later she jumped when Charla yanked up the dryer hood.

"Come on out sleeping beauty."

"Thanks," Tracey mumbled, pulling her shoulder bag off of her lap and sliding up out of the chair.

Charla rinsed out the deep conditioner then blew out Tracey's hair. Maybe she should go on and talk to Charla about their sex life? Tracey kept her voice low because two more women had entered the shop. They waited in the plush red chairs along the wall.

"Um . . . what you were saying earlier . . . about our sex life . . . " Tracey whispered as Charla's swift hands combed through locks of her hair and snipped the ends.

"Yes . . ." Charla said with a long drawl.

"What sex life?"

Charla clucked her tongue.

Tracey shrugged. "It is what it is."

"Which is how often?" Charla asked.

Tracey sighed.

Charla put her hand on her hip. "You're coming with me next month. We're going down to *The Romance Place*."

"The Romance Place? Do I even want to know?"

"'Course you do. It's a little place down in Westchester. They sell the usual . . . games, lingerie, toys, all kinds of stuff for couples—but it's classy and discreet."

"I'm supposed to buy what while I'm there? A lace nightie. Some candles? Silk sheets?"

"You can, but that's not the main reason for going there. The place has an upstairs where they hold classes in the evening. They have two instructors who teach belly dance, lap dance, erotic dance, and pole dancing." Charla said, her face lighting up brighter than a Christmas tree.

"You took the classes?" Tracey asked.

Charla nodded. "Absolutely. Gabriella helped me create my own personal lap dance routine with my own music. She even helped me pick out the clothes and the right items to decorate my bedroom to make it more romantic. I did the dance and, let me tell you, it spiced things right up."

"Really?"

"Yep. I did it for his birthday last year and he loved it. He asks me to do it all the time."

"Well, how often have you done it since then?"

"Once a week or so."

Tracey whipped around in her chair. "Every week?"

"Sure. We even have a name for it. We call it the Friday night special." Charla beamed a saucy smile.

"No wonder I can't get you on the phone sometimes," Tracey laughed, shaking her head. "You two are on another level."

"What's the point of being married if you aren't going to have a good time? We're having a great time."

Tracey winced. Charla didn't know anything about Brian and Lisette, but the comment still stung. Having fun. Being carefree. A marriage should have those moments. Tracey and Brian Jones? Definitely stuck in a rut, and oh how deep the rut seemed after hearing about her sister and brother-in-law's escapades.

"Trace, you and me, we are going to *The Romance Place* and you are going to come back and blow Brian's mind."

"You think so?"

"Oh, I know so."

Tracey started to tell Charla she would take her up on the offer when her phone buzzed. She reached in her bag and pulled out the device. She'd missed a call as she dozed beneath the dryer hood, and now she saw a text message from her brother Jamal.

Sis! Call me back. Urgent!

She speed-dialed him. "What's wrong? What's so urgent?"

"Dad's in the hospital," Jamal said.

"What?"

"Again."

"For what?"

"Blood pressure. You know how he is. He doesn't take care of himself like he should. Come pick me up. He's at Temple."

Tracey's head started to throb. "How is he?"

"He's stable for now. We'll know more when we can talk to his doctor."

"I'll ring you before I get to Overbrook. Be ready."

Tracey put the phone away. "Char . . . my Dad's in the hospital."

"Oh my goodness! How is he?"

"I don't know. Jamal said blood pressure. He's probably in there for observation. He's been blessed he hasn't had a heart attack or a stroke by now."

"Here, let me brush the rest of this hair into a bun for you, all right. I'll have it done in a second. You can come by later and I'll finish it."

"Thanks."

All thoughts about Brian and Lisette vanished from Tracey's mind. Her father needed her. She had no time to sit around being melancholy about two people she couldn't control. As soon as Charla finished, Tracey jumped up, pressed two twenties into her hand, grabbed her jacket from the wall hook and hustled out the door.

CHAPTER
Seven

TRACEY SPIED Jamal pacing back and forth on the porch as she eased the Volvo up to the curb in front of her mother's house. Jamal's hair had grown much longer than she'd seen him wear it in a while. It was styled as a neatly trimmed, textured afro framing his mocha-colored face, and looked great with his thick black eyebrows and mustache. Tracey started to tell him he looked nice, but she choked back the compliment when he glared at her as he climbed into the car.

"You know why you had to come pick me up? I still need to get my car fixed."

Tracey pulled off and headed down the street. "I asked you to call me back and you didn't. I got busy and forgot about it."

"I still need it though. My money is funny right now. Even with my certifications, I'm only getting a little over minimum wage."

"What about your private clients?" She remembered him telling her he could get as much as sixty dollars an hour traveling to wealthy client's homes and training them privately on their own equipment.

"I only have two of those right now and my gym clients are dwindling. This year isn't like last year. Last year we started a campaign for new people to come in and get ripped in time for summer. I think they cut money from the advertising budget this season."

"Really?" She raised an eyebrow.

"Yeah. Less people are there looking to work out. Plus, I get people who say they want to lose weight. Then I take them through a trial session and they don't return."

"I told you about pulling that boot camp routine on people. You're not in the Army anymore. People don't want you to make them drop and give you twenty push-ups between each exercise," Tracey teased.

"Results. High intensity gets results."

"Remember the guy you told to give you fifty push-ups, then three sets of mountain climbers, and then burpees — and he threw up? Didn't he cancel his gym membership after that?"

"Anyway . . . I still need the loan for my transmission."

"We can talk about that later." Tracey shifted the topic. "So do you know yet, what's going on with Dad?"

"He's having trouble and he's under observation," Jamal sighed.

Tracey fell silent, keeping her focus on navigating the car through the city streets. In less than four hours she'd been granted her silent prayer to stop thinking about Brian's interest in Lisette. But now concern over her father filled her mind.

She prayed silently as she stepped on the gas and sped faster into the city.

WHEN THEY WALKED into Pernell's hospital room, they spied him sitting up in bed watching TV. He turned and smiled wide displaying two gold teeth glittering from the side of his mouth. A faded blue hospital gown sagged on his robust body. He'd kept his watch on. Tracey recognized it as the rose gold

Breitling Starliner she and Brian had given him two Christmases ago.

"Hi, Dad," Tracey said, moving close to his bed.

"Hey, Dad," Jamal said.

"Hey now. Here's my kids!" he announced to his roommate, an older Asian man in the bed next to him. "Man I made some beautiful kids in my day, I'm telling you. They're smart too."

The man paid no attention.

Tracey sat down on the side of her father's bed. She grabbed hold of his rough wrinkled hand dotted with brown age spots. "A stroke?"

He looked at both them with his eyes wide. A frown creased his face. He shrugged, then gave a slight nod.

"Baby girl, don't worry about me," he said, looking down at the bed. "I felt bad there for a minute. But I'll be out of here in a few."

"A stroke, huh? And you'll be out of here soon?" In her head she ran down a list of things to ask his doctor. Questions about c-reactive proteins, cholesterol levels, blood pressure numbers, and homocysteine.

"Doc told me it was a mini-stroke. Transient attack or something," he sighed, running a hand over his face. "Darling, this body of mine is something I gotta live with."

"What happened this morning?" Tracey asked, clutching his hand tighter.

"I got dizzy and had a hard time getting up and moving this morning. I wish your Uncle Ray hadn't called Jamal telling all my business. I'll be fine."

Stubborn. Tracey's father had never been big on wellness. He enjoyed drinking, but Tracey never considered him an alcoholic in the same way her mother had let drinking ravage her when Tracey was a teen. She'd never seen her father drink before or while he worked and he'd been a bus driver for nearly forty years. But she'd called him enough in the evening times to know he drank after hours. He liked to spend Friday and Saturday nights at his brother's bar in North Philly, sitting on a barstool sipping Remy Martin, letting the intoxicating liquid magically erase anything he didn't feel like thinking about.

"Have you been seeing your doctor regularly?" Tracey asked.

Pernell looked away. "When I can."

"What about your blood pressure meds?" Jamal questioned.

"Now I do take my pills. Every day," Pernell insisted. "Ask your Uncle Ray."

Tracey and Jamal glanced at each other, frustrated.

"Come on now, y'all, don't look like that," Pernell said.

Tracey looked back at Pernell. "Like what, Dad?"

"Like I have one foot in this hospital bed and the other one in the grave. I follow up with a specialist next week." Pernell's voice started out strong, but wavered as he continued. "I'm here under observation. What I gotta do later . . . "

Tracey changed the subject. "Brianna has a dance recital next month. If you could manage to take care of yourself, you might be able to make it to see her dance."

Pernell grinned. "Where's the recital?"

"Up around our way. I'll get you the information. She'll dance ballet and tap."

"Do you think she'll be a professional dancer when she grows up?" Pernell probed.

"No. She mostly does it because her friend Jayda does it."

"Hey, how come you didn't tell me she had a recital?" Jamal asked.

"Lately I keep forgetting to tell all the right people." Tracey had forgotten all about the recital when the mess with Brian started.

"It's a shame you don't get over to North Philly to see me and Ray. Ever since your Aunt Zee passed, seems like none of y'all can manage to come over and pass the time with me or your uncle."

"It's still hard for all of us. She was gone so fast," Tracey said.

Aunt Zee was Zehendra Mae Watson. She'd been married to Pernell's brother Ray for more than thirty-five years when an aggressive form of breast cancer claimed her life three years back.

"You know I'm up there all the time," Jamal joked.

"Well I want the kid who comes over *not* wanting money all the time to visit."

Tracey and Pernell laughed as Jamal rolled his eyes and looked out the window. "Yeah, all right. I see how y'all are."

Tracey's heart beat fast at the thought of her father's blood pressure not being under control. "Dad, you need to take this episode seriously. And you're blessed Uncle Ray got you over here in time. Most times folks have these small attacks, forget about them, and then they have a full-blown stroke." Tracey put her purse strap back on her shoulder, moved over to his bedside table and poured her father a cup of ice water from the beige plastic pitcher.

"Where's your doctor?" she asked.

Pernell crossed his arms on his chest. "Now you don't have to talk to him. I'll do the right thing. I'm not a child."

Tracey and Jamal glanced sidelong at each other again. From the look in Jamal's eyes, their thoughts must have matched. They'd seek his doctor the minute they walked out of the hospital room.

"How long will you be here?" Tracey asked.

Pernell grimaced. "Not sure yet. Most likely for another day. Then I'm 'sposed to follow up with a neurologist."

"Count on me taking you to that next appointment. You don't have a choice." She fluffed up his flat pillow and kissed him on the lips. "I love you."

"Love you, too."

A tired look settled on Pernell's face and he didn't talk much more. Tracey stayed close to his side, watching a court show on TV for a while. An hour passed before he closed his eyes and drifted off to sleep. When Pernell's breathing grew even and he snored lightly, they tiptoed out into the hallway, closing the room door behind them.

Jamal spoke first. "A stroke."

Tracey echoed her brother. "A stroke." She craned her neck around as her eyes scanned the sterile cold hallway. "I don't care what Dad said, we are talking to his doctor."

Jamal blew air out through his teeth. "Yeah, I'm going to find out about that now." He turned and headed for the nurse's station.

Left alone for a moment, Tracey dug her phone out of her purse and dialed Brian on his phone. It rang several times before going to voice mail. She hung up then entered the speed dial number for Germantown Family.

"Germantown Family Medical."

Relief flooded her body when she heard the deep female voice on the other end of the line. "Ruthie. I'm glad it's you."

"Yes, can you hold for a moment?" Ruthie asked, her voice crisp and professional.

"Certainly, I . . . " Tracey didn't finish before the phone went mute. She peered down the hallway. Jamal pointed in her direction as he talked with a short Indian man with thick black hair. Tracey held her phone, leaned against the wall and waited.

Ruthie came back, but this time her voice was lower and she sounded tense. "Tracey, hi," she said.

"Yes, I'm trying to reach Brian."

"I figured as much." Ruthie paused. "He's not in."

Tracey straightened up like someone had pricked her skin with a hot needle. "You mean he's at the hospital?"

"No, sweetie. I mean, he left at eleven. Dan's taking his appointments. Brian's not available unless there's an emergency. His specific request."

"And . . . ah . . . " Tracey pushed the words out of her mouth. "Is Lisette there?"

"She's not here today, either."

Jamal and the doctor started walking toward Tracey. She'd have to hang up.

"Thank you, Ruthie. I'll talk with you later."

"Everything all right?" Jamal asked as he approached.

Her heart banged in her chest like a gong and she'd broken out in a sweat, but she put on her game face. "Fine."

"You sure about that?"

"That's what I said." Tracey directed her attention to the doctor in front of her. "Hello. My father is under your care?"

"Yes he is. I'm Dr. Srinivasa. Good to meet you."

"Good to meet you, too." Tracey got straight to the point. "What exactly happened to him?"

As the doctor proceeded to launch into the definition of the transient ischemic attack and what it would mean as far as her father's future health was concerned, Tracey listened closely, but her heart fluttered as she thought of Brian. This was not fair. Not fair at all. Her dad needed her to be there for him. Her feelings were torn now. One part of her wanted to stay with her father, and the other wanted to dash out of the hospital, jump in the car, and search for her husband.

Dr. Srinivasa finished his talk with, "Are you going to assist with your father's care?"

"Uh . . . yes, definitely." Tracey stammered.

"He will need to follow up with a neurologist. His appointment will be scheduled before his discharge tomorrow."

When the doctor headed into the room to take a look at her dad, Tracey stayed in the hallway. Jamal shot her a puzzled look. "Go on in. I'll be there in a minute."

Jamal shook his head as he went inside, while Tracey whipped her phone back out.

She dialed Brian's on call phone, leaving a 911 message, then leaned on the wall and waited. It took only a minute before he called her back.

"Brian," Tracey said flatly.

"Tracey, you know this phone is for emergencies only. Why didn't you call my personal phone?"

"I did. You didn't answer it."

"I must not have heard it."

She ignored that statement and pressed on. "My dad had a mini-stroke. I'm over here at Temple Hospital with Jamal visiting him. He's under observation."

"No way! When did all this happen?"

"He woke up this morning having a hard time talking and couldn't see straight. Uncle Ray called an ambulance and they rushed him here."

"How is he?"

"Right now he's resting. He sounds normal, but we don't know all the damage yet. He'll be released tomorrow and has to see a specialist."

"They've done all the necessary scans?" Brian asked.

Tracey sighed. "I don't know. His doctor came down the hallway a few minutes ago. I'm about to go find all that out. Look, I need to spend some time here so I need you to make sure the kids are squared away of this afternoon. Call and make sure Ty goes to pick up Brianna from Jayda's after school. And when you get home, let them know about their Pop-pop. Oh, and see what they want for dinner tonight."

"Tracey, that's your job."

Tracey pursed her lips. She'd let that comment slide. She clutched the phone tight in her fist and swallowed hard. "Yes. And today it's yours."

"Tracey." Brian said, his voice dripping with displeasure.

"My dad had a mini-stroke. A stroke! I need you to see about our children this evening."

She paused to see if he would offer a lie about working. He didn't.

"See you at home later," his voice trailed off.

Tracey ended the call, then squeezed her eyes shut and counted backwards from a hundred. She got to ninety before she stopped and took a deep breath. She hadn't meant to make Brian take over the house and kids that afternoon, but she decided to use the one thing that could keep him from going out to be with Lisette. That's if he wasn't with her already.

Jamal peeked his head out of the room door. "Will you get in here?"

Tracey turned and put her hand on the room door. "I had to take care of something important."

"Well, is it taken care of?"

"For now."

CHAPTER

Eight

"SISTER JONES, IS SOMEBODY DEAD?" Pastor David Downes's deep southern drawl stretched the words as far as they could go, looking like he wanted to make Tracey smile.

"No." Tracey frowned, far from ready to laugh. Instead, she sat stiff in a chair in her pastor's super clean office, trying to figure out how to ask for advice for her marriage while revealing as little as possible about the situation.

"Is someone sick or critical?"

"No."

"Excellent. Everything else can be worked out." He gave a warm smile. "Let's pray, and then put your worries on pause and tell me what's going on. Heavenly Father, we adore you and give you all the glory. We bless your name Lord, for you are worthy to be praised. As we talk together, may your presence be known. Guide our thoughts and our words. Please provide comfort and hope for Sister Jones at this time. We love and honor you Lord. Thank you Lord. In Jesus Christ name we do pray. Amen."

"Amen," Tracey said.

Pastor Downes ran a hand over his bald head as he reclined

in his chair. "I'm here to help. Please share what's on your mind."

"Well," Tracey cleared her throat, then continued. "There's a situation in my marriage right now. I confronted it and I thought everything would die down, but . . . " She paused. She might as well put it out there. "Brian is cheating on me."

Pastor Downes raised a bushy eyebrow. "He's admitted this to you?"

"Yes and no." She directed her gaze to the top of the pastor's desk. "I've asked him about his relationship with a nurse at his practice. He said they're only friends. I don't believe him." She lifted her eyes to meet the pastor's, and repeated herself. "I don't believe him."

"Why not?"

"He and this woman, they call and text each other a lot. So, I confronted him about their conversations, but then last week I caught him rearranging his schedule and taking time off without telling me, on a day when the nurse was also away from the office. Pastor, I was so mad! I shut down for a couple of days to keep the peace. There's something going on, but I can't get to the full truth with him."

"Do you know the woman?"

"I met her once," Tracey said, quickly adding, "and I don't care to know her."

"Sister Jones, has your husband known her for a long time?"

"Not very long. About five months I think. That's how long she's been working at the practice."

"I see. Are you concerned about anything else you experienced with your husband?"

The skin on Tracey's face burned as she recalled Brian's words, which she was about to repeat. "He admitted to me he's grown close to her. He likes her. He enjoyed his conversations with her, and I'm not totally convinced he didn't enjoy anything else with her."

Pastor Downes leaned in, understanding coloring his face.

"You're nervous because there could be a threat to your marriage. I know you, so I know you've prayed about your marriage. But you think you may need to do something more. Is that correct?"

"Exactly."

"All right. Wait just a minute." Pastor Downes stood up and shuffled out of the office. In less than a minute he returned with a small book. He passed it to her before he settled behind his desk. "Take a look through it."

Tracey turned it over in her palm. The cover had fancy black script text written over a faded gray picture of an empty bedroom. *Letting Go and Letting God Work in Your Marriage* by Dr. Frank H. Dockens, PhD.

The pastor nodded at her when she looked up again. "Go home and read that. Meditate on the scriptures in there. Incorporate the prayers into your private time with the Lord. Follow the guidelines in the book. Your situation isn't very different from what I've seen with other couples throughout the years. This book helped them. It can help you."

Tracey frowned. "Pastor, no disrespect to you, but this is—"

"Not what you're looking for?" he asked.

Tracey let the book drop to her lap. "I'm not having problems with my spiritual disciplines. I read my Bible. I spend quiet time with the Lord. I pray daily. None of it stopped my husband from outright lying to me." She took a deep breath, exhaled and tamed her voice before the heat of her frustration continued to push it higher. "I think I need more than this."

Pastor Downes's voice was warm but firm as he leaned in again. "Sister Jones, I hear you. I want you to know I didn't pull out any random marriage book. There are exercises for you in there. If you want your marriage to improve, you should use it."

Tracey nodded.

He settled back in his chair. "Now, I'm going to ask you some questions and I'm trusting you to answer honestly."

"Okay."

"When was the last time you spent private time with your husband?"

"That depends on what you mean by private."

"Honesty, please," he reminded her.

"A couple of weeks ago."

"When was the last time you went out to have a good time together, just the two of you?"

Tracey had to think on that for a minute. When was that? Oh, right. The kids had been hanging out with Ricky and Charla that weekend. Tracey and Brian had gone to Sunday brunch. She remembered wearing her favorite red wool dress to match Brian's red sweater. "Early December. We went to the jazz brunch at Relish."

"Has he tried to take you out any other time recently?"

"No."

"All right," he said, pausing for a moment. "Do you have a lot of family in the area? Any people around to help you so you can get out more often?"

"Sure. Well, my parents, they're in Philly. His parents are over in Voorhees. My brother is in Philly. Brian's two brothers and their wives, they live in Conshohocken. My close girl-friends are in Delaware County. But they all have their own lives. My teenager's life is full because of school and sports teams and his study groups. Everyone's so busy. Though I guess I should make an effort to search for a regular babysitter for Brianna."

"Okay. Big question for you. Has your husband tried to be affectionate with you?"

"Yes. But he did that after an argument."

"Did you go along with him, or did you push aside his affection?"

She did the uncross and re-cross thing with her legs. Laced and unlaced her fingers. "I told him I didn't want him in my space."

"I see."

She looked up at her pastor. "So, you probably think I deserve what's happening, don't you?"

Pastor Downes's brown eyes connected with hers. "I'm not here to judge. I'm serious when I say I'm here to help. It doesn't matter what I think."

She offered a half-smile. "But I want to know what you think."

He chuckled. "Well, now that you're asking. I'm only your pastor. I might as well give you my humble opinion."

Tracey allowed a small laugh. She sat up straight and stopped fidgeting. "Go on."

"An actual affair is a big charge. But there are some things I do know from what you've told me. You and Brian need a regular date night each week, even if you stay in the house. Spend more time together. I know he's busy, but he can manage something. Around here, my schedule stays packed. But when it's time for me to be with Sis. Downes I block out the time."

She crossed her arms and made a face. "Why do I have to ask him for time he should be giving me already?"

"Do you want your marriage to get better or worse?"

"Better."

"Good." He took a sip of water from the bottle on his desk. "Sister, yes—you are right. He should be giving you his undivided attention. But since he isn't, you'll need to pursue him. And pray for him daily. Call up some of those folks in your family, or get a regular babysitter for your daughter and get out with him."

"Okay."

"The exercises in the book will help you formulate specific prayers for your situation. Remember, at this point you're seeking truth and at the same time trying to reestablish bonds in your relationship. Don't alienate your husband. You want to draw closer to him and rebuild trust so you can walk together."

"And if this thing is deeper than he's told me about?"

The pastor's eyes still brimmed with kindness, but his smile faded. "If that's the case, you'll have a battle on your hands. Brian could be emotionally enmeshed with this woman, have a hard time letting her go, and both of you might think about divorce."

Tracey kept quiet as she allowed those words to do cartwheels around in her brain, then fall down and sink in slow.

"But as you know," he cleared his throat, "we don't do divorces here at Rise. I haven't lost a couple yet and you two are not going to mess up my record. Let's pray and you can go home and do your homework."

Tracey waved the book at him and sighed. "I start reading this, and . . . "

"Do the exercises. And before this day ends, schedule a date with your husband. Make inroads to clear the air and talk openly with him. Try to listen to him without judging."

"Okay."

"Last thing. You have an enemy. But the enemy is Satan. Not Brian. Not the nurse." He leaned back in his chair. "Now, let's pray."

A minute later Tracey headed out of the office. She stood in the hallway, the book resting in her hands. She flipped through the pages and read the introduction. Verses. Prayers. Chapters ending with a list of questions and action items. It seemed like a condensed version of *The Love Dare* nearly every Christian couple she knew completed after the *Fireproof* movie came out a few years back. All the same nuts and bolts. Maybe it would help. She zipped the book into the front pocket of her bag and headed out. Time to see about her father.

TAKING Pernell to see the neurologist was crazy. Tracey bit her tongue and stayed silent as Pernell dragged his feet and stalled for time. He pouted like an overgrown baby while he shadowed her into Dr. Remir's office.

"You know, I feel great today," Pernell reassured Tracey as she opened the car door and took his hand right after they pulled up to the hospital.

"Terrific," she said. "Keep right on feeling good while you get these instructions and plan to follow them."

In the office, Dr. Remir spoke plainly. "Mr. Watson, ministrokes are definite warning signs for a full-blown stroke."

"Does that mean it will happen to him soon?" Tracey asked apprehensively, reaching out to touch her father's hand.

Dr. Remir held his hands up as if to say he couldn't make a prediction. Then he looked over at Pernell, whose eyes were downcast, and spoke about debilitation, paralysis, and diminished quality of life. Tracey looked over at her father and noticed his stillness. He sat wordless in the molded blue plastic chair. No blinking. No movement. He did not ask any questions. Tracey stared at her father's face for a long moment. Immobile like granite. He must be getting the point.

When Tracey dropped Pernell off at home, he tried to reassure her again. As he got out of the car, he told her, "This old man will be fine."

"Yes, because this old man will listen to his doctors from now on."

Driving toward home, Tracey's thoughts darted from Brian, to her father, to her mother, to the kids, and back again. When her phone chimed, she ignored it. Instead, she took a moment to pray. *Lord, whatever else is coming across my path, give me your grace and provide me with the courage and strength to handle it. Amen.*

Tracey didn't bother to pick up her phone to find out who'd called. She'd get to it when she got in the house.

Her phone chimed once again, jolting her out of her thoughts. This time she focused her eyes on the road and put the device on speaker.

"Hello."

"You felt the need to talk to Pastor Downes, huh?" Brian didn't yell, but he still sounded ticked off.

Tracey focused on keeping the car straight while she drove. Why lie? She didn't do anything wrong. "Yes, I did."

"You talked about me?"

She cleared her throat. "Of course I talked about you."

"Now Pastor Downes wants me to meet with him tomorrow. He also asked me to stop teaching the Men's Wellness class on Sunday afternoon, effective immediately."

"Did he say why?"

"Said he had concerns about my home life. He doesn't want anyone serving if it's taking away too much time from their family."

"Oh."

"Yeah."

"Listen, we were just talking."

"I thought you and I were clear everything is fine. There should have been no reason for you to discuss our private life with that man."

Everything's fine? Had Brian taken a couple of whiffs of laughing gas that morning?

"First, that man is our pastor, and I trust him. And second, I do not feel fine, Brian. Not at all. You hurt me, and I'm not sure where our relationship is going, and I chose to talk about it with someone who could give me some sound guidance."

"Without asking me?"

"I don't need your permission!"

"Tracey, all I'm saying is if you wanted to go see a counselor, that's a discussion we should have had before you talked about this with anyone at church."

Traffic on the road grew thick. A huge semi whizzed past her window and she eased off the gas, keeping the Volvo from drifting too close to the truck. This was insane. If Brian wanted to fight with her he needed to do it face to face and not smack dab in the middle of gas-fumed gridlock.

"Tracey, are you there?"

She gritted her teeth as she tried to keep the Volvo away from the heavy crush of cars that followed the trucks. "I'm here. But can we talk about this when I get in the house. I'm almost there."

"No, we'll talk about it later tonight." The phone clicked off.

That's it. Once she got close to Chestnut Hill, she turned the car in the direction of Germantown Family. The place was probably filled with patients but who cared? Not Tracey. Up until now, she couldn't tell if Brian told the truth or not about things being over with Lisette. But if Tracey showed up and viewed Lisette and Brian's body language, their movements would tell her the truth.

Reading the marriage book would have to wait until after her visit to Germantown Family.

CHAPTER
Nine

TRACEY PARKED RIGHT in front of the office building. She'd probably end up with a ticket. Whatever. She grabbed her purse, locked the car and dashed inside. Ignoring the elevator, she climbed the stairs two at a time to the second floor. She pushed the door that lead into the long, narrow hallway, made a sharp right, then opened another door into the Germantown Family waiting room.

Quiet. One elderly man waited there, sitting in a chair in the corner. Tracey spied Ruthie behind the glass partition separating the waiting room from the nurses' area. Ruthie, with green-rimmed reading glasses perched on her nose, looked up and nodded toward Tracey, but didn't rise to greet her. Instead, the older lady kept silent as she thumbed through multi-colored file folders. Whatever Ruthie thought about Tracey showing up out of the blue, she wasn't going to say anything about it.

As Tracey hung her brown leather jacket on the wooden coat rack she felt a swift breeze behind her. She whipped around in time to see a woman hurriedly pushing her arms into a white down coat, her petite body clad in light green scrubs, white nursing clogs on her feet.

Lisette! She moved so fast the white canvas bag slung around her body was airborne as she opened the door and let it slam shut behind her, making the front wall vibrate.

Tracey glanced sidelong at Ruthie behind the glass, as if to say, *Did I see what I think I saw?* Ruthie gave Tracey a fast nod. That was all the information Tracey needed. In less than five seconds Tracey zoomed out the door, down the hallway, and stopped five feet away from Lisette, who stood in front of the elevators.

"Lisette Santana," Tracey said as she approached the young woman. "Right?"

Lisette pressed the down button for the elevator. She turned her head and looked directly in Tracey's eyes but didn't utter a word. She had small eyes and wavy light brown hair flowing to her mid-back. Slender. Strikingly pretty. Could pass for J. Lo's sister.

Tracey reached out and knocked Lisette's hand away from the elevator button. "I'm talking to you."

The young woman finally spoke back, her voice raspy and slow. "I see you. I don't have anything to say to you."

Tracey stepped closer. "Oh, I think you do. You certainly have a lot to say to Dr. Jones, since you call him more than I do each day. And by the way, in case you don't remember me, I'm . . ."

"I know who you are." Lisette scanned Tracey's body up and down before she slowly turned her gaze back to the silver elevator doors.

Tracey leaned in close enough to catch a whiff of Lisette's spearmint gum. "I don't appreciate you calling and texting my husband the way you do. Stay away from him unless you need to interact with him in a professional capacity. He has a wife. Have some respect!"

Lisette stared right back into Tracey's eyes as she chewed her gum and hitched her bag up higher on her shoulder. She looked . . . bored. The raspy voice came out again. "That's the best you can do?"

"Pardon me?"

"Stay away from my husband. He has a wife." She mimicked Tracey's words in a high-pitched tone. She even yawned and rolled her eyes.

Tracey talked louder. "Woman to woman. I'm telling you . . . back off!"

The elevator door opened and Lisette walked in and turned around. She pushed the button to hold the door open. Looking right in Tracey's eyes, she smiled wide, both rows of straight white teeth on full display.

"I hope you're enjoying the leather jacket you got for your birthday. Nice, isn't it? No need to thank me for picking it out. And isn't Relish a phenomenal restaurant? I hope you loved going there because it's my absolute favorite place to eat and Brian loved going there with me. You take care now."

The elevator doors slammed shut as Tracey realized the bomb Lisette had just dropped. Tracey loved that jacket. She'd been so surprised Brian had picked out and wrapped something so stylish and instead of having the usual crystal vase of red roses delivered to the house. She'd actually praised him. Thought he'd been paying more attention to what she liked.

She'd thought wrong.

The hallway seemed gray and narrow—more than usual—and smelled stale to Tracey as she stood there dumbfounded and alone. And for what? Lisette had totally missed the fact she was being confronted. Tracey could have asked her about the weather and her face would have looked exactly the same. No remorse. No shame. Nothing. And to make matters worse, the chick had the nerve to mock her!

Maybe Tracey hadn't been direct enough?

She bolted for the stairs and scrambled down them so fast her boot heels clicked the concrete sounding like a wild castanet orchestra. Her heart galloped while her brain telegraphed staccato messages. *Stop. Don't do this. Go back. This is not a wise thing to do.*

True. A wise woman wouldn't run out of a building, push

open a door and stand out on the street, wild-eyed, looking up and down the sidewalk like her purse had just been snatched and she was searching for the assailant. The Christian thing to do would have been to remain calm and centered, pray for strength, and ask God for guidance for the next thing to do.

Trouble was, Tracey couldn't see praying.

She saw red.

Especially when she squinted and saw Lisette had made it all the way down to the end of the block and was standing at the corner waiting for the light to change, holding a cell phone in front of her face, yakking away.

Christian. Wise. Stop. Right. Now.

No!

Tracey had never been so glad she'd shoved her car key in her pants pocket. She fished it out in a flash, ran over to her car and jumped in. A freshly minted ticket decorated the underside of the windshield wiper. She ignored the ticket, turned the ignition and threw the car in drive so fast it jerked. She stomped on the gas pedal and the Volvo shot out of the parking spot, down the street and closer to Lisette on the corner—closer and closer—until Tracey stopped the car with a screech just as Lisette stepped off the curb.

Tracey kept the Volvo still. Long enough to stare Lisette in the eyes. *You see me now right?*

She hit the gas, jerked the wheel, and the car flew right up to Lisette's body before Tracey hit the brake. If Lisette hadn't jumped back suddenly, fallen to the sidewalk, and landed on her butt, the car would have knocked her so hard she'd have flown down the street a few yards and landed on the pavement, broken and oozing.

Tracey turned the car back toward the street and accelerated into the flow of traffic. The rhythm of traffic calmed her. She would keep driving for a few minutes then go back to Germantown Family to see Brian.

At a traffic light, Tracey stared at her hands on the steering wheel. They were shaking. But Tracey hadn't hurt anyone. Scared someone, yes. Hurt someone? No.

Short telegraphed messages ran through her head once more. *That. Was. Not. Wise. That. Was. Not. Loving.*

This time she answered herself out loud.

"No. It. Was. Not. But. It. Felt. Good."

"HAVE YOU LOST YOUR MIND?" Monica yelled.

"Monica, I swear, I don't know what came over me." Tracey held her phone in front of her, rubbing the dust out of her eyes as she sat, pulled over in the Volvo, a few blocks away from the office building.

"Well, did you hit her?" Monica asked.

"Of course not."

"When she fell, did she hurt herself?"

Tracey paused for a second. She replayed the sight of Lisette tumbling to the pavement and falling on her behind. "I don't think so, no."

"Good, because I don't want to see you get sued for damages by some nutcase because she dissed you in a hallway and you had to teach her a lesson."

"I know."

"It's not worth that."

"I know," Tracey repeated. "Thank you, Jiminy Cricket. I promise you, I am not going to take a trip to Muncy over some nurse."

"Good."

"Girl, please tell me something to take my mind off of all of this? I gotta go back and try to get a hold of Brian and talk to him, and I need to clear my mind before I get there. Help me think about something else. What's going on with you this week? Are you dating anyone new?"

"Are you kidding me? Girl, do you know you almost got mixed up in a homicide!"

"I'm trying not to think about that. You wanna come visit Rise on Sunday? I'll probably need someone to talk to because I doubt Brian will be in great spirits."

"Absolutely not!"

"Why'd you say it like that?"

"There's no choir! Where's your choir? Why do you all have a house band like on *The Tonight Show*? And your pastor doesn't wear a robe. And for Bible study you have to meet in house groups."

"Life groups."

"Give me a good old-fashioned church with choirs and building fund thermometers on the wall and ministers in fancy robes and flowers on the altar and Sunday fried chicken dinners and missionaries named Bertha and Beulah. Now that's church!"

Tracey laughed. "You made me laugh so I'm giving you cool points."

"Thank you."

Tracey sighed. "I gotta go figure out more about this mess."

"Try not to run over anyone this time."

"I won't. I think."

CHAPTER

Ten

TRACEY LET thirty minutes pass before heading back to Germantown Family. As she walked from the main waiting area down the narrow hallway to Brian's office she debated in her head as to whether or not she should tell him she'd nearly mowed Lisette down on the street on purpose. She decided against it. Why waste time talking about that when there was the big issue she needed to discuss?

"We can keep talking now," Tracey announced as she entered his office, shutting the door behind her.

Brian looked up from the files on his desk. "I told you I'd talk with you later."

She planted her bottom in the chair in front of his desk and stared at him without blinking. As far as she was concerned, they were going to get to the bottom of things right there in his office. No matter what happened, she would not allow them to get into a full-on fight at home with the kids. The thought of that brought back flashbacks of being nine years old, huddled in her rickety twin bed with the lights out, afraid she would wet the bed but too scared to tiptoe into the hallway and go to the bathroom. Her stomach always twisted in knots back then when she heard Alice and Pernell cursing and yelling at each other like they hated each other.

Not in the Jones's house.

"I didn't like the tone you used when you hung up," Tracey reprimanded Brian, gritting her teeth. "Now you tell me about you and Lisette."

"What do you want me to tell you?"

"The truth." She gazed long and hard at their family Christmas picture in the silver frame on his desk, then looked back at him.

Brian stared back at her. Silent.

Tracey sighed. "I just talked to her in the hallway. I take it you asked her for help on my birthday present and she made a suggestion. I like the gift though. I'll keep it. Oh, and she made sure I knew you took me to her favorite restaurant. Sounded a lot like someone trying real hard to point out you and she are pretty close."

"I'd hoped it wouldn't come to this. Lisette and I became friends. We aren't anymore. I guess you want to know everything else?"

"That would be nice!"

Now why did his face look like that? With his mouth downturned and his eyes scrunched up all weird. It freaked Tracey out. His face showed sorrow mixed with remorse and confusion and she had the crazy urge to place her arms around him and comfort him. Try to stop him from hurting. Must have been a reflex emotion. Something she felt because she loved him. Then she remembered she was hurt too. So she stayed put and kept her arms crossed in front of her.

"I'm not sure where to start," he said.

"At the beginning."

"Honey, I can't," he stammered. "This is . . . I can't."

Now Tracey was "honey"? Oh, please! Now she had to become the Oprah Winfrey of the room, asking simple and direct questions. Back straight. Shoulders steady. Here we go.

"Do you love her?" Tracey asked.

"Of course not."

"When did it start?"

"January."

"Where?"

"She worked here late one night when it was icy outside. I dropped her off at her apartment. She invited me in for coffee to thank me and I went in with her."

"And you had sex?"

"No."

"No?"

Brian shook his head. "No, but we were attracted to each other and I could feel it. We . . . got together two weeks later when I drove her to her apartment again. I skipped going to the gym."

"I see," Tracey said, her heart sinking with the magnitude of her husband's admission. Her eyes shifted down toward her lap.

"Do you want more details?"

She paused for a second then shook her head. "No. Not right now."

"Are you okay?" He reached out for her hand.

Tracey pushed her chair back to maintain distance from him. "I'll be all right."

Amazing. She didn't feel like slapping, kicking, or throwing anything at him. The truth had come out. She felt oddly at peace. Free from wondering.

He looked puzzled as he scanned her face. "Do you want me to go on?"

"Yes." Tracey could take it. "Go ahead."

Brian took a deep breath. "It happened maybe a couple more times . . . same situation."

Tracey's eyebrows shot up. "A couple?"

"Two more times."

Silence for a moment. Tracey uncrossed her arms. "Where was I?"

"What do you mean, where were you?"

"I mean, where was I when all this happened? Did a time warp of some sort occur?"

Brian looked away. "These were regular weeknights. You were at home with the kids."

"When you were supposedly at the gym working out?"

He nodded.

"What happened after that?"

"Nothing. I never went to see her again."

He leaned over and grabbed some tissues from the box on his desk. He pressed them against his eyelids then wiped his nose.

"What about the day you left the practice early?"

"That was for me. I needed some time by myself to think and pray, but I did call Lisette and talk to her. I'd already told her we couldn't continue what we started and I needed her to accept it and move on. But breaking it off with her had caused new problems. She started getting angry with me and calling my phone all the time. She let things slip out and started talking loud around the office. When Ruthie talked to me . . . and then Dan brought it up . . . " Brian shook his head and sighed.

"It must have really upset her, you ending it," Tracey said.

"I'm married."

"Probably blew her mind when you decided to act like it."

"Sounds like you feel sorry for her?"

"I feel sorry for both of you," Tracey snorted. "All she had to do was chat you up a bit and pour you some Folgers and you're willing to break your vows? Really? Seriously."

"Tracey, please. If we're going to talk about this like adults, no sarcasm."

She swallowed, pausing for a moment to look away, then looking back at him.

Brian continued. "Since Lisette and I didn't do anything the first time I visited her apartment, I dropped my guard. I didn't even think she was interested in me like that. She sees a lot of guys—she's always going out with someone and meeting up with people she's seen on Tinder. I'm fifteen years older than her. I thought I could serve as her mentor."

"Mentor?"

"That's how we started talking so much. I gave her my personal phone number when we she told me she was thinking of applying to medical school."

"Med school? Come on."

"No, seriously. She told me she'd always dreamed of being a pediatrician and opening a clinic in a low-income neighborhood. She loves kids and she's got a good work ethic. When I told her about my experience at UMDNJ she had a lot of questions. I thought I could . . . I mean . . . I wanted to help her out."

"Why'd you lie to me then?" Tracey asked.

"When?"

"The night we drove to Walgreens, I asked you if there was anything else I should know. You told me no."

"By that time what she and I had done had been over. I didn't want to hurt my marriage by talking about it."

Tracey watched him search her face for a reaction. She didn't give him one.

Brian continued. "Look, there was no way I was going to destroy my family for something stupid, incredibly brief, and completely over."

"Oh." What else could she say to a husband who provided half-truths and pretended they weren't outright lies? He'd had no intention of telling Tracey about this. If not for Ruthie, she wouldn't have known a thing.

"I didn't want to hurt you," Brian said.

"Stop saying that! Stop insulting me!" Tracey's words dropped like ice cubes. "You had no business . . . "

She shut up. What was the point? Why preach about adultery to a man who'd been a born again Christian for nearly two decades? He knew better.

Brian nodded, opening and closing his hands toward her, as if to say, *Well, yes, but what can I do now?* He looked dejected, like he would do anything to escape the office, rewind the events of the winter, and travel to a different space and time.

Too late.

"I'm sorry," he said. "Well, she's gone now."

"Gone?"

"She resigned. She came in late, turned in her letter, gathered her things and left. I haven't heard from her since."

"And you probably won't again," Tracey mumbled.

"What did you say?"

Tracey refused to repeat herself. She sat stiff in the chair, her arms across her chest. Where were they going to go from here? She was glad she had more insight into how everything happened, but she didn't know what to do next. Sure, she envisioned a future with Brian in an intact, loving family. She was relieved her husband had the sense to end the affair quickly. But on the flip side, every cell in her body throbbed with anger.

Brian got up, moved away from his desk and stepped toward her, his arms open to embrace her. Tracey crossed her arms tighter and leaned away.

"Don't touch me." Her skin had turned cold and her stomach churned. She rubbed the goose bumps emerging on her arms.

He rubbed his hands over his face as he moved away.

She wiggled to try and relax her rigid shoulders. A headache was forming and the harsh fluorescent light in the room made it worse.

"I was wrong and I'm sorry and—" he started.

Tracey stopped him. "I know where you're going and don't even ask. You were sleeping with your nurse. Your nurse! You can't push us past this and go on like before!"

"I'm not trying to speed you past your feelings. I'm asking you for forgiveness because I need your forgiveness."

She couldn't say yes or no at that moment. She stood up and leaned forward. Her stomach did a double-flip, then a half-twist, and the slightly-off kilter feeling propelled the contents of her belly out of her body and onto the floor in front of his desk with a wet splat.

He jumped. "Are you all right?"

Tracey pulled back from the mess and sat back down, grateful she'd managed to keep liquid bitterness from splashing onto her pants and boots. "No. I'm not."

Brian backed away, walked over to the door and gestured toward the hall. There was a rest room outside.

"I guess I'll get something to clean up this mess." He mumbled.

She rested her back on the chair and closed her eyes, concentrating on keeping the sick feeling down. "I guess you will."

CHAPTER
Eleven

TWO DAYS past the affair revelation and Tracey's mother called to talk. Still weary and in a foul mood, Tracey didn't want to chat with anybody, but what could she do? She'd been in the middle of preparing Sunday dinner when Tyler answered the ringing phone. She frowned as she slowly took the receiver from him and said hello.

Alice got right to the point. "You ever find out what my son-in-law was up to?"

"Yes, I did." She cleared her throat and grabbed a knife to trim the fat off the slab of steak on the cutting board in front of her. "And he did. And it's over now."

"Are you all staying together?" her mother asked.

"For now we are," Tracey said.

Alice offered her wisdom. "Then you two are staying together for good. If you were really upset, you would have left him five minutes after you found out the truth. So, he got a little off-course, but he didn't get away with it. That should be enough to scare him away from ever trying it again."

Tracey rolled her eyes, said goodbye, and hung up fast. She turned her attention back to cooking. Her wounds, as raw and bloody as the meat beneath her hands, were too fresh for her to think about what staying together with Brian meant.

To say Tracey was angry was an understatement. Her own rage actually frightened her. Anger bubbled up like hot lava inside of her at odd moments of each day, forcing her to sit down and gain control of her emotions. She endured it by staying silent. Other than venting during her phone calls to Monica, Tracey simply refused to talk about the affair with anyone. Not her other friends. Not Charla or anyone else in her family. Not her life group. Certainly not Pastor Downes. He would probably ask about those assigned exercises, and Tracey didn't have the heart to tell him there was no way she could force herself to dig that boring marriage fixer-upper book out of the bottom of her purse.

Every time she bent her knees to pray, she couldn't find the right words to offer up for her and Brian. She'd ask for peace, grace, and mercy, but that's all she could manage.

It turned out there were way too many questions to ask him at one time. And each time he answered two of them, three or four more flooded her mind. She'd ask whenever he was alone with her, which was not often because they slept in different rooms now. The room they used for a house office contained a small black convertible futon. Brian slept there, night after night. It became a pattern neither Tracey nor Brian was willing to break. When Brianna noticed and asked about it, Tracey quickly changed the subject. If Tyler noticed, he didn't say anything. The cold iciness of the abrupt end of February gave way to the long blustery weeks of March. Snow and ice melted away from the streets, but the chill in the air remained. Brian and Tracey lived together. And apart.

One night Tracey showed up in the office after the kids were in bed and sleeping and after Brian had taken a shower and changed for bed. She stood awkwardly next to the small black futon.

"What was the sex like?" Tracey asked.

"Physical," Brian said.

"What's that supposed to mean?"

"Honey, I don't want to dish out explicit descriptions to you. It was a connection that happened three times. I can tell you what we did wasn't anything out of the ordinary."

"Talking about it bothers you?"

"Yes." He stood up from the futon and sat down in front of the computer, reaching over to click on the monitor. "And dwelling on it bothers me even more."

Tracey still had questions. Was Lisette more flexible? More exciting? Did she satisfy him in ways Tracey could not? Then there was the safety aspect of her husband's escapades.

"Did you use protection with her?" Tracey asked.

Brian nodded. Tracey read his body language. The rigid set of his bare shoulders. His back positioned straight in the chair. He didn't want to talk anymore.

She left.

Days and nights passed like that. Tracey asked different questions. Brian would answer using as few words as possible.

March dragged on. Brianna's dance recital came and went. So did basketball games for Tyler. They were still a family. Ever since the big reveal, Brian worked and came home every evening right on time unless an emergency didn't permit it. He was still apologetic. Every Friday evening, he brought her a fresh bouquet of flowers and placed them on her nightstand. But in the house, they saw each other and didn't see each other. They spoke to each other, never really saying anything. She didn't say anything about forgiving him. He didn't ask. He looked tired and forlorn most evenings. Tracey still cooked his meals and served him. Did his laundry, picked up his dry cleaning, and had his car serviced. A glorified housekeeper. No personal connection at all. It was like they were standing across a cold, icy lake, looking at each other from different shores, wondering who was going to care enough to jump in and swim across so they could be together again.

BY LATE MARCH Tracey decided it was time to stop moping around the house. Sure, she and her husband were barely speaking but the rest of her life didn't have to be on hiatus. So one blustery Saturday morning she called Monica and drove out to pick her up so they could go walking down by the Art Museum.

Out of the car and onto the sidewalk, Monica moved more briskly than Tracey. Sweat beads dotted Tracey's forehead and she wiped them away with the back of her hand. No talking from either of them for the first twenty minutes. Monica barely broke a sweat by race walking—typical for a woman who worked out regularly. Tracey looked at her, pumping her arms to her side, her head raised high and her feet moving steadily, hitting the pavement so evenly it was like she was marching to a beat.

"You want to slow up a little bit?" Tracey puffed, reaching down to pull the drawstring waist of her pants tighter.

Monica smiled and walked even faster. "There are pregnant women at my gym who run twenty miles a week. What's your excuse?"

Tracey pushed her white Nikes to hit the pavement even faster. She struggled to keep up with Monica's pace. "You're getting on my nerves!"

Monica grinned, nodded, and took a sip from her water bottle. "Keep up. We're in training now anyway."

"Training?"

"Yes. The Sickle Cell Walk-a-Thon is in the Fall and you and I are going to walk it and finish at the same time. If you start walking now, you'll be able to walk it fast. We're going to walk this for Mark," Monica said.

Mark Bonner was Monica's baby brother. He died four years back of complications from Sickle Cell disease shortly before his thirtieth birthday.

"I'm good with walking it. But can I walk it slowly?" Tracey puffed.

"Nope. You are going to walk fast," Monica said, still pumping her arms hard.

They were two miles away from where they started when Monica slowed down. They'd reached an area with a bench under a red sugar maple tree. Monica gestured toward it and Tracey nodded gratefully.

"You were trying to kill me back there!" Tracey groaned.

"No way!" Monica shook her head. "I wasn't going fast enough, and we were only walking. When is the last time you went to the gym?"

"The year after Brianna was born. After I lost the baby weight I never went back."

Monica made a face. "Every woman needs a daily exercise program. Even if all you do is walk for forty-five minutes a day. You need to get your heart rate up every day."

Tracey looked out over the withered yellow grass. Right in front of where they sat, two black squirrels played, chasing each other back and forth. She had to admit, the fresh air hitting her lungs felt great. And the squirrels made her smile. She was out with a friend. She was alive. She had a family. How was it possible to feel thankful and free and scared and confused all at the same time?

Tracey sniffed. "Brian gets on me all the time about having a daily workout. Or, I should say, when he talked to me regularly, he would tell me." She shrugged. "Guess it is what it is."

"It is what it is?"

Tracey took a sip of water. She turned the bottle over and over in her hands. A clear bottle with hot pink writing on it that said SturdyGirlCycling. "I can't stop reading blogs and articles about adultery. I read sometimes an affair happens once and it's over, but then sometimes it happens on and off through the whole relationship."

"It's hard to trust men sometimes."

"You're telling me!" Tracey agreed.

"Being single isn't the worst thing in the world. At least when I close my door at the end of a night no one's coming through it later to hand me a basket of lies," Monica said.

Monica didn't lack attention from men. She received phone calls from men on the regular, and often went out to restaurants, plays, concerts and museums. She even flew down to South Beach once, when a Cuban man she met during a conference sent her some tickets to fly down and visit him one summer weekend. She always told Tracey she enjoyed the dates. But they never amounted to much more than a collection of dates. Often, Monica would find the man wasn't interesting enough for her to consider as more than a friend. She said it kept her out of trouble. And it certainly kept her away from the realm of broken hearts and bitter tears.

Tracey chuckled. "I married for better or for worse. Single is not an option."

"Cheating isn't a deal breaker for you?" Monica asked.

Tracey gazed out over the grass. No more squirrels at play. "I always thought it would be, but there's so much to consider. The kids. The time we've invested in our relationship and our home. We're a family."

"I see," Monica said. "At least you didn't tear him to shreds. If it were me, I don't know. I'd have packed his things and thrown him out the house."

Throw him out. Divorce. All those thoughts had crossed Tracey's mind a million times, but there was no point in putting him out now. He'd stopped the affair by himself, repented, and apologized. Putting him out would tear apart their family, and she'd only be doing it out of anger, not because she didn't love him or want to understand him. Still. Tracey doubted her husband's desire for Lisette disappeared overnight. Brian liked Lisette's motivation and passion for life. Passion. Just thinking about it stirred up the hot lava feeling in Tracey's chest. She pushed herself up from the bench.

"Let's walk, Monica." Tracey grabbed Monica's arm and tugged her to her feet. "It's better if we walk."

They picked up the pace, moving from a slow stroll into a race-walk. Tracey looked at the pathway curving in front of them and quickly assessed she was not fit enough to continue the way Monica could.

"We're going uphill now?" Tracey asked.

Monica had already quickened her pace and pulled away from Tracey. "Absolutely. That's the only way to get there."

"Get where?" Tracey muttered, moving her feet faster. "And why does it have to be uphill? Are uphill battles a way of life?"

Couldn't life be simpler? Or could she at least grow more prepared for the challenges ahead of her, like she was while she walked? The two moved uphill, putting one foot in front of the other. Tracey forced herself up the steep incline her bestie climbed with fury. Why keep going?

She answered herself five minutes later when she reached the top of the hill. Because when you stop, you're dead. The climb gave Tracey an epiphany. She caught up with Monica and stopped her for a second.

Tracey puffed. "Charla told me about this place in Westchester, where uh . . . there's classes . . . stuff for women. She said it spiced up her marriage." Tracey took a few seconds to catch her breath. "We need to get the ball rolling again. Someone has to—it might as well be me."

"And you think this place can help you?"

"I don't know. It's something new. It can't hurt."

Monica smirked. "Let me guess, I have to come along?"

"What else is a bestie for?"

CHAPTER
Twelve

THE ROMANCE PLACE. A simple neon sign perched above the door stated the name and ensured no one mistook it for an office building. Heavy, dark glass doors and tinted windows kept the inside a secret from prying eyes. When Charla pulled open the door and ushered Tracey and Monica inside, the sweet aroma of vanilla, strawberries, and honey floated through the air so rich Tracey yearned to nibble on it. And the music. Gentle strings. Distant bell chimes. Water rushing. The music enveloped Tracey like a warm cashmere blanket. Instant relaxation.

Tracey and Monica traipsed in behind Charla, whose hair was now a short, chic cap of platinum-colored curls. She led them down a wide hallway. Wrought iron wall sconces held flickering faux candles that provided enough light to keep the women from bumping into each other. Tracey stopped when she reached a carpeted staircase. A huge store stood on one side, right before the staircase started.

Tracey rushed over and looked into the store. "Char, what's in there? It's beautiful. Is that a fireplace burning on the side wall?"

"That's the Love Shop," Charla said. She stopped a few paces behind Tracey. "We'll go in there later."

"Forget the fireplace. What's a mahogany sleigh bed doing in the middle of the floor?" Monica peered over Tracey's head.

"That bed is for sale. But it's been for sale for as long as I've been coming here," Charla said.

"Oh I know! We get to see live demonstrations, huh Charla?" Tracey teased.

Charla linked arms with Tracey and guided her away from the glass doors. "What kind of a freak do you think I am? It's just a sales gimmick. When you touch the sheets and pillows on it and feel how soft they are you'll probably buy some."

"This looks like something out of 1001 Arabian Nights. I love the smell," Monica mused.

"The candles. I buy some each time I come here," Charla said.

They climbed to the top of the stairs where Charla led them down another hall before opening a heavy wooden door. Tracey stepped inside and took a look around. She'd expected a dark room. A stage. Maybe couches or something. Instead she stared at a large dance studio. Overhead fluorescent lights. Hardwood floors. Mirrored walls. Two straight-back wooden chairs propped against one wall. In a corner sat a large wicker basket filled with fabric, scarves, and several different colored feathered boas. Another corner held a pile of plush pillows. Tracey twirled around staring at everything. Nope. No poles.

Women of various ages and races milled around toward the back of the room, hanging their bags and coats on hooks and changing their shoes. Talking. Laughing. Tracey's eyes widened when she realized she saw only three women who looked to be in their twenties. The rest appeared to be in their mid-thirties and mid-forties. Some looked to even be in their fifties. Maybe they were attempting to get their groove back, too?

Charla tapped Tracey on the shoulder, knocking her out of her thoughts. "Did you bring your heels?"

"Yeah." Tracey unzipped her shoulder bag and pulled out a pair of tall black high-heeled shoes. "If I have trouble dancing in them, do I have to keep them on?"

"No. If you feel uncomfortable take them off."

"Oh my goodness." Tracey dropped her heels on the floor and turned Charla around so she could see Monica.

Monica had already changed into a pair of silver open-toed sky-high stilettos. The shoes and her height made her look like a super-sized runway model.

"Dang. Skyscrapers and everythang girl." Charla stared down at the silver shoes.

"All you need is some lingerie and fake wings on your back and you could be an angel in the VS Fashion Show!" Tracey said.

Monica pivoted, walked, and then pivoted again. "Don't hate me because I'm beautiful, darlings. Tracey, you better get up on those heels and learn you something you can take home."

Charla held on to Tracey as she slipped on her heels. "She's gonna to do just that. Here come our teachers."

Charla had told Tracey the teachers would instruct them on erotic movement and dance. So Tracey figured the instructors would be young, lovely, long-limbed, lithe women capable of moving their bodies with seductive grace. She smiled when across the floor walked a pale, petite, steel-haired, middle-aged woman wearing black yoga gear. The woman beamed as she took long strides to the center of the room, then greeted the class.

"Hello everyone! I'm Meredith. Glad you could make it to this afternoon's class." She peered around the room. "I see we have some new people here and a few 'returners'." Meredith pointed enthusiastically and Charla and two other women waved back. "Excellent. First-timers, I hope you enjoy yourselves, and returners—I think you'll find a few new things to incorporate into your routine. This is my assistant, Susie, and she'll be helping me demonstrate the moves."

A young redhead with freckles grinned at the crowd. She wore a tight white fitted t-shirt, black leggings and red platform heels so high Tracey hoped she wouldn't fall and break her neck.

Meredith raised her hand. "Let me see the hands of all the wives here. Oh, and all the moms."

Tracey thrust her arm in the air in concert with seven other women.

"We're so glad you're here. Welcome." Meredith nodded at them. "One of the reasons we put together these classes was to help you get reacquainted with your intimate self. Yes, you're a wife or a mother or both, but you are also a woman. In the hustle and bustle of your daily life, you're probably used to tending to everyone else and shoving yourself aside, right? For example, all my mommies, how many of you have danced this week?"

No one raised their hand.

"Any of you taken a long hot bubble bath this week? With fragrant candles placed around the bathroom?"

Again, no hands.

"Anyone undressed seductively for your partner and allowed them to enjoy seeing your body move before exploring it?"

Crickets.

"Well then, this is the right place for you. This class is all about learning movements that will help you appreciate your bodies and connect with your intimate self. This is not a pole dance or strip dance class. It is a movement class, and many of the moves will teach you how to get out of your clothes in a more seductive manner," Meredith pronounced.

Tracey rubbed her hands together and looked down at the floor. She adored making love with Brian, but she'd never danced naked for him, not even on their honeymoon. Sliding out of her clothes as a way to entice him? Never. Their sex life was enjoyable and warm, but she'd never thought to stage any sort of show, not even when the frequency of their sex started to dwindle. No candles or baths. And definitely no erotic movement involving stripping, chairs, fuzzy fabric, or feather boas. Maybe if she had been doing that, the door would not have been cracked open for Lisette to entice Brian? Oh, whatever. Just concentrate on learning new moves, Tracey thought.

"Ladies, before you leave here today you will have created

your own movement routine step by step." Meredith moved over to Susie and put her hands on Susie's shoulders. "Susie here is going to put on some music and show you a sample routine. Everyone, take a seat. Relax, listen to the music, and have a look."

Tracey eased down on the floor and pushed her back up against the mirrored wall. She leaned over toward Charla and whispered. "She's not going to be naked at the end of this, is she?"

"I keep telling you this is not a freak show. Just watch."

"This is like the routine you do for Ricky?"

"Sweetie, I've got many routines."

Tracey gave Charla a playful shove. "You make me sick."

Susie dimmed the lights and fiddled with buttons on the stereo system. She lit three candles and placed them on the shelf next to the stereo. Then she moved to the center of the room. The music started. Luke James. "Make Love to Me." Mild and slow. The class watched carefully as Susie listened to the music for a few beats. Then she began to sway. Slow. She rolled her hips to the music, and then moved the rest of her body into the act. By the time she sank slowly to the floor and slithered across it, it looked like she melded with the song, illustrating each note with her body movements. She used her arms, her legs, her hips. In the dance, Susie moved from a standing position, to the floor, to a chair, and to the mirrored wall behind her. By the time the song ended, she was seated in a chair, beckoning to an imaginary lover with a come-hither gesture.

The class clapped when Meredith brought the lights back up.

"Thank you Susie," Meredith beamed as Susie put the props back and clicked off the stereo. "Now everything Susie demonstrated was a different move. She strung all the basic moves together and performed them in different places."

Seductive, sexy movements. Tracey could do that. Nothing in the routine required her to be a contortionist.

"Okay, now we're going to get right into it. Everyone come

on out to the floor and find a spot. We're going to work on the very first move. Your walk." Meredith said.

Tracey jumped to her feet. She was the first one out on the floor, standing right behind Meredith. Charla and Monica rolled their eyes, but she didn't care. Something inside of her yearned to learn something new. To move. To dance. To have something she could show off with when she decided to use it. It sure would surprise Brian. She missed making love with him, and even though she wasn't sure when that would happen again, she felt warm inside thinking about it. If he was going to be surprised, she'd have to reconnect with him at some point. Some time when her anger and frustration subsided. But she wouldn't worry about it now.

Susie changed the music on the stereo. This time the sweet voice of Sade filled the studio. Tracey followed Meredith's instructions on how to execute the sexy walk in time to the music, and how to add sexy arms with the walk. When the music changed to Luther Vandross and Tracey started rolling her hips back and forth in time to the music, she felt like a pro—a seductive, fun-loving, hip-swaying, hair-shaking pro. By the time she slithered across the floor on her knees and turned over on her back she was really into it. She caught a glimpse of herself in the mirror. Sweaty. Serious. T-shirt moist and sticking to her chest and shoulders. Her face flushed with color. Brown body moving in curves. Arms and fingers inviting someone to play— to come into her world. She felt sexy again, for the first time in a very long time. Something Brian would want to see. Yep. Probably what he needed to see.

"WHERE IS EVERYBODY?" Tracey called out when she sauntered in the house that evening.

"I'm in here." Brian answered from the family room.

She went to the family room and saw Brian sprawled across

the couch with a throw pillow clutched against his chest, watching basketball. "March madness?"

Brian yawned. "Yeah. It's that time again."

"Kids?"

"I put Brianna in her room. Tyler went to hang out at Jonathan's house. He'll be back by ten."

"Oh." Tracey put her purse down on the couch table and unzipped her jacket. "Why'd you send her to bed so early?"

"She whined and complained too much about not having pizza tonight. I gave her a few minutes to get herself together, and when she looked like she was going to throw a tantrum, I sent her upstairs for fifteen minutes. I went to check on her when her time was up and she was fast asleep."

Tracey chuckled. "Sounds like our favorite kindergartener." She pulled off her leather jacket, took off her gloves, and unwrapped the soft pink pashmina from around her neck. She stood looking down at her husband as he stared at the TV and watched a couple of college boys rush for the ball.

"You eat?" She asked.

He shifted on the couch. "I heated up some leftover lasagna and made us some salad. I tried to wait for you but I didn't know you were going to be out past eight."

Tracey rubbed her neck. Shifted her weight from foot to foot. "No, that's fine. I'm not hungry, anyway."

Brian turned from his game and gave her a deep look. "Eat a little something. You've been out all day. Bring your plate in here and hang out with me."

"Sure." Why fuss about it? The t-shirt sticking to her back reminded her she'd missed him. He'd been on her mind as she'd danced that afternoon. Eating dinner with him on the couch wasn't much, but it was a start.

Brian had sat up, scooted over, and made room for Tracey at the end of the couch by the time she came back with her plate and a glass of ice water. She put her drink down on the side table, balanced her plate on her lap, and settled in. He must have cleaned up the family room because there weren't any games, puzzle books, PlayStation controllers, dolls or other mess scattered around, and no dust on the tables or specks of dirt on the floor. He knew she liked the rooms to be picked up in the evening time. She appreciated it.

On the TV, the college hoops crowd screamed, each side trying to motivate its team to trump the other one. If she were there, she'd be jumping and screaming, dropping popcorn on the floor and acting wild. When they were newly married they used to attend at least three Sixers games each season. Used to.

"Still a Sixers fan?" She asked after swallowing a mouthful of tomato and pasta.

"I have to be, I grew up here and those are my boys."

"You're better than me. I turned to Miami Heat last year."

"Traitor."

"Yeah, well, I want my team to win for a change."

"I like rooting for the underdog. They can still pull through."

She sipped some water and cleared her throat. "Don't count on it."

He laughed. She smiled. They kept watching the game while she finished her food.

College boys ran up and down the court while the sounds of the ecstatic crowd rose and fell with every one of their attempts to steal, shoot, or pass the ball. But they kept going. No matter how many fouls were called or baskets were missed. No matter how many times a player tried for the ball and ended up sweaty and sprawled on his backside on the floor, he'd get back up. Shake off the sweat and pain and embarrassment. Jump back in game. The athlete was part of a team, and the team had one goal. Win the game.

Tracey needed to shower and shampoo. Her hair had unraveled out of a messy bun. Her t-shirt stuck to her back and her yoga pants clung to her butt and thighs. But she didn't care. This was the closest she'd been to Brian for a month. She guessed she'd finally cooled off because being next to him didn't give her those hot lava jolts of anger anymore.

She rested her head on his shoulder. Closed her eyes and breathed in deep as she snaked her arms around his waist. "I'm tired."

Brian put a hand on her arm. Rubbed it gently. Then moved it upwards. Rubbed her shoulder. "I'm tired too."

Tracey kept her head on his shoulder. He smelled yummy. Like soap and cologne. Boy, it felt good to hold him again. To be close again made her feel precious. She nudged him. "So where are we going?"

"Upstairs when the game is over."

"No," she said with her eyes still closed. Her arms tight around his waist. "Where are *we* going?"

He sighed as he let his head drop down. He kissed the top of her forehead. "You're holding the answer to that."

Betrayal? Ugh. It made her want to destroy everything in sight, stopping short of her own marriage. But that was over now. Today his strong arms held her as they sat in the family room he had cleaned up. Eating lasagna she'd cooked. In their warm house. Back to normal. Almost as if nothing had ever happened. This was Tracey's husband. And though someone had tried, no one had taken him. He wasn't leaving. He apologized. He'd asked for forgiveness. And he was here now, with his arms around her, squeezing her, making her feel safe and protected.

Safe plus protected equaled love.

Tracey raised her head and looked Brian in the eye. "We've got a nice bedroom."

"I know."

"We're supposed to stay in it at night. Together."

"I know." Brian scooted closer to Tracey.

"So," Tracey said. "Let's start there. We'll work the rest out in time."

He squeezed her even tighter. "Sounds good to me."

CHAPTER
Thirteen

"MOM! SOMEBODY'S AT THE DOOR!" Tyler called from the downstairs hallway.

Tracey's fingers were covered with hair moisturizer. She sat with an irritated Brianna between her knees as she combed, parted, and moisturized the girl's hair. "Well did you answer it? Who is it?"

"Yeah. A lady says she's looking for Brian," he yelled back.

Tracey's spine stiffened. Drops of moisturizer flew off the tips of her fingers and landed on her dark jeans, her shoes, and the wooden floor. Uh-uh. It couldn't be . . .

"Ty, what's she look like?"

"Latina lady with long wavy hair."

Tracey pushed Brianna out from between her legs and ignoring the girl's yelp, told her to stay put. She tossed the comb and brush on Brianna's play table, ran out of the room, flew down the stairs—barely righting herself when she tripped and slid across the front hallway—and shoved her son aside at the front door.

No mistake. There stood Lisette, in neat black pants, a lime-colored button down shirt and a short black jacket. She appeared business-like but Tracey seriously doubted the woman had secured a job with Publishers Clearinghouse and had come there to deliver a million dollar check.

Keep your head, Tracey. *Keep. Your. Head.*

Tracey backed away from the door, partially closing it while she used her other hand to snatch Tyler to the side.

"Mom! You almost fell. Who is that?"

Tracey spoke fast. "She worked with Brian at the practice for a few months. I need to speak to her. Do me a favor and go upstairs and keep Brianna from coming down here!"

"Nah. Uh uh. I'm not leaving!" Tyler said.

"Ty, please. This is something I have to deal with."

"Forget it, mom. You don't look right . . . and . . . you want me to get rid of her? Because I can get rid of her!"

Listen to this kid sticking up for her. But now was not the time. She squeezed his hand then gave him a push toward the staircase.

"No, please do what I say. Upstairs. Distract your sister and make sure she doesn't come walking down those steps." That was all Tracey needed—to get Tyler and Brianna mixed up in some mess she'd been praying was over for good.

Tyler grumbled and grasped the doorknob. Tracey grabbed his arm, pursed her lips and stared into his eyes, telegraphing her serious attitude to her son. She breathed a sigh of relief as he let go of the door and turned toward the stairs. As soon as she heard his feet on the staircase she opened the front door.

Lisette stood there on the porch. Quiet. Pretty face made up to perfection. Perfect full lips. Small cold eyes.

Tracey took a quick deep breath. Blew it out. Then she pushed open the screen door and stepped out onto the front porch so fast Lisette had to double step backwards to avoid being whacked by the door handle. "Can I help you?" Tracey said.

Lisette recovered fast. "Yes. I'm here to talk to Brian. Is he here?"

"No, he's not." The nerve of this woman. Like Tracey would tell her anything, even if he was in the house.

"When will he be back?"

Tracey snorted, "That is none of your business."

"Well I have some business of my own, and I need to speak to him."

"That's too bad." Tracey shook her head. She let her words drop slow enough to sink in deep. "Not. Gonna. Happen."

"You've got some nice porch furniture out here. May I have a seat and wait for him?" Lisette asked.

"May I call the police and have you arrested for trespassing?"

"You don't want to talk to the police, unless you want to tell them how you nearly drove over me."

"That's a matter of opinion. I was in my car, on a public street, I turned the corner and you happened to be stepping off the curb. If I really wanted to run you over, the car would have been on the sidewalk where you were walking."

Lisette held up a hand. "Look, I need to speak with him."

"About what?" Tracey asked.

"A personal matter."

Tracey rolled her eyes. "I see. Well, he has office hours. You're well acquainted with where and how long he works."

"I need to talk to him privately."

"Gee, that's too bad." Tracey said as she willed herself avoid dwelling on what the private matter could be. That hot lava feeling darting up her spine and traveling through her chest told her it was best to stay as neutral as possible. The kids were in the house. This was not the time to do something she'd have to repent about later. Peace had to rule the moment. The Lord would provide peace in her heart if she needed it. Now was definitely the time to start asking.

"He blocked my numbers from his phones. Now I need to see him in person."

So Brian *had* been serious about cutting off all contact. Serious enough to provoke this lady into going somewhere she knew she shouldn't. Either that or the chick was a garden variety nutcase. Wait a minute. Was Tracey dealing with a crazy person? That purse Lisette held definitely looked big enough to hold a gun. Husband's jilted lover shoots wife? No way! Lord, protect this woman because if she made one fast move toward her purse Tracey refused to be held accountable for beating her senseless.

Tracey pulled herself up to her full height, crossed her arms beneath her chest, and spoke in a loud, clear voice. "Lisette, you have two options. You can either tell me what you need to speak to my husband about and leave, or you can just leave. Either way, you are leaving."

The front screen door swung open fast behind them. Tracey whipped around but not quickly enough to stop Tyler from taking one long step out onto the porch and standing right behind her. One look at his steeled face and clenched fists told Tracey he was not going to step off the wooden boards of that porch until Lisette left. He had to have heard at least the last few moments of their conversation.

Tracey turned back around and fixed her eyes on Lisette. Her voice ratcheted down to a more subdued tone. "It's time for you to go."

Lisette's eyes bounced from Tracey to Tyler and back to Tracey. Tracey watched her clutch her bag tighter to her side. Whatever nerve Lisette had come there with appeared to have drained out of her now pale face.

"Tell Brian he will hear from me," Lisette said.

Tyler stood so close behind Tracey she could feel his shoulder right behind her neck and she could smell his Axe body spray. Neither one said anything as they watched Lisette leave the porch, walk down the stairs and travel along the sidewalk. She walked at a leisurely pace, past the trees and the driveway, down the lane and finally out of Tracey and Tyler's line of sight.

"Where's her car?" Tyler asked.

"She doesn't drive. Apparently that makes it easy for her to ask people for rides," Tracey sighed. She turned and looked up at him. "We should talk about what just happened here."

Tyler shook his head and twisted his lips in disgust. "No. I figured it out. Brian?"

Tracey placed a hand on Tyler's arm. "Let's talk."

He shook her hand from his body. "I'm going out. Brianna's upstairs with her coloring books."

Before Tracey could utter another word, Tyler vanished, his legs carrying him back into the house in a split second. She didn't have to follow him to know he was gathering up his keys, his jacket, his phone and iPod before leaving out the back door. She'd wait a half hour before calling him. If Tyler did figure out Lisette had been intimate with his stepfather, it was best to just let him walk out and blow off some steam.

Tracey didn't have that luxury. Hair washing and braiding was a regular Saturday chore. She had to carry herself back upstairs and go cornrow a head full of soft brown tangled hair on a five year-old who had no idea why her mother had run out of the room like a nut. Tracey formulated her plan as she reached the stairs. Get to the girl's room. Put a Disney DVD in the player. Gather up the oil, comb and brush again. Settle Brianna in her little wooden chair again. Tell her the truth. Mommy had to go handle some mess. *A big mess.* Yes. *Did it matter who made the mess?* No. *Was someone being punished for it?* Yes.

All of them.

"THAT'S the chick Brian's smashing, huh?" Tyler smirked.

"Watch your mouth! We don't talk like that in this house, or for that matter, anywhere," Tracey chided.

He shrugged. "Sorry."

Tyler had returned to the house two hours after he'd left. He'd trudged back upstairs and passed Brianna's room on the way to his bedroom, a blur in a gray hoodie with white head-phone cords dangling from his ears.

Five minutes later she had knocked on his door, pushed her way inside and sat on the edge of his messy bed. Tyler was parked at his computer desk, his open laptop in front of him. At sixteen he knew more about technology than she did, and came and went from the house more responsibly than she'd seen any other teenager. He had a good amount of freedom, mostly because he'd never caused them any problems. Tracey hated that he knew about the affair, but what could she do? He'd walked right into it when he answered the front door.

Tracey leaned back on her elbows and stared at the quilted pattern on his wrinkled blue comforter. "Her name is Lisette. She was a nurse over at Germantown Family."

Tyler turned to face her. "I'm right then? He cheated on you with her?"

Tracey sighed. "Yes, but don't start acting a fool in the house just because you know."

"Yeah . . . okay. He's still with her? That's why she came here?"

"No. It's over now. I don't know why she stopped by here to see him."

"You don't want to find out?"

She shrugged. "If it's important enough for me to know, the Lord will reveal it. I've already spent way too much time and energy thinking about her and Brian."

Tyler's clenched jaw and rigid posture transmitted his disapproval. "Mom? You're not gonna divorce him?"

Tracey sat up and focused her eyes directly on Tyler's. She had to make her words as clear as glass. "We're a family. We're going to stay a family. It's over. We are moving on. God is still in control here."

He nodded slowly, but Tracey watched questions dance behind his eyelids. His jaws? Still tight. Tracey averted her eyes and stared out the window. She had no more words and even the ones she'd just spoken sounded contrite and corny, so she concentrated on staring at the silky blue sky and the rays of sunshine. Clues of springtime arrived more each day. The icy winter had faded away. Thinking of it gave her the hope that came with knowing time moved on no matter what.

How in the world could she expect a teenager to understand that?

She turned her gaze back to Tyler. "You're disappointed in him?"

"Yeah . . . you know . . . "

She knew indeed. "Want to pray about it?"

"Now?"

"Yes," she stretched a hand out to him.

He shook his head and swiveled his body around in his chair until he faced his computer screen. "Maybe later."

Tracey took the hint. She rose to leave, for a split second considering putting her arms around him like she did when he was a skinny, big-eyed, crooked tooth kid in elementary school—when the issues he dealt with were no more serious than rips in his pants from playing too rough on the playground, forgotten lunch money, and always needing new sneakers. That was then. Now, in the chasm between childhood and adulthood, he had to make sense of the craziness that happens in the adult world—as confusing and sinful as it was.

She decided against hugging him but reached over to give his shoulder a squeeze.

He surprised her by reaching up to catch her hand. "I want to go live with Dad."

Tracey stopped. "Kyle?"

"Yeah."

"Wha?" Her breath disappeared, making it hard for her to speak. "When . . . ah . . . you've been thinking about this?"

Tyler stayed focused on his computer screen. "Me and Dad have been talking about it for months now."

"Really?"

"He hasn't said anything to you?"

"No."

"Call him."

"Is there something wrong with being here? This is your home." Tracey's heart thumped in her chest. She grasped the back of his chair.

"Call him."

Tracey nodded, and turned to leave. What more could she say? She'd always had custody of Tyler, but it wasn't like there'd been a big dispute about that to begin with. She'd left Syracuse pregnant, gave birth to a baby boy months later, and he'd been living with her ever since. True, Kyle was in Tyler's life and talked to him on the regular, but she'd had no idea her son toyed with the idea of leaving home before he went to college. Call Kyle? Absolutely. But she'd do it when she wasn't tempted to yell at him for not communicating with her first about bringing Tyler up to New York.

A knock vibrated Tyler's bedroom door as Tracey placed her hand on the doorknob. Before she could stop him, Brian poked his head inside.

"Hey Trace, do you know Brianna has all her Barbies stripped and lined up in the hallway? She told me she's getting ready to run a whirlpool bath for them. Did you tell her she could do that?"

"I'll get her." Tracey looked back at Tyler. He'd put his headphones on and turned his face toward his computer screen, but not fast enough for Tracey to miss the angry glare he shot at his stepfather.

Tracey pushed Brian backwards out of Tyler's room and shut the door firmly behind her.

"What's that about?"

"He needs a minute to himself right now, okay."

Tracey shoved her feelings into her gut, jumped into autopilot mode and started moving. She could feel Brian's eyes on her as she hustled toward the hall bathroom and the sound of running water.

"Trace, stop!"

Tracey, kneeling, briskly gathered up dolls from the floor, securing them in the crook of her arm. "Yes."

"What's going on?"

"Wait a second." She raced to the bathroom, dumped the dolls on the counter, told Brianna to let the water out of the tub and forbade her to turn on any jets before rushing back into the hallway and straight over to Brian.

She folded her arms across her chest. "Lisette paid us a visit today. She came and stood right there on the front porch."

"Oh," Brian said in a low voice. His face drooped. "I had no idea."

"I figured you didn't. But you're missing the worst part. Tyler answered the door."

"And?"

"And from the way she looked and how she asked for you, the kid is smart enough to put two and two together."

"So he knows . . ."

"Right."

"And he's . . . "

"Sitting there. He needs a minute to think so leave him there." Tracey stopped for a second. "He just told me he's been thinking about going to live with Kyle. I don't think that had anything to do with what he saw this morning, but he decided this was the right time to tell me."

Brian turned toward Tyler's room. "I'll go talk to him. Man to man."

"No, he needs a minute. Try to talk to him later. Look, find out why Lisette came to see you. I don't want to see her show up again."

"Okay, come on. I'll call her right now." He turned towards their bedroom.

Uh-uh. No. Tracey was sick to death of reacting to drama.

Especially when it was caused by a pretty lady who seemed intent on causing trouble and probably expected to get a call from Brian immediately.

"No. We'll call her when I'm good and ready." Tracey walked backwards toward the hall bathroom. "Right now I'm going to help clothe some naked dolls and possibly have a tea party afterwards."

CHAPTER
Fourteen

TRACEY SPEED-DIALED Kyle from her car. Might as well call him as she drove to the grocery store. She didn't feel like having one more heavy conversation in the house.

Kyle picked up after one ring. "Hi Tracey," he said, flatly.

"We need to talk," she said.

"I figured I'd hear from you soon. Hold on."

Tracey kept driving, waiting until she heard Kyle's voice again.

"I had to find the remote to turn my music down," he said.

"Where are you?"

"In the office trying to finish some work. I'm traveling all next week." Kyle owned a sports agency business. He was always on the go.

"Ty," Tracey paused for a second, then got to the point. "Uh . . . today he said something about living with you?"

"Yes, we talked about him coming up here."

She wheeled her car into the grocery store parking lot and scanned the crowded area for a place to park. "Not cool. You should have talked to me about that first."

"I didn't plan on talking about it. Tyler brought up the idea."

"Really?"

"Yes, he did. And I agree with him."

Tracey sighed. "I don't know why he started talking about living with you, but I am not about to stop on a dime and hand you over the keys to my baby boy like he's a Chrysler 300."

"Of course not. Now, if he was a Bentley," Kyle chuckled.

"No jokes." She pulled into a parking space. "Not today."

"Let me be serious then," Kyle said as the faint sound of Kem crooning in the background ceased. "I have the right to try to make life better for him, even if it means moving him up to New York."

Tracey was adamant. "He's my son. He's always been with me and until he goes to college, he stays with me."

"Sounds like you've got your mind made up, huh?"

"Sounds like I'm telling the truth."

"He's not happy. Conversation after conversation, every day after school he calls me. He told me he's an afterthought in your house and you and Brian barely speak to each other or to him. So talk to your boy about how he feels, because when he talks to me, I get the impression he'd rather be somewhere else."

Tracey's face grew hot as she gripped the steering wheel. "We have a few issues to work out."

"How many times this week did you wave Tyler to the side and tell him to watch his sister? When do you connect and talk to him? Oh, I know, when you have time left over after taking care of Brian, Brianna, and who knows what else."

If Kyle had snatched Tracey and pushed her headfirst into a scalding hot shower it couldn't have made her wince more than hearing those words. She mashed her tongue between her lips, holding back acid words threatening to spill out if she didn't control them.

"It's not really your business, but Brian and I are going through something right now."

"I know. Tyler called me an hour ago. You had a surprise visitor this morning?"

Tracey hadn't exactly told Tyler to keep his mouth shut about Lisette's appearance. "I'm not going talk about that right now," she said.

"You don't have to."

Tracey massaged her right temple with her fingertips. "How Ty feels? We'll talk to him. He doesn't need to pack up and move to New York because he's feeling shut out."

"That's not all of it, he's also been thinking of coming up here because . . . " Kyle paused. "Did Tyler tell you about my Pops?"

"Not recently."

"Pop's been on a few different medications and none seem to be working that well. He has his good days and bad days, but his quality of life is disappearing fast this year."

Kyle's father, Thaddeus Addison, had been diagnosed with Parkinson's disease ten years earlier. From what Tyler had told Tracey, she gathered the disease stayed under control with the help of medication. At the end of last summer, Tyler had come back to Pennsylvania with stories about how his grandfather's trembling grew so bad he sometimes had trouble feeding himself. When he retired years ago, the former lawyer and judge had plans with his wife, Celeste, to travel the world. That was before Parkinson's set in. Two years ago, Kyle sold his home in northern New Jersey and his parent's home on Long Island, combined the money from both home sales and bought a larger house in Long Island. That was where he and his parents lived now, and where Kyle had designed a private area for his parents with a special bathroom and a chair lift in case his father ever needed additional help. It was the most selfless thing Tracey had ever heard of Kyle doing.

"My Pop's challenges are getting worse," Kyle continued. "Years ago the doctors told my Mom the disease might not progress for decades. They must have told her that just to get her out of the office. All I know for sure is my father wants to spend more time with Tyler."

Tracey blinked at the rows of cars in the lot until they

confused her. Her appetite disintegrated. What was she planning to cook for dinner again? "I'm going to have to talk to Tyler some more."

"I'll be in Miami this coming week. Call you in a few days?"

"That's fine."

Tracey ended the call. Forget the grocery store. She'd order take. Her baby boy might leave the nest sooner than later but for a reason deeper than escaping the Jones home. A problematic former mistress still had to be handled. And Tracey hadn't checked on her own father in more than three days, even though she'd vowed to help him take better care of himself.

Leaning over a stove was the last thing she wanted to do.

Things were getting hot enough.

"TRACEY, did you order food? There's a delivery guy at the door," Brian called out.

Tracey yelled back from the bathroom. "Yes, I did. Can you get the food and let the kids eat, please?"

"Aren't you going to eat?"

"Not right now."

Tracey did her best thinking while sitting in the first floor bathroom. No one thought to look for her there. And even if they did, no one would barge in on her. She could sit there and pray long and hard. Clear her head. Figure things out.

She stood up from the floor and gazed at herself in the full length mirror behind the bathroom door. Dark circles had taken up residence under her eyes. Faded jeans hung loosely around her waist. She pulled her leather belt tight. Her white and maroon t-shirt sagged around her chest and shoulders and frayed around the bottom edge. She reached up and tugged off the black elastic band from her ponytail. *Get out of the bathroom and go deal with life, Tracey.*

Brian walked toward her as she stepped into the hallway.

"Eat something," he said. "If you don't want chow mein or sweet and sour chicken, I can make you something else."

The idea of swallowing anything made her want to gag. She reached out and tugged his hand. "Kids are chowing down?"

"Yeah."

"Then let's go make that call." She pointed to the upstairs.

"You sure?"

She nodded. They needed to get it over with.

Upstairs in their bedroom, she tucked her legs underneath her on the bed, and perched beside him as he dialed Lisette first on her cell phone. She didn't answer. Tracey watched as Brian dialed another number. She guessed it was Lisette's apartment. Tracey refused to dwell on the fact that he knew both numbers by heart.

Tracey listened as Brian said, "Lisette . . . I know . . ."

Tracey picked at her fingernails for a moment before she leaned over and grabbed an emery board from the top of her night stand to channel her energy into something constructive.

Brian stayed silent for what seemed like a long time before he spoke again. "I'm not agreeing to . . . no . . . no, you can tell me right now."

Tracey raised her hand in the air, waggled her newly filed fingernails then pointed to her face.

He wiped his forehead before switching the phone to the other hand. "Meet me? I can't." Quiet once again. "Um hmm . . . no . . . it won't be like that." Long pause. "That's the way it has to be. I can get you what you need, all right. You don't have to make threats." Pause. "I'll let you know."

He clicked the phone off.

"So?" Tracey asked.

"She wants a recommendation for a new job. She's applied for a position at one of the Children's Hospital network offices."

Tracey stifled a laugh. "A recommendation? You're kidding. She stood on our porch today for a recommendation?"

Brian shrugged. She studied his face. He looked weary, like

he was tired of surprises and wanted some rest for his soul. Join the club.

Tracey stopped filing her nails. "Are you going to let her list you as a reference?"

He shrugged again. "If it will stop her from showing up here and help her move on with her life."

"It sounds like an excuse to me so she can stay connected to you. But you know what? Let her go ahead and list you as one of her references and let that be the end of it. Has she asked Doug or Dan for personal recommendations?"

"No. She wants me as a reference. She wants me to meet with her to talk about it."

"Why doesn't that surprise me?" Tracey rolled her eyes. "I'm not accepting you going face to face to talk with her about jobs."

"I figured that." He paused. "But she said something about a case for sexual harassment. That she could make things difficult for me if I didn't do what she asked."

Tracey stared in Brian's face. Not a trace of a joke. He dropped his gaze to the floor, his face slack.

Tracey rubbed her face, smoothed her hair with her hands and breathed out slow. "This means . . . ?"

"I should meet with her and hear what she has to say. Let her know she has my approval to list me as a reference and I'll help out if anyone calls me. If I don't, there's no telling how far she'll go to get my attention."

Tracey snorted. "Unbelievable. Sexual harassment? I thought everything was mutual with you two?"

"She was my subordinate, and I had the advantage. If she hires a lawyer and drums up a case, it would be her word against mine about how it all started and if she says she felt pressured to do what I wanted—"

Tracey finished his statement: " . . . even if she didn't have much of a case, it would be enough to cause trouble and ruin your reputation as a professional."

"Yes." He nodded as he looked in her eyes. "I'm sorry. A thousand times. A thousand different ways," Brian said.

Tracey believed him. She studied his face. He looked every bit as stressed as she was. "I know."

"And did you really try to run her over with your Volvo?" He asked.

Tracey was so not in the mood to discuss that bit of history. "No. But I came close." She ran her hands through her hair again. "Look, I need a minute to myself. I'm going back downstairs."

"If you need to vent, go on and vent. You don't have to run and get on the phone with Monica, Charla, or your mother."

She cocked her head to the side. Amazing. After all these years he still didn't trust that when she said she needed a minute to herself, that's exactly what it was. No phone calls. And no talking unless it was to the Lord.

Tracey slid off the bed, and pulled her jeans higher up on her behind—they'd slipped down low again. "I need to go pray. Is that okay with you?"

She watched his eyes. They were squinted with hurt. She'd spoken the wrong words with the wrong attitude again. But why didn't he get it? Why was he so disconnected from her feelings? She stood in front of him now, starving but too ticked off to eat anything. Hair a hot mess. Shirt wrinkled. Weighed down. Everyone had needs. She had to keep on keeping on.

"So you know where I'm going and what I'll be doing." She stalked out of the room, giving herself a mental pat on the back as she successfully forced back the urge to throw in the words, "And maybe you should do the same."

Tracey marched back downstairs, made a pit stop in the family room to grab her Bible and purse, and headed down the hall to the tiny bathroom and shut the door. She dropped to the floor. Stone tile dug into her knees, but she didn't change her position. Head down. Muscles tight. Quiet. She clasped her hands. Kept her head bowed.

No words would come. Nothing.

She changed her position, taking her Bible down from the edge of the sink and sitting down hard on her butt to page through it. Page after page passed under her fingertips but frustration kept her from resting on a specific verse and meditating on it. She couldn't concentrate enough to read anything, not even a psalm. She pulled her purse over and rummaged through it. In the bottom was the marriage booklet Pastor Downes had given her. She hadn't bothered to do anything with it, so it rested stiff and new in her hands.

She flipped through the book for a minute before pitching it into the wastebasket next to the toilet. Stupid book! Who the heck was Dr. Frank Dockens, anyway? And where was the chapter on how to deal with beautiful fools who threaten to sue your spouse for sexual harassment?

On second thought, she should keep the book. Maybe she'd use it one day. She leaned over and reached into the wastebasket, fished the book out, and pushed it into the bottom of her purse again. Her purse? Stuffed full of papers, appointment cards, and who knew what else. Barely any room for anything. When she shoved in the booklet, a page from Alice's overdue Verizon phone bill popped up. As she slid the bill back in, a card for Pernell's neurologist stuck out the top.

Tracey sighed. This was not the time to let her marriage fall apart. Too many people were depending on both of them. She peeked at the cover of the booklet again, Pastor Downes's words resonating in her head:

Do you want your marriage to get better or worse?

Better of course. But this was not going to be as simple as forgive and move on. Not by a long shot. A week earlier she had allowed herself to hope. Felt a little joy about the possibility of forgiveness, healing, and fresh beginnings. Pushed herself to take a risk and learn how to dance for Brian. She'd seen herself as a woman in motion, capable of resilience and rebirth. It took one day of strange events to murder that vision.

If Brian played a sultry slow jam for her right now, it wouldn't matter.

She'd forgotten where she'd stashed those sky-high heels and she couldn't remember one single move.

CHAPTER
Fifteen

TRACEY HAD SUGGESTED to Brian that he meet Lisette in the Starbucks at Target on City Avenue. A busy, public place with a huge plate glass window looking right out onto the parking lot. No way would she let Brian go alone to meet up a woman he'd stopped an affair with, no matter what the circumstances. So he agreed to drive to Target that Thursday evening. Tracey would follow him, stay in the parking lot, and watch all their interactions from her car.

"Are you sure you're going to be okay seeing us talking?" Brian asked as he closed the back door and followed Tracey down the steps to the driveway.

She thought about that for a second as they traipsed to their cars.

"Let me put it this way," she yanked her car door open. "I'd rather see the two of you talking than not see you."

They headed out.

She'd shifted roles again. First she was the betrayed wife. Then the forgiving wife. Then the potential dancer. Now what? Wannabe spy?

By the time they approached Target, Tracey felt itchy, hot, and jumpy. She reached down and turned the heater off, right before turning into the parking lot. She positioned the car as close to the store as she could without illegally parking in a handicapped spot, turned off the ignition, and settled in to wait.

"Lord, if there is a pathway out of this nutty situation that leads to some peace in our relationship please show me where to find it. Thank you. Amen," she prayed.

A clear evening. Tracey could see right into the Starbucks, all the way to the counter where Brian stood ordering a coffee or tea or something. She craned her neck around and scanned the area. No Lisette so far. Brian walked over to one of the condiment tables and put something in his drink, turned and took a few strides over to a table pushed against the front window. Excellent. Now when Lisette came in, Tracey would be able to see the whole thing from beginning to end.

And if her marriage disintegrated, at least she could contemplate becoming a private investigator.

Tracey rubbed her eyes. When she opened them she felt a teeny electric shock shoot up from her gut. Good Lord! In two seconds Lisette had materialized out of nowhere and now she stood right next to the table where Brian sat. She wore a short black trench coat and dark jeans. Wonderful. At least she wasn't wearing a tight halter top and hot pants or something skanky. *Stop it, Tracey. Be still and watch.*

Tracey dared her eyes not to blink as Lisette sat down opposite Brian and started talking. From what Tracey could observe from the parking lot, all they did was chat—though it appeared Lisette led the conversation. She was a movement talker. She waved her hands in front of her face and gestured a lot as she yakked away. Brian sat rigid. Shoulders set. Face motionless. Mostly nodded and let Lisette talk. When he did move his lips, it was brief. Probably one word answers. It was the same thing he did with Tracey when he wanted to escape a conversation. Occasionally he would pick up his cup and take a few sips, but he didn't do much else.

Tracey couldn't remember ever watching a silent conversation between two people so intensely. Well, maybe once. She was seventeen and studying at the library after school. That time, she'd been the one sitting inside by the window. She had looked up from her geometry book for a moment and found herself staring at a couple standing on the sidewalk. Arguing. They had to have been in their early twenties. The man, broad and beefy, looked about a hundred pounds heavier than the thin pale brunette who stood in front of him. His arms were crossed tight across his chest. The thin woman stood with her arms akimbo, her mouth moving a mile a minute. The man said nothing. But he kept inching closer and closer to her. She talked. He moved. She talked. He moved. Finally, the man let his arms down, reared back and pushed the woman so hard she stumbled back and fell to the pavement. He said something to her as she lay there weeping and dejected, and then he stalked away.

Watching Brian and Lisette from her parked car was worse than seeing two strangers in a violent argument. But seeing them aroused the same feeling inside she'd had back then—a sickening awareness that she should not be watching, but unable to turn away.

Why *did* she need to watch, anyway? To make sure Brian didn't go waltzing off with her? To be certain they didn't hug or kiss? Tracey's phone buzzed, jolting her out of her thoughts. She didn't intend to talk unless it was someone important. She yanked it out of her coat pocket, checked the caller ID, then answered it.

"Hi Ma. What is it?"

"Is Brianna allowed to eat ice cream with chocolate syrup in your living room?"

"No. Tell her to stay in the kitchen until she's finished."

Tracey had brought Alice to the house earlier that day to watch Brianna while Brian and Tracey went out that evening. Ever since Tracey's talk with Kyle, she went out of her way to make sure she didn't rely on Tyler to watch his sister all the time. At least tonight he could enjoy his Friday with his friends.

"All right, I'll corral the little chick," her mother said. "Oh, and I need to ask you something when you get back."

"Sure thing. Ma, I've gotta go."

"Bye."

She clicked off, shoved the phone back in her pocket, and focused her attention back to the Starbucks window. This time she saw Lisette with her mouth shut and her eyes turned down, staring at the top of the table. Then Lisette looked at Brian as he leaned on the table with both elbows, shoulders still rigid. It looked like he was letting out more words than he'd uttered during the entire conversation. He pointed at Lisette, said something else, smacked the top of the table with his hand, and sat back in his chair.

Tracey guessed that was the end of the conversation when she saw Lisette get up, walk out of Starbucks, and make a beeline for the front door of Target. Her face was rigid as she pulled a phone out of her purse, pressed a button and started talking. She clicked off, clutched her phone in her hand and stood there. Half a minute later, a red Mustang whipped down the driveway and right up to where Lisette stood. She climbed in and the car sped away.

When Tracey looked over at Brian through the window, he sat there with his arms crossed, looking at nothing. Tracey was torn. Should she go in and see him? Pull out her phone and call him? What?

Nothing, it turned out. Brian grabbed his coat off the chair and walked out of the store. He moved so fast he was in his car and about to drive off before she could react.

Her eyes felt full of sand and the skin on her face tight. She probably hadn't blinked during the entire exchange. And now, seeing Brian back up and drive away fast, almost as if he'd forgotten she was watching, her backside felt welded to the seat and she lost the ability to turn the ignition key.

Two seconds later she came to her senses and turned the car on. "This better be good and over now," she muttered.

BACK AT THE HOUSE, Tracey faced her mother. "Brian's not here? Did he come through here at all?" Tracey stood unbuttoning her coat in the family room.

Alice reclined on the couch in the family room, with Brianna laying across her legs fighting sleep. They were watching *Garfield* on the large-screen TV.

"Nobody came through here 'cept Ty, and he's upstairs," Alice said. "How come you're back so soon? I thought y'all would be out till late. And how come you're here and he isn't?"

Tracey reached for her phone as she backed out of the room. "It's a long story. I'll be back in a minute."

Where in the world? What in the world? And why now, doggone it? Tracey paced back and forth in the dining room, her cell phone to her ear. Brian's phone rang seven times before he answered it.

"Brian, I'm home. Now where are you?" Her voice rose an octave. She had one hand placed on her hip, the other gripped the back of a dining room chair. She dug her nails into the fabric.

His voice sounded curt and grim. "I'm in Germantown driving around. I was thinking about stopping by Ricky's house for a minute."

"Everything's taken care of now right? You don't need to talk about anything else with her do you?"

"Right now I need to think. I need to blow off some steam."

"Steam?" Something had definitely changed. "Tell me right now what's wrong."

"That whole scene was wrong! Arguing in public! People standing around listening, and my wife spying through a window like some double-agent watching my every move."

"And?"

His voice elevated. "I'm getting pressure from you, pressure from her, and I'll be home later!"

Tracey pressed the phone closer to her face. Her fingers

closed tight around it. She willed herself to keep her voice low while talking through clenched teeth. "Why are you mad? You don't have the right to be upset about something you behaved your way into!"

"Stop telling me what I already know! Stay in the house. I'll be there *when I get there!*"

The phone clicked off.

Tracey stared at her phone in disbelief for a moment before she tossed it onto the dining room table and watched it slide to the middle and smack against the bottom of a cut glass bowl full of lemons and oranges. She peeled her jacket off and threw it over the top of a chair, and snatched her shoes off dropping them on the floor. Leaving everything there, she plodded back to the family room where she peeled fifty pounds of Brianna off of her mother's legs and gathered the girl into her arms. She sat on the couch and buried her nose into Brianna's braids, breathing in the soft scent of her hair oil. Brianna's tight corn rows had held up nicely over the week. At least Tracey had done something that had lasted.

"Whassamatter with y'all now?" Alice twisted around to look in Tracey's face.

"Don't ask," Tracey glanced sidelong at her mother. "And don't even think about lighting a cigarette in here."

Alice dropped the crushed pack of Virginia Slims and a red plastic lighter back into her purse. "Tracey, where's Brian?"

"I don't know!" Tracey automatically stroked Brianna's back and rocked her after the girl jerked. "I don't know."

"The side chick in the picture again?"

"I really, really do not want to talk about this right now, okay? Let me go lay Brianna down and I'll be back."

Tracey stood with Brianna in her arms and pressed her cheek against the girl's head. She wrapped her arms tight around Brianna's body, grateful to feel someone's warmth as she carried her down the hallway and up the stairs to her bedroom. She pushed four naked Barbies and two picture books out of the way before yanking down the covers and nestling Brianna inside her sheets.

Tracey sat for a moment looking at peaceful, sleeping Brianna. She adored watching her kids while they slept. They looked so serene. Tracey had loved only two men in her entire life and each one had given her a healthy child. She could at least thank God for that.

Brianna flopped over and started to snore. Tracey tiptoed out of the room and headed back downstairs.

When she reached the family room, she heard her phone buzzing from the dining room. Probably Brian. *Whatever.* She'd leave the phone right there. No more drama. Not tonight.

"Let's talk," Tracey said to her mom, sighing as she dropped down in her chair.

"Huh?" Her mother lay on the couch, flipping from channel to channel with the remote. She finally settled on *Top Chef* and let the remote drop to the floor.

"You said you had something to talk to me about," Tracey reminded Alice.

"I'm going to need your help I think," Alice said, her words flowing out like molasses.

Why all the mystery? Tracey shifted her weight and tucked her legs up underneath her. "Ma, it's okay. Go ahead."

"It's the house."

That's what Tracey figured. Alice probably needed a repair done or her washing machine replaced or something like that. "Got it. The house. What do you need done?"

"Nothing needs to be done to it. We're about to lose it," Alice confessed.

"Lose what?"

"The house."

Tracey put her feet back down on the floor, sat straight up and leaned toward Alice so she could hear better. "You're about to lose the house? Wait, Ma, you mean you got a foreclosure notice?"

Alice shrugged and nodded, reached into her purse, fished out an envelope and passed it to Tracey. Tracey pulled out the letter and speed read it. Lots of legal words. Default has occurred. Missed payments. Fees. May lead to foreclosure. But nothing noted that it was an official notice of foreclosure. This was a letter from the mortgage company.

"How did you get this letter?" Tracey probed.

"This is the third letter. It came in the mail."

"So no one delivered this officially, right? Did you have to sign for it?"

"No. I didn't have to sign for the other ones either."

Tracey decided to skip over the fact that this was the first time her mother had mentioned missing any mortgage payments. "How long have you and Jamal been having trouble making the mortgage?"

Alice shrugged again. "Since the late fall. I thought we'd be able to get it together and make up for what we missed but now there are fees and all our other bills have been so high. You know Jamal hasn't had a lot of clients."

Her brother needed to get up off his butt and either drum up some business or teach classes somewhere, but now wasn't the time to blurt that out to her mom who looked kind of embarrassed. Tracey walked over and sat next to her. She held the folded letter in her hand. This was bad, but it wasn't something she couldn't handle. And she'd had enough of being the moral police—telling people when, where, and how to manage their issues. Alice and Jamal's situation involved throwing money at the bank and making plans for the future. Compared to her current marriage woes with Brian, money problems were simple.

"I can help you out, but you both are going to have to make plans for how you're going to handle the future."

"Thank you." Alice nodded.

"You're welcome." Tracey was used to the lack of emotion. Alice wasn't a hugger or kisser, so she stayed silent and still.

Eyes forward, concentrating on *Top Chef* contestants running around a massive kitchen, cutting up trout.

They watched the rest of that *Top Chef* episode and two more. Tracey's eyes had started to droop when she heard someone open the back door and come inside. She bolted awake. She looked over at her mother, who had fallen asleep and was lightly snoring, her head resting on one of the couch pillows. Tracey slid off the couch, pulled her mother's legs up and over so she could lie down on the couch fully, and covered her with a light blanket. Then she meandered through the living room, past the dining room and into the kitchen.

No Brian. Where'd he go that fast?

She padded up the stairs and down the hall to their bedroom and pushed open the door.

He sat on the edge of the bed in the dark. If the curtains hadn't been open and the moonlight streaming in, Tracey wouldn't have been able to see him at all. She went over and stood close enough to smell him. She peered in his face. Nothing. She sat down next to him but didn't force a conversation.

Eventually he sighed and rubbed his face with his hands, sighed again, and finally asked, "What do you want me to say?"

"Whatever you want."

She watched him unbutton the top of his shirt, scratch his neck and his ears, and stop moving again.

"There's not going to be any issues with sexual harassment."

"No?"

"None. I'm positive."

"You agreed to recommend her for jobs?"

"Yes."

Tracey braced herself for the answer to her next question. "Is there anything else I should know about?"

His reply came quick. "No."

She didn't bother to ask anything else. What on earth for? He could have said yes, no, or maybe. It no longer mattered. Her level of trust in him had sunk so far beneath sea level she'd have to rent a submarine and shine a searchlight to find it.

CHAPTER
Sixteen

TRACEY SPENT the next two weeks tracking Brian.

She found nothing, even though this time she was unrestrained and unrepentant in her fact checking.

Each night she grabbed his phone and scrolled through it while he showered, but she never found any calls, texts, or new phone numbers in question. Out of desperation, Tracey called Ruthie twice. Ruthie told her Lisette hadn't been to the office as far as she knew, and Brian spent all his time with patients or in his office.

Other than the night of the Starbucks visit, he didn't seem to have any unaccounted for alone time. Germantown Family. Home. Church. Gym. Ricky's house. Tracey guessed she could relax.

Except for one thing.

Brian barely talked. He moved through the house like he was in a daze. Time passed and Tracey tested him.

One week she ordered takeout every night. Pizza. Chinese. Hoagies. Fried chicken and french fries. By Thursday Tracey expected Brian to pull her aside and give her a lecture admonishing her of the dangers of eating too much fast food and reminding her about their family commitment to good health and nutrition. But when Thursday evening came, Brian made a beeline right to the dining room where he sat down devoured every bit of the food she put in front of him.

No fussing. No lectures. And for the first time in three months, Tracey had nothing to bring up or discover about him. Still. The vibrations between them seemed off and distant. She could at least discuss that with him.

While they dressed for church Palm Sunday morning, Tracey stopped him. "Brian, what's going on with us? Seriously?"

He stood in front of the full length mirror, looping a yellow and navy blue striped tie around the collar of his shirt. "Nothing."

"I didn't cook a thing this week. You didn't notice?"

He shrugged as he pulled his Windsor knot tight. "Maybe I did. Maybe you were tired. You decide what we eat. Why should I complain?"

"It wouldn't have been a complaint. Just a discussion."

Her eyes tracked him as he crossed to the bed and picked up his navy blue suit jacket. He tugged at the buttons before putting it on. "Well I've had enough hard discussions to last me a while."

"Really?"

Brian pulled himself up to his full height and adjusted his shirt sleeves inside the suit jacket. He smoothed the lapels and checked the way his pants hung and the way his shirt was tucked in around his trim waist. Buttoned the jacket. Approved his look in the mirror. Then he turned back to her. "You ready?"

Tracey sat fully dressed in a yellow linen suit with matching heels. Her anniversary diamond earrings hung from her ears. Her makeup was done and her hair was flat-ironed to perfection. All she needed to do was put on her hat.

No fighting. No sins to confess and no forgiveness needed. Nothing to complain about.

But still no connection.

Tracey stood up and walked out of the bedroom door her

silent husband held open. How did it feel not to care anymore? Relaxing? Freeing?

Maybe she should try it.

A CLEAR BLUE sky and saffron sunshine rays brightened up the Monday morning, making it so much easier for Tracey to proceed with her plans. She stood in line in the Commerce Bank less than fifteen minutes after the bank opened. Wearing jeans, a white fitted t-shirt and Keds, her hair up in a ponytail, she must have looked younger than her years when she handed the teller a slip to make a withdrawal from a CD.

"Driver's license please," the young red-haired woman said, her eyes narrowing.

Tracey slipped her ID under the glass transom and waited.

The red-haired lady took the ID and scrutinized it, staring at the signature, before entering the account numbers into the computer in front of her. She clutched the ID and the slip in her hand.

"Just a moment."

"Certainly," Tracey acknowledged with a blank look on her face.

The redhead stepped back a few paces, walked over and tapped the shoulder of a larger blonde-haired woman wearing a grey suit. The blonde looked at the slip, then looked at the ID, then looked back over at Tracey.

Blonde lady stepped up to the window and addressed Tracey. "Did you really want to withdraw from your CD? Or from your regular savings?"

"From my CD."

The lady looked out over her wire frame glasses. "You'll have to pay a penalty for breaking the CD before the maturity date, based on the interest already paid on it this year."

"I know. That's fine."

Blonde lady typed information into the system and asked, "Would you like that in large or small bills?" The younger red-haired lady stood behind her, watching.

"Large bills, please," Tracey said.

After that, there was nothing further, other than the customary *have-a-nice-day* when the teller passed her the envelope holding the money. Tracey turned to leave, taking her sunglasses from the top of her head and pushing them onto her nose.

And in less than ten minutes, in the tan Fossil bag hanging from her shoulder, Tracey had $10,000 tucked in a white envelope. Her plan for the morning was to deposit $3,000 of it into Alice's bank account to help pay her mortgage company, and give $4,000 to Jamal so he could fix his car pronto and secure some more work. In the late afternoon she would take Brianna to visit Pernell over in North Philly.

The rest of the money? For Tracey.

Two words: Retail therapy.

Time for her to take a moment in the early afternoon and click her mind off while shopping. Stop thinking about Brian, Lisette, Tyler, Brianna, Alice, Pernell, Kyle, affairs, and all the other stuff jiggling around in her brain. Besides, she needed new clothes anyway. None of her clothing fit her well anymore, and she was tired of slopping around during the week in baggy jeans, shapeless t-shirts, and college and sorority sweatshirts that now hung on her frame like oversized paper bags—even if they were comfortable.

A twinge of guilt pierced her like a splinter as she drove away from the bank on her way to Overbrook. She hadn't bothered to talk to Brian about her mother's mortgage, Jamal's car situation, or her need for new clothes. *Who cared?* Not a mature or godly way to handle things. Siphoning money away from the jumbo CD where they kept emergency cash? Major marriage violation. Dishonest. Sneaky . . . even if she had good intentions for most of the money.

Tracey stepped on the gas, accelerating fast enough to push those bothersome thoughts out of her head. Why should she tell Brian?

He'd find out . . . eventually.

IT WAS incredible how much furniture Tracey's mother managed to cram into her small bedroom. King-sized bed. Two armoires. Two nightstands. A dresser. A couple of footstools. All of it heavy and dark, and blocking windows and closet doors in some way. Good quality, but too much of it. Some of this stuff could go into other rooms in the house. But Tracey wasn't there to do interior decorating.

She stood in the bedroom doorway and watched while Alice, wearing beige slippers and a zippered maroon housecoat, a brown towel thrown over her shoulder, rummaged through her dresser. Tracey had managed to catch her right before she started getting ready for the day.

"Ma, we're going to take care of the mortgage this morning, all right?"

"You know I have to send the money right away."

"Right. So get dressed and we'll go by your bank, do the deposit, get the certified check and be done with it in time to get you to work."

"You could have written me a check," Alice chided.

Tracey shook her head. "No. It would take like a week before your bank would clear my personal check. A cash deposit is better. And a certified bank check won't pose any problems with your mortgage company."

Alice straightened up, clothing draped over her arm. She looked at Tracey, her head cocked to the side. "Thanks."

Those words were as close to *I love you* as Alice would ever get. Tracey accepted the words gratefully.

"Where's Jamal?" Tracey questioned her mom.

"Upstairs. I'd be surprised if he's awake."

"Yeah, well, he'll wake up when I get up there." Tracey left the doorway and headed down the hall and up the stairs.

Tracey knocked on his bedroom door. No answer. She peeked inside. No Jamal.

"Jamal! Where are ya?"

"In here." Her brother's voice boomed out from the room on the opposite end of the hallway. Tracey tapped on the door then peaked her head inside.

"You're up?"

"Yeah. I don't lay around all day every day." Jamal lay on the bench in a black t-shirt, shorts and sneakers, doing chest press repetitions. Different sized weights littered the floor, along with a jump rope, several towels, and three different sized exercise balls.

Tracey stepped in and sat on the floor next to one of the exercise balls. "I hope you don't jump rope up here."

"Nah, I take it outside." He pushed the barbell up from his chest once more, rested it on the metal hooks, and sat up. "How come you up here so early? Something going on with Dad?"

"Not that I know of, but I'm going over check on him later after I pick up Brianna from school." Tracey looked up at him. "I stopped by to check on you and Ma and this mortgage issue."

He grimaced. "Yeah. We have to figure something out. My training hours aren't making it, and Mom's hours keep getting cut every month."

"Could you do more if your car was up and running?"

He grabbed a towel from the end of the bench and wiped sweat from his face. "Yeah."

"Well, I've got the money for you to get your Honda fixed, so can you get your car towed to a shop today?"

Jamal leaned up from the weight bench, grabbed a faded grey sweatshirt off the closet doorknob, and pulled it over his head. "No thanks, I don't need it."

"What are you talking about? You've still got your car. I saw it parked by the curb."

He shook his head. "It needs to be fixed, but I'm not taking money from you. Keep it. I'll figure something out."

"Jamal, you asked me to help you back in February."

"I know."

"So what's up?"

He gazed at her for a moment. "Ma told me you'd be helping us out with the back mortgage. I understand you stepping up to help her. She's our mother. But I don't need you saving me."

Tracey hadn't expected Jamal to reject the money offer. She glanced at him sitting on the weight bench. He'd cut off the cool and funky afro he'd been growing and his black hair was now in a short, sharp Caesar cut. Up in the morning? Refusing money? Looked like someone was changing.

"Are you sure? I mean, you can fix the car and then pay me back," Tracey offered.

"I don't wanna be on the hook to pay you back."

"So what are you going to do?"

"I still train clients. Plus, I'm thinking about finishing my degree, getting a teaching cert and becoming a gym teacher. In the meantime, I have my fitness certifications. I'll drum up some business at the gym. Because, as far as I'm concerned, with me being here, you shouldn't have to break out your checkbook."

She smiled and crossed her arms. "You've been making plans."

"I've always been making plans. Until I have a reason to move out, I'm here to help her. The mortgage thing?" He shrugged. "It was a tough winter."

"Tell me about it," she cleared her throat.

"Hey," Jamal gave a slight nod toward her. "What's up with you?"

"Huh?"

His voice softened. "You and Brian. Everything okay? Ma mentioned . . . "

Pin pricks needled her spine. "I don't want to talk about it," Tracey said, clearing her throat again. "I'm going to bug Ma to get a move on it because we have to hit the bank before she starts her shift. Then I'll spend ten extra minutes convincing her not to smoke in the car or bank."

Jamal chuckled as he tugged on gray sweat pants over his shorts. "Good luck."

"DAD!"

"Tracey, get out of our kitchen! You don't need to be fooling around in there," Pernell called from the living room.

She yelled back. "Your recycling bin, Dad. What's with all the Pepsi bottles?"

"'Cause that's what Pop-pop likes to drink!" Brianna called out.

"That's right, sugar, you tell your mama for me!" Pernell laughed.

Tracey stood in the middle of the kitchen floor of Pernell and Uncle Ray's row house in North Philly, surveying the landscape. It should be against the law to allow two sixty-something bachelors to live in the same house unless they had enough money for a housekeeper. In addition to the empty Pepsi bottles overflowing from the recycling bin onto the floor, a stack of cardboard pizza boxes leaned against the battered green trash can in the corner. The room smelled stale, but at least it didn't have the stench of rotting garbage.

She held her breath as she opened the refrigerator and peered inside. She didn't need to though. Nothing in it besides an open box of baking soda, ketchup, mustard, soy sauce bottles, and Pepsi and Mountain Dew. No milk, lean protein, fruit, or vegetables.

Tracey ambled back to the living room where Brianna grinned as her Pop-pop set up a small black card table so they could enjoy their favorite activity together: Pop-pop teaching Brianna how to play cards.

Tracey watched and waited as Brianna set up her own folding chair, climbed up on it and rolled up her sleeves. Their routine was always the same. Her dad would deal the cards and he would attempt to teach Brianna how to play: usually Uno, followed by several rounds of I Declare War. Then he would try to teach Brianna how to play Tonk. She usually giggled the whole time and never learned anything except that her grandfather loved her smile.

"Dad?"

"Yes, baby?" He snapped the rubber band off the deck of Uno cards and started shuffling.

"Soda and pizza? That all you're eating around here?"

He shrugged, dealt cards and winked at Brianna who wiggled in her seat, anxious to start their game. "You know we aren't hardly in here. I eat breakfast at the spot on the corner before I go in to work. And the cooks come into Ray's Place on the weekends, so I eat platters when I go there."

"I'm hoping those platters come with vegetables?"

"Oh, you know Towanda makes the collards so good they make you want to slap a homeless person."

"Ooh," Brianna giggled. "Pop-pop said you could slap a homeless person!"

"That's a figure of speech. You're not supposed to slap anyone!" Tracey raised an eyebrow at her smiling father.

"Baby, don't worry about me. I'm getting by. Once a week, Julia stops past and makes us some dinners for the week. It's not always this empty in here."

"Dad, your doctor recommended a balanced diet for you. Low cholesterol. More fruits, vegetables, and whole grains. Lean protein. Remember?"

Pernell nodded, laying down a Draw Four card and changing the color to blue. "I've got the information sheets in my room. I never seem to have the time to read it all."

"Dad, you're going to have to make the time."

He reached over and tickled Brianna, who had crossed her arms and made a face after he slapped a Draw Two on top of the pile.

"You like playing with your grand baby?" Tracey asked.

"I love it."

"You won't be able to play cards with her anymore if you have a stroke."

Pernell sat back in his chair, arms folded across his belly. Tracey watched him as he gazed at Brianna. She watched him take in the smooth brown twisted braids with navy blue barrettes on the ends. Deep set eyes and missing front tooth grin. He sighed and nodded.

Tracey felt for Pernell. She hadn't come over that evening to lecture him but to spend time and let him clown around with Brianna. Still, no way could she ignore what she saw in that kitchen. It made her stomach twist in knots to think breakfast for her father would be cold pizza and Pepsi out of a plastic tumbler.

She reached out and rubbed his shoulder. "You need a wife."

"I had one," He frowned as he leaned up to get back in the game. "I gave her all I had to give and it still wasn't enough to keep her away from the bottle. I'm not capable of loving anyone like that again in life." He winked at Brianna. "UNO!"

Why was love so draining?

Because there was no way to avoid becoming attached to an imperfect person, no way to provide them with everything they needed for success in life. But giving up on a marriage meant what? Living without love, without anyone to help balance a budget or pay a mortgage off before old age set in. Lonely nights. Dirty dishes.

Cold pizza washed down with Pepsi and no one around to care.

CHAPTER
Seventeen

"MOMMY, HURRY UP!" Brianna called.

Tracey scurried down the church hallway with her right hand gripping Brianna's hand and her left arm cradling her purse and Bible as Brianna rushed them toward the Rise Theatre.

"Girl, why are we running?" Tracey asked.

"There's a worship band this morning! We get to play the tambourines and shakers! I want a tambourine!" Brianna weaved her way around families and friends greeting each other in the main hall.

Tracey breathed a sigh of relief when they finally reached the theatre at the end of the corridor. Brianna bolted for the glass door to the theatre and ushered herself inside and down the stairs. Tracey shook her head as she signed the attendance sheet at the desk. Sunday school and children's worship had sure come a long way. When Tracey was little and made trips to church with Aunt Zee's family, children's church was a basement affair with rickety chairs and ditto sheets handed out by a church volunteer. Dry cookies at snack time and several choruses of "Jesus Loves Me" before praying and leaving. Brianna's worship experience at Rise? A full-fledged children's worship service in a small carpeted theatre with surround sound, flashing lights, and a contemporary Christian band. Twenty-something youth pastors and their assistants in jeans and Scripture-scrawled t-shirts ushered the under-fourteen crowd through praise and worship, testimony, prayer, giving, a Scripture lesson, and a message.

She'd finished signing in Brianna when Tyler tapped her on the shoulder. He'd been a few yards behind her the whole time.

"Same place as always?" Tracey asked him.

"Yeah. Meet you right outside the main sanctuary when we're done," Tyler said before turning and heading toward two male figures standing six feet away from him—his friends, Jonathan and Bryce.

"See you later." Tracey watched him walk away. In the past month they'd had two more discussions about his moving up to New York with Kyle, and he hadn't changed his mind. But anything could happen before he packed up and went away for the summer.

With Brianna signed in at children's church and Tyler sitting with his friends in the balcony, Tracey headed to the sanctuary. Her Bible dropped to the floor with a thud when she suddenly bumped hard against a solid muscled chest. The crash took her breath away.

"What the . . . " Tracey cha-cha stepped backwards, shook her head, blinked and found herself staring at Brian.

"Kids are all settled, right?" He stared down at her.

"Yes, but—"

"Then come on," Brian said firmly.

He reached down, scooped up her Bible in a flash, handed it back to her and grasped her hand, jerking it so hard she figured he meant business. Tracey's mouth dropped open but she couldn't find any words. Where did he come from? She'd left him at the house because he'd said he wanted to sleep in that morning. Now he popped up at Rise wearing wrinkled jeans and a polo shirt, pulling her behind him fast enough for her to understand something was wrong. Tracey dropped her head rather than meet the eyes of the people they zipped past. She had no choice but to dart along behind him, becoming more infuriated by the second.

"You're not going to service this morning," He growled, holding open the glass front door for her.

Really? Like he even needed to tell her. She'd figured it out already, considering the vice grip he had on her hand.

Outside Tracey quickly breathed in the dewy grass scent of the late May morning. She breathed out. She breathed in again. The oxygen flowing down to the pit of her stomach gave her the strength to snatch her hand away from him and double-step backwards so he had to turn toward her to grab her hand again. She caught his eye and fixed him with a fierce *if-you-grab-me-again-you'll-see-the-white-light* and *the-gates-of-heaven-today* look.

"Don't touch me!" She stumbled back again.

Fire in his eyes, he dropped his arms to his sides and stayed in one spot, shifting his weight from one foot to the other.

Stay calm and cool, Tracey. "You better give me a good reason why you dragged me out here!"

Brian's nostrils flared. Jaws tight. "A reason?"

She rubbed her arms through the sleeves of her white silk blouse. "Yes, a reason!"

"All right." He stepped in close enough to kiss her. "Ten thousand dollars missing from our bank account! Is that a good enough reason?"

Suddenly the damp May air seemed a lot less fresh and much more chilling. She backed away from him once more. Rubbed her manicured hands together. Bit her lip and tasted lip gloss. So he found out. Gee. Bizarre to be on the other side of the table of deception.

"Is this how you fight back, Tracey? Stealing from us?"

"I didn't steal anything. I was going to tell you!"

"When, huh? After you'd spent your way through all our savings?" He pointed at her. "I should have known. Look at you.

Where'd you get that skirt? And that silk shirt? And I didn't buy you those silver bracelets."

Two people passed Tracey and Brian as they stood at the top of the steps. Tracey shut her mouth and willed herself not to look in their faces. Her cheeks burned hot, her skin itched and her scalp prickled with heat.

Deep breath. Seven counts. Good girl. "Can we go and talk about this like adults?"

Brian was silent as he turned and stalked down the steps and into the parking lot. She followed a few yards behind him. Easy steps. Maintain enough distance. Far enough that if he decided he didn't want to remain civil, she had a split-second chance to run.

Brian opened the passenger side door of his car, let her drop inside, slammed it shut and race-walked to the driver's side.

He dropped into the driver's seat in a flash. "So what happened to the money?"

"Can you at least drive us out of here? Someplace where we can talk privately?"

Brian turned the key in the ignition, backed out of the parking spot, and drove out of the lot. Tracey kept her lips sealed to allow the angry energy to die down as he drove them away from the church. She rubbed at the goose bumps that refused to go away on her forearms. She should have brought her trench coat, or at least a pashmina to throw around her shoulders, but this was no time to think about that.

He stopped the car two blocks away, right next to a small children's park. Tracey jumped out and headed to a park bench.

Brian came and sat next to her. "Ten thousand dollars! I've seen the online bank records. And you're walking around the house each day like nothing's wrong!" He whistled. "Just tell me . . . I can handle it. Is there another man in the picture?"

"Are you nuts?" Tracey felt like punching him. She'd never been unfaithful to anyone in her life.

"Then what?"

Tracey sighed. "Ma was months behind on her mortgage and probably a few weeks away from getting an official foreclosure notice. Jamal couldn't get out and work as much as he needed because his car was busted. I figured I'd help him to get his transmission fixed."

"All of that couldn't have been ten thousand dollars! Ma's house mortgage isn't that high, and I know how much transmissions run. And you never said a word to me about your family needing anything! What did you do with the rest?"

"I spent it," Tracey mumbled.

"What?"

She turned and stared him in the eye. "I spent it."

Brian shook his head. "On what?"

"Myself."

He kept shaking his head. "I knew it."

She might as well go on and hang out all her dirty laundry. "Okay, I should have told you Ma needed help with her house. And Jamal didn't take the money from me because he didn't want to owe us. I kept his portion. Before Monday was over, I bought myself some things at the King of Prussia Mall."

Silence. Tracey stared at Brian for a moment, then turned to gaze at the brightly colored playground equipment. His silence was more unnerving than if he'd been screaming. Tracey's insides felt glued together and she suddenly hated the silk blouse and black pencil skirt ensemble she wore.

Tracey glanced down at the silver bangles on her wrist. Delicate and pretty. They matched the silver triple ring necklace she had on. She'd bought all of it at the Kenneth Cole store. But the shopping spree which netted her the jewelry, four pairs of Michael Kors skinny jeans, four Ralph Lauren blouses, a Louis Vuitton clutch, two White House Black Market skirts, and three pairs of shoes – only made her feel guilty. Five days later she returned everything to the stores she'd visited, keeping only a few dress items for church and the jewelry, which the store would not accept as a return. She'd stashed the cash back in the white bank envelope and buried it under her worn copy of *The Purpose Driven Life* inside her nightstand. She'd planned to deposit it to the CD account but hadn't gotten around to it yet.

He stared her up and down with disgust in his eyes, then he looked away. "You don't love me," he said.

Now where was this coming from? "Of course I love you. I'm always here for you."

"No, you're not," he said. "I'm your security blanket. I give you a comfortable lifestyle so you can take care of things for the kids. For the house. For your mom and dad. For yourself."

"Brian!"

"No." He cleared his throat and his voice came back stronger. "I love what I do. I love to help people. I work hard day in and day out doing that. But I come home to zero affection or attention. You walk around the house like a robot. And Tyler? He passes in the hallway like a zombie, barely speaking to me. My baby girl is in her room when I leave, asleep when I get home, and dancing and playing with her friends on Saturday afternoon. We're at church on Sundays. Who's there for me, Trace? Who?"

Tracey's mouth flew open to mention his cold demeanor for the last month, but closed her lips before the words could escape. Arguing back and forth competing about who exhibited the worst behavior wouldn't help. She reached out to touch his shoulder. He brushed her hand away.

"This morning I checked the accounts to see how we're doing. Money is flowing out like water! Bills for the house. Shopping. Private camps for the summer. Tuition for private school."

"Kyle pays Tyler's tuition."

"I know, but I cover all his extra fees and uniforms. And tuition for Brianna? Why? What kindergartener needs to go to private school? Now you're paying for housing for your mother and brother and having shopping sprees on the fly? Seriously, do I exist just to bankroll your lifestyle? And if that's all I'm here for, why did you force me to tell you about what I did with Lisette? Especially since I knew I was wrong and I ended it myself."

Oh no, he didn't throw Lisette's name in her face! Tracey burned to make a nasty comment and send it zinging right back at him. How dare he bring Lisette up? *Never mind. Let it go.* Tracey's eyelids throbbed as his words resonated in her head. He sure was making a big stink about money, but he still hadn't talked with her about what happened that night at the Starbucks in Target. It seemed like he might never mention it.

Tracey objected. "After Brianna was born you and I agreed it would be best if I stayed home until Brianna entered middle school. I worked when we met and I've never had a problem working so if this is about me not spending money and getting a job..."

She stopped talking. *Do you want your marriage to get better or worse? Warm partnership or cold pizza in the mornings?*

Once again, they teetered on the edge of their relationship. Any words they spoke would be moving pawns in a chess game.

Make the wrong move . . . too many losses.

Make the right move . . . be a champion.

Sure, Brian was behaving like a victim, but if she called him on it what would that do except push them further apart? She heard the words loud and clear in her head. *I am the Lord your God who teaches you what is best for you, who directs you in the way you should go.*

The best way out? Follow God's commands. Be humble. Be repentant.

"Pray with me? Please." She leaned over and touched his hands. "Lord, in Jesus name, forgive me for taking family money without discussing it. Forgive me for the attention I didn't give my husband. Forgive me for my rebelliousness. I turn to you and submit to you for I know you will guide me to do what is right. Amen."

Tracey opened her eyes. Brian was looking right at her, astonishment in his eyes.

"I returned everything except two outfits for church and the jewelry because the store wouldn't accept the return. And you know about Ma's mortgage. The rest of the money is in our bedroom and it's going back to the bank tomorrow. Forgive me. I'm sorry." She squeezed his hands.

"I forgive you," he said.

A long pause hovered between them before she asked, "What do you want, really?"

He spoke slow. "I want my wife back. And I need all this craziness to stop right now. I'm so sorry about what I did and for the fallout afterward. If I could take it back, I would!"

Tracey looked down at her lap. She hadn't appreciated the cold shoulder she'd received after his meeting with Lisette, but she needed to let that go for now. Make a decision and stick by it. *Better or worse. Partnership or cold pizza.*

"Maybe we can go somewhere. Do something nice for a change," she said.

Brian let out a soft chuckle. "That would be good."

"Ma wouldn't mind hanging out with her grands. Where do you want to go?"

He placed his hand over hers. "Surprise me."

CHAPTER
Eighteen

PLUSH.

Tracey took four steps into the suite and let the door swing shut softly behind her. She glanced around, grasping the key card tight in her palm. Not too big. Not too small. A window view of the whole city. She craned her head around and peeked in the next room. King-sized bed with huge pillows. Soft colors. Nice. The Ritz Carlton.

The perfect place to rekindle romance.

Or set the stage for a devastating separation?

Who knew at this point?

Tracey let her bags rest on the carpet, reached her arms out, stretched and smiled. After Brian told her to surprise him, she didn't waste time trying to come up with ideas. That would have been amateurish. She'd gone home after church, changed her clothes then pulled out the big guns.

She'd called Charla and the guru of all things romantic had delivered wonderfully. One phone call to her had netted Tracey information about every one of the Ritz Carlton room specials. She'd picked the Bed & Breakfast package, called the hotel and made the reservations, and quickly dialed Charla back.

"Go on and drop that hairdresser act, sweetie. You need to write a book. How do you know about all these places?"

"Ricky and I make a game out of it. Each month we come up with something new. Each person tries to top the other person. Five years of that adds up."

"Write that book. And what am I taking with me? See-through nightie? Candles? What?"

"Use your imagination," Charla had advised.

Thank God for her sister-in-law. The suite was beautiful. Tracey paced around the carpet for a minute, and then walked into the bedroom and let herself fall onto the bed. Soothing. Her muscles were grateful. The room smelled fresh and inviting. Just what they needed. A change of environment. Something different from their everyday grind.

After a few moments of letting herself float on the cloud that was cleverly disguised as a bed, she stood up and walked back to where she'd dropped her bags. She dug her phone out of her purse, sat on the couch and called Brian. He answered after one ring.

"Hey Tracey."

"Hey, yourself. I'm here."

"Are you ready to tell me where 'here' is?" He teased.

All during the week, each time she'd tried to tell him where they were going that weekend, he'd rushed out of the room, telling her he didn't want to know. At first, she thought he was being cold, keeping his mind focused on other things, but he joked about it with her every day that week. That started to excite her. By the time he'd left the house that Saturday, he didn't know where he was headed that evening. They'd made a deal that she'd have to call him and tell him where to meet her.

"Ritz Carlton. Rittenhouse Square."

"Classy!"

"I know. We have a suite."

"What's the room number?"

"Come find out. Go to the front desk. Identify yourself and ask for Mrs. Jones. They'll tell you where I am."

"It's like that?"

"No, it's more than that. Much more." Tracey clicked off the call.

Ooh! Now that felt good. Like back when they were newly-weds. Under the right circumstances, he could still make her insides feel like hot melted marshmallows. She couldn't deny it —she missed being intimate with him. Sure, they'd been sleeping in the same bed for weeks now but they didn't make love because she'd told him she needed more time to get over the affair. Well, she still wasn't over it completely, but she did want to enjoy her husband again. And why shouldn't she? Brian was *her* husband.

Time to get ready. Let's see. Dinner. When should they go eat? Hmm. She wouldn't worry about it. They could decide together once he arrived and relaxed with her for a while.

Music. The day before Tracey rooted through the CD orga-nizers in the family room and collected all of Brian's Motown CDs, lugged them upstairs to the office then loaded her iPod with slow songs. "Distant Lover," "Quiet Storm," "I Want You," "Ooh Baby Baby," "You Make Me So Very Happy," "Since I Lost My Baby," "Baby I Need Your Loving," "I Call Your Name," "Rocket Love," "All This Love," and "If This World Were Mine." Brian loved Motown. It was all his parents played when he was a kid and he couldn't get enough. She'd have added "Neither One of Us Wants to be the First to Say Goodbye" to the playlist, but that was too darn painful considering all they'd been through in the last few months. She also left off "Let's Get It On," a song so obvious it was cheesy. She set up the mini-speakers on the nightstand, attached the iPod to it, dialed to the playlist, clicked play and adjusted the sound. Perfect.

Ambiance. The room already smelled pleasant, but candle-light would be pretty. She envisioned them holding each other, flickering light surrounding them. So she placed six lavender vanilla pillars on brass holders to catch the wax.

Dancing for Brian? She'd practiced a little during the week so she'd brought along her heels. If the moment was right, she'd do a small routine and see how he liked it.

Clean up. It was just after five in the afternoon. Brian would likely arrive at the hotel in less than an hour, and she still needed to shower. She ran her fingers through her hair. Clean. Still smooth from when Charla had flat ironed it a few days earlier. The shower steam would mess it up, but she didn't care. What was the point of protecting it? If things went well for them her hair would get messy anyway. She left her shower cap in her overnight bag, stripped off her clothes and headed to the bathroom.

While she adjusted the water temperature she heard Marvin Gaye's voice singing away in the background. Distant. So many ways to be distant and not all of them had to do with geography. There she was in a hotel suite trying to reconnect with someone she saw every single day. He was the one who hurt her to begin with, but now she was the one buzzing around a hotel room, lighting candles, playing music for him? She sighed and shook off the negative thought. She had to get past it immediately. Romance and resentment? Not good bedfellows. She wrapped a towel around her torso and left the bathroom long enough to crank up the volume on the music and grab more vanilla candles to burn in the bathroom as she showered.

SKIN SLICK AND SOAPY. Water, warm and steamy. Tracey kept her eyes shut and listened to the music. Smokey was singing now, his voice like a feathery caress. Quiet Storm. Tension melted away, sliding in a mass from her neck, down her shoulders, over her back and down the drain. She pushed every-thing off her mind as she washed and rinsed her skin. The affair.

Family troubles. Tyler's decision. Brian's attitude. The money thing. She envisioned all of it flowing down, down, down. Dissolved into the mass of shea butter scented bubbles floating around her feet. She tilted her face up towards the spray and let the water droplets dance against her face. Massaging. Then she stepped back, squeezed liquid soap into her wet hands, lathered her body all over and started again. Troubles gone away. All that was left was the warmth. A wet cocoon shielding her from her own memories.

"Lovely," a man's voice purred.

She opened her eyes and gasped, startled. She'd been so into her shower she hadn't heard Brian come in.

"When did you . . . "

"You look absolutely beautiful." His voice was deep. Low. Sounded like he was seeing her for the very first time. He stood with his face peeking inside the ghost-white shower curtain. Not moving, just looking at her, wide-eyed. She stood still and nude and met his gaze. Butterflies turned cartwheels inside her belly.

"Thank you," she smiled.

"You've lost some weight. You looked great before. But now you look so smooth."

She looked down at her feet. Water and white bubbles swirled around her toes. The weight loss was from stress. But telling him so would have broken the mood.

"I'm finished. I'll get out so you can come in." She moved to the back of the shower and pulled at the curtain from the other side.

"No." The mesmerized look remained in his eyes. "Stay there. Don't move."

He was gone in a flash, then back to the bathroom, a stripped down brown and smooth muscled version, stepping into the shower spray and letting water splash down and around him. She reached back and grabbed a fresh washcloth from the bar, handing it to him with the bottle of shea butter soap. Then she stepped back and watched him do the same thing she'd just done. Listen to music and clean up. The song had changed and now Brian sung along with The Four Tops, "I Believe In You and Me." Reminiscing probably. That was their song, the song had been playing on his car stereo when he proposed to her. He hadn't had a ring with him. Only a promise of one as he'd taken her hand, traced circles around her ring finger and blurted out, "Marry me?" His voice sounded as good as it did that day. Tracey couldn't sing a single note, but she wanted to join him in song and be a part of his melody. She put her hands on his back, slid her fingers down and washed off the rivulets of soap. Moved closer and wrapped her arms around his strong body, slick with clean water. He broke the embrace. Turned and kissed her. Took her breath away. His eyes were closed. She shut hers and let her body mesh with his.

Melodic.

TRACEY HELD Brian's hand tight as they lay together between the sheets, warmed by each other's body heat. The candles still let off their light but the room was darkened as sunset faded into night.

She felt so light she would have floated off the bed if not for the weight of his body as her legs intertwined with his. The music continued to play. This time it was DeBarge serenading them with "All This Love."

"This is really nice. The room smells great and I love the music," Brian said, his voice smooth.

"Thanks, I thought you would."

"You took care of everything."

"I know."

He let go of her hand and reached down to start caressing her hips. "Seems like you always take care of everything."

"Well, I try . . . "

"You do a great job. I appreciate it."

"You're welcome," Tracey whispered. Two words of response was all she allowed herself to say. If she said anything else, flames of resentment would rise up inside her and kick her out of the dreamy feeling they'd managed to create together tonight. A week earlier he had called her a robot. That hurt. Lisette probably hadn't been a robot during their time together.

"Trace?"

"Umm hmm."

"What's the matter?"

"Nothing. What makes you think something's wrong?"

"You're digging your toenails into my ankles."

She pulled her feet back.

He kissed her on the forehead. His lips lingered there for a moment, making her warm. "Tell me?"

She sighed. "You called me a robot."

"Huh?"

"Last week when we had that argument. You said I walk around the house like a robot."

"I actually used the word robot?"

"Brian, you were right there with me."

He held her tighter. "I'm not a woman. I don't remember every word I've said. If I called you a robot and it hurt you, I'm so sorry baby."

"I take care of business around our house. I cook. I clean. I budget. I organize. I drive the kids where they need to go. I make sure everyone has everything they need. I'm no robot, I just get all the thankless jobs done," Tracey said. "You know I could have gone back to working in marketing after I had Brianna. I liked it and I was good at it. We both decided it would be better for me to support everyone by being available at home."

Now they laid there as stiff as cadavers. Tracey dropped her head back on the pillow. Why couldn't she have kept her mouth shut, on the one night that whole year they'd been blessed enough to step out of their regular roles and routines and come together like they should? It had felt phenomenal earlier that evening in the shower, and then in the bed together. So good to know her desire was still there and Brian still had the power to make her heart beat fast. The last thing she wanted to do was complain about being a housewife.

Brian caught her hands and trapped them in his. "Wanna trade places?"

"Quit playing," Tracey said.

"I'm serious. You want to do something different. I'm listening to you. You want to go back to work?"

"I think about it sometimes, but, no." She nestled deeper in the sheets. "I'd still have to be available for all the kids' school and activities and home chores and everything. A job on top of it would make me more tired."

"Then what do you want?"

She had no clue. In the past few months all she'd prayed for was peace and reconciliation in their marriage. Now it looked like they were at a place to start over again. She hadn't thought of asking for much else. One thing at a time.

Tracey moved her head closer to Brian's. "I'm getting what I want right now."

"Intimacy?"

"Exactly."

The music changed again. Brenda Holloway sang, "You Make Me So Very Happy." The room grew darker. They listened to the whole song together without talking.

"How're things going with you?"

He shrugged. "You really want to know?"

"Yes," she answered, meaning it.

"I'm frustrated. School was much harder than my day-to-day right now." He dropped her hands and rolled over on his side, pulling her arms around his body so she lay tight against his back. "I'm not making a difference. Not like I thought I would," he snorted. "I can't get to know any of my patients better because I only get ten minutes with each one before I move on to the next one. Then the insurance work gets worse every year. I'm spending four hours in health care paperwork for every hour I spend actually treating patients."

"Your evenings are getting longer."

"That's where all my time is going. It's ridiculous. I'd be of better use if I was a missionary doctor in Africa. At least then I'd be hands on, getting in there and helping a community in a way that makes an impact. I pushed through school and residency to get to this? Spend a few moments with a patient, recommend them to a specialist or change their medication, then move on? Who am I helping?"

"You're helping more than you know. Want to teach me how to do what you do?

He laughed and pulled her arm tighter around his torso. "If having a different career would give me a chance to sing regularly, or teach more wellness classes, or get in a basketball game with my buddies more often, I'd do it."

The only light left in the room was the candlelight, and a few of those were fading. The music stopped. Tracey looked over at the nightstand and realized she hadn't set the playlist to repeat. When she tried to roll over to turn it back on, Brian pulled her back to him, face to face.

"Stay close to me." He kissed her lips.

"But the music?"

"Forget about it. Stay with me." He squeezed her even tighter. "I don't want us to grow apart again. Do you hear me?"

"I hear you." She kissed him, then looked in his eyes. "But I've got something for you to see."

"What is it?"

Tracey smiled as she pulled away. "I need to turn some lights on. These moves involve high heels."

CHAPTER

Nineteen

"MOM, someone's at the door for you!" Tyler called out.

Tracey sat on Brianna's bedroom floor, teaching Brianna's friend Jayda to play *Memory*.

"Don't leave, Mom!" Brianna said as Tracey jumped up.

"I'll be right back, I promise," Tracey said, rushing out of the room. She rounded the door, flew down the hall, then stopped. Wait a minute. No. Uh-uh. She would not run down the stairs or slide across the front hallway again no matter who might be at the front door.

When she reached the downstairs hallway, she passed Tyler ambling back toward the kitchen, cell phone in his hand, texting as he walked. Cool. He wasn't concerned about who was standing on the porch. A good sign.

Tracey opened the door and stepped out on the porch. A tanned woman smiled and extended her hand. She wore a navy blue polo shirt, khaki pants and brown loafers.

"Mrs. Jones?"

"Yes."

"Hello, I'm Rose Esper, from The Clean Team. How are you today?

Tracey raised an eyebrow. "Good?"

"Ma'am, your husband told us this would be a good time to visit and take a look around the house for an estimate. May I come in?"

"My husband? Did you say estimate?"

"Yes ma'am." Rose glanced down at a white notecard on her clipboard. "Four bedrooms, two bathrooms upstairs. Kitchen, half-bath, dining and two living areas on the first floor. I'm here to take a look at your room sizes. The estimate will be based on that. Oh, and he also said you would decide on frequency."

"Frequency?"

"Yes ma'am, how often you'd like the team to come clean your house. Twice a week, once a week, once a month? However you'd like to customize the visits, we can accommodate you."

Brian? No way! Yes, way! She could kiss him for this.

Tracey grinned as she opened the door. "Please come on in. Can I get you a cup of coffee before you take a look around?"

"No, but thanks for the offer."

"All right, I'll show you the upstairs then."

Tracey led Rose to the second floor where the woman took notes on the size of the hallway and the main bathroom before poking her head into Brianna's room.

"This is my daughter Brianna and her friend Jayda. Say hello, girls."

"Hello!" the girls chorused and grinned.

Brianna was wide-eyed. "Why are you looking in my room?"

Rose winked. "Oh, I'm taking a look at the furniture and shelves and windows and floor space. My team members are coming to clean here each week."

"Really?" Brianna squeaked.

"Ooh, you're getting a maid?" Jayda's eyes followed Rose as she walked across the floor.

Tracey corrected her. "Not a maid. A cleaning service comes to clean the rooms."

"How is that not a maid?" Jayda scrunched up her face.

"A maid would be here every day for cleaning, laundry,

putting away items, organizing our clutter. A cleaning team won't do all that. They'll come in and clean things like the floors, bathrooms, and furniture, then leave after a few hours."

"Oh." Brianna stood up. "Can we come with you while you look at the other rooms?"

Tracey glanced over at Rose. "Do you mind if the girls watch?"

"Of course not. Come on," Rose said.

Brianna and Jayda, all grins and giggles, clasped hands and skipped out of the room behind Rose and Tracey. Little girls always seemed to be full of dance, movement and wonder about the smallest things. And little girl energy was contagious. With the girls giggling and whispering behind her, Tracey walked with a bounce as she led Rose from room to room and answered questions about things that were cleaned each week, problem areas and such.

Downstairs, Tracey led the small parade from the hall to the living room, family room, and dining room. They ended up in the kitchen where they ran into Tyler.

He looked up from pouring himself some iced tea. "What's going on?"

"It looks like I'm getting some help for cleaning the house."

"You asked for a housekeeper, Mom?"

"No," Tracey said, smiling to herself. She reached out and tapped Brianna's shoulder, then shook her finger to warn her to stop chasing Jayda around the kitchen island. "But Brian sent a cleaning company to do an estimate."

Tyler nodded, a gorgeous white smile creasing his face, his braces removed in May. "That's what's up." He grinned. "Changes, huh?"

"Yep, and I like it!" Tracey said.

He was talking about more than The Clean Team. Two weeks prior Tracey had come home from the grocery store and found a crew of landscapers ripping out weeds, mowing grass, pouring mulch and planting flowers on the front and side lawns. Brian had sent them as well. The black-eyed susans and petunias they had planted looked great. A few days later, Tracey arrived at the house after dropping the kids at their schools and was blocked from parking in the driveway because Brian had called contractors to repave and seal it. The chips and cracks? A memory.

Rose looked up from scribbling notes. "Mrs. Jones, I'm going to take a look at that half bath and that completes the downstairs, so we can go over the estimate in a few minutes. Okay?"

"Certainly." Tracey flashed Tyler a wink and a smile. He returned both.

Tracey followed Brianna and Jayda back down the hallway, then motioned for them to go back upstairs. She turned into the living room and sat on the couch.

Rose strolled in and sat in the upright chair across from her. "You have a beautiful home."

"Thank you."

"How often would you like a team to come in?"

Tracey paused for a moment to think. It would be nice to walk around a spic-and-span house at least once a week. "Once a week."

"Okay." Rose penciled in something on the sheet on her clipboard, checked a few things, then handed the blue paper to Tracey. "Take a look and tell me if this is reasonable for you."

Tracey looked at the amount scribbled on the sheet. "Sounds fine to me. Let me call my husband for a minute and run this past him."

"Sure."

Tracey grabbed the cordless extension from the side table and speed-dialed Brian's phone.

He answered and talked like he'd been in the house with them the whole time. "Whatever you decide is fine."

"But . . ."

"Are you surprised?"

"Yes. All this from the man who said money is coming out of the accounts like water?"

"Will this help you? Take an item off your to-do list at least?"

"Of course."

"Then that's what I want. So take care of your business." He hung up.

Tracey clicked the phone off, shrugged and smiled. She glanced down at the paper. "I see a signature is needed here. May I borrow your clipboard?"

Rose handed it to her. "Here you are. Oh, and see the line at the bottom for "Day"? Write in which day you'd like a team to arrive. And we'll need a key for your house. The key stays in a secure lock box and is only removed when a team is sent to your home. Our company is bonded and insured."

Tracey wrote down Friday, then added her signature. "I'll get a key for you right now. Can they start next week?"

Rose took the clipboard, smiling. "A team of two cleaners will be here next Friday morning."

"Excellent."

BEAUTIFUL DAYS CONTINUED. The warm temperatures grew even warmer. Tracey and Brian managed to get out and have a few more dates together. They were so relaxed around each other by mid-June Tracey didn't anticipate Brian would turn cold on her when she brought up the subject of Tyler moving to New York permanently.

They were in bed on a Friday night, holding one another and resting. Tracey felt Brian's muscles tighten as soon as she started talking about Tyler leaving.

"No," Brian said firmly. "Absolutely not. He can visit as many times as he wants, but he's not living up there."

Tracey sighed. "Would you at least think about how he feels? His grandfather is getting worse. "

"Yeah, but Kyle, as a full-time dad? Come on." Brian removed his arms from around her body and put his hands behind his head. "The man drinks too much and smokes cigars every night. He runs through women like it's going out of style and he hasn't set foot down here in the last ten years. Makes Ty come see him, like the world should cater to him on everything."

"Maybe things will be different with Ty up there?"

"And what happens when his grandmother starts spending more time at doctor visits with his grandfather, and Kyle travels every other week? Who's going to be there for Tyler? Tracey, God gave you and I the responsibility of raising him right."

Should she tell Brian the full story about Tyler feeling stressed staying in his current situation? If she brought that up it would make it seem like she was blaming Brian for Tyler wanting to leave their home. Skip it. What mattered most was talking about it and making a final decision.

"The more I think about it the more it irritates me," Brian snorted. "Where was Kyle when we got Tyler's braces put on? What about all the ball games he's missed? The report cards we had to sign? When we found out Ty was allergic to pumpkin and his face swelled up like a grapefruit, I was the one who stayed in the emergency room and made sure he was treated properly."

"Why are you making this about Kyle?" Tracey asked. "This is about Tyler. If we make him come back home at the end of the summer and his grandfather's health takes a turn . . ."

"I can't flat out agree to this. If Kyle's lifestyle was more in keeping with what we are trying to show Tyler as faith-filled parents, there wouldn't be a problem. We'd be turning the boy over to negative influences."

Brian had a point, but it wasn't like their own home was the perfect Christian household. In the past year Tracey could count on one hand the number of times she'd seen Brian praying or doing devotions. As a matter of fact, her own devotion times had all but limped to a halt since life started throwing hand grenades in February. Except for good morning and good night prayers with Brianna, there were no family prayer times. And they'd skipped out on life group for three months. Witnessing to others and sharing their faith? Please. Tracey and Brian had just weathered tsunamis in the form of deception, unfaithfulness, anxiety, and more. And Brian was worried about Kyle not modeling a proper lifestyle? Really?

"Tyler's leaving next Thursday. We need to say something," Tracey said.

"When I get up in the morning, I'll talk to him."

"Fine." Tracey rolled over to her side of the bed, pulling her pillow behind her head. No need to discuss anymore. If it wasn't for the fact that they needed to make a decision, she wouldn't have brought it up at all.

Brian rubbed her shoulder. "We've got unfinished business," he continued.

"Really?"

Brian moved his body down lower in the bed and held onto her again. "Let's drive down to Atlantic City and stay at The Borgata next weekend."

"But we don't gamble," Tracey said.

"We don't have to gamble. We can still enjoy the place. They have four-star restaurants and I heard the rooms are fantastic. A quick getaway outside of Philly. You and me."

"And Brianna?"

He nuzzled his face against the back of her neck. "Rick and Charla can keep an eye on her. It's only two nights. We'd be back on Sunday in time to pick her up and go to evening service."

His hands caressing her body did a lot of convincing on their own. A whole lot of convincing. Very nice. Their local getaway back in May helped to heal their connection to each other. Another getaway? Tyler would be in New York with Kyle of course. Sending Brianna to stay with Charla might mean coming back and seeing her daughter with pink and purple yarn braided into her cornrows, or possibly a newly constructed fake fourteen-inch long ponytail grazing her back, but that was a minor issue. Hmm. Tracey could practice forgetting the past. Focus on the pleasure of being with her husband. Show off more moves she learned from *The Romance Place*. Brian could spend time running his hands all over her.

Oh, yes. Another getaway sounded like something the doctor ordered.

"DO YOU HAVE EVERYTHING?" Tracey stood in the doorway of Tyler's bedroom surveying the messy landscape. His train to NYC would be leaving in an hour, so it was too late to complain about the way he'd destroyed his room while packing. He seemed in good spirits considering they'd told him they had reservations about letting him live in New York permanently.

Tyler hitched his backpack on his shoulder, gripped the handle of his black rolling duffel bag, and offered her a half-smile. "Yeah. But can you pack up my computer and printer and ship them to me tomorrow? Thanks!"

Tracey put her hands on her hips and smirked. "Yeah, I'll get right on it."

"Mom, I'm just playing."

"Mm-hmm. Come on. Let's go. And make sure you take your iPod because I'm not mailing that either."

They were on the road heading toward 30th Street Station when Tyler asked, "You gonna be okay this summer?"

"Of course."

"You *and* Brian?"

Tracey pressed her lips shut for a moment as she eased her foot off of the gas pedal to keep from speeding around the curve of the road.

"Mom?"

Tracey scratched at an itch on her cheek, then concentrated on keeping the car steady moving in the flow of traffic. What could she say? Things had gotten a lot better, but her internal feelings were . . . complicated. Not a day passed when Tracey didn't think about Brian's affair. Sure, love still existed between her and Brian, but there were still twinges of resentment and mistrust. How could she package that all up and make adult issues sound sensible to a sixteen-year-old who realizes he's blessed to live in a well-to-do household with two parents and probably didn't care to hear that his world could collapse right around him if his mother and stepfather decided to dismantle everything and walk away?

She kept it simple. "It's not easy, but there's nothing too hard for God. Both of us want you to enjoy your vacation and while you're gone we'll keep working at things."

"What about a marriage counselor?"

Tracey shrugged. "Maybe. Who knows?"

"You know, if you want, I can stay here this summer. I can call Dad and tell him I'm not coming. If you need me to, I'll stay," Tyler said.

A lump lodged in her throat. "You're going," she insisted. "Besides, your granny called today and told me she can't wait to see you. That's your family, too."

She didn't say much else until they reached the train station and parked. When they scrambled out of the car she ran around to the other side, reaching out and hugging him long and hard before releasing him. Their hugs felt different each year. He'd been growing up and further out of her arms since he'd learned how to walk.

"Uncle Jamal told me that he might come up and visit some lady he met who lives in Harlem. He might stop through and see me next month," Tyler mentioned as they walked to the electronic ticket kiosk.

"Don't bet on it. I'm pretty sure he's going to have his hands full here. Anyway, you've got everything you need and you know the routine."

One more quick hug and a kiss on the cheek before Tyler turned and started pushing buttons on the machine, running through the prompts to retrieve his ticket.

"Bye. Call me when you get there." She stepped back and

winked at him. "And I don't care what your dad does on Sunday
—you go to church with your grandparents."

"You know I will." Another shy grin before he hitched his
backpack higher on his shoulder and headed over to stand in
line for the Northeast Regional that would deliver him straight
to Penn Station.

Tracey found an empty space on a bench, whipped out her
cell phone, and speed-dialed Kyle.

He answered on the second ring. "Tyler's on his way, right?
I've got Sonia driving out to the station to pick him up in an
hour and half."

"Relax. Your child will be on the train in fifteen minutes."

"Good." Kyle sounded like he was fumbling with something.
"I have to meet with a new client in about thirty minutes. After
that I have two more meetings then I'll be home to see him
tonight."

"Who's going to be home for Tyler before you get there?"

"Mom and Pop. Mom's making dinner for everybody. I
smelled cobbler baking before I left the house this morning.
She's making all his favorites: baked ham, potato salad, peach
cobbler. When my son gets here we're fitting to tear something
up!"

Tracey smiled. Same old Kyle. Bad boy exterior covering the
heart of a man who loved his family to death. "Sounds nice. Give
my best to your parents and try not to corrupt my kid too
much."

Kyle laughed. "Talk to you later."

Tracey clicked off and slid her phone into her shoulder bag.
She waited and watched as Tyler kept moving in the line until he
reached the front, where he turned and waved back at her. Then
he disappeared down the escalator with the rest of the crowd
ready to board the Northeast Regional. She stayed still for
another minute, watching all the people move around her. Not
too crowded for an early Friday afternoon. The crowds would
grow bigger and louder as the Friday commuters made their

way into the station after 3:00 p.m. She breathed out a sigh of relaxation, grateful she'd managed to put Ty on an earlier train and that Sonia would be able to pick him up.

She eased up off the bench, pulled the keys from her purse and headed in the direction of the car. Even in the cooler air of the train station, sweat formed on her forehead and her skin felt moist beneath her t-shirt and jeans. An early heatwave. One hundred degrees in the shade. When she reached home she'd have to change into a tank top and shorts. She'd throw some items for the weekend into Brianna's overnight bag, pick her up at day camp, and drop her off at Charla's salon.

Bright and high in the sky, the sun scorched everything that lay beneath it on the city streets. She cranked up the air conditioning as soon as she turned the key in the ignition. Hot or not, she smiled, looking forward to the weekend away. Who knew when the heat wave would break? Saturday? Sunday? Oh well. Hopefully her brand new plants and flowers wouldn't wither and die in the heat.

CHAPTER
Twenty

LATE SUNDAY EVENING.

At Rise Church, streams of people headed out of the building after evening service, walking in small groups across the parking lot to their cars. Tracey stood at the bottom of the stairs right in front of the church, waiting for Brian to bring the car around from the overflow parking lot in the back. She held sleeping Brianna to her body.

Brianna was exhausted after running around with her aunt and uncle all weekend. And like Tracey had anticipated, Brianna sported a new hair style by the time they picked her up Sunday afternoon. It was pretty though. Tons of box braids all the same size and length with multi-colored beads on the ends, pulled up onto a ponytail on the top of her head. Her head rested on Tracey's shoulder as she snored. Sweat trickled from the back of Tracey's neck down her spine. The heat wave had not yet broken. Where was Brian?

Relax, Tracey. Relax. What a wonderful weekend! Though they'd seen precious little of The Borgata. Tracey could only remember the restaurant, lobby, and their luxurious room. Their time together? More reminiscent of their honeymoon than recent times. She'd enjoyed being alone with Brian. Now she craved time with him even more. But even better than that, a lot of Tracey's resentment over the affair began to fade. She hadn't thought about it at all while they were away.

Ten more minutes passed as Tracey waited. The parking lot in front of the church was practically empty now. The back lot had to be deserted. So where was Brian? Tracey's arms ached from holding up the weight of her sleeping daughter. Tracey hitched her up even higher. Forget waiting. It would be better to walk the shortcut down the small pathway around the church to the overflow parking lot behind the building.

She'd gotten the hang of keeping both her hands laced under Brianna's bottom with the bulk of the child's weight balanced on her shoulder. Her purse weight balanced her other shoulder. Good. She would make it to the parking without waking up Brianna.

Tracey turned into the lot behind the brick building, and heard Brian talking.

Wait. A female voice?

Brian's voice was deep and hushed and the female voice was shrill. Tracey clutched Brianna tighter and she walked forward as fast as she could. The click of her heels wasn't enough to drown out the argument going on now barely fifty feet away from her.

Brian and Lisette.

Together.

Fighting.

"Calm down! Keep your voice down," Brian insisted.

"When are you going to tell her? If you don't tell her, I will. I don't care!"

"We'll talk about this later! Not now!"

"Yes now!"

Brian pleaded, clearly trying to keep his voice down, but Tracey heard every word. "Lisette, my family is here! You have to leave right now!"

Lisette's voice was filled with fire and tears. "I am not going anywhere!"

Tracey stood ten feet away now barely breathing with Brian's back to her.

It had been nearly three months since she had last seen Lisette. Now here she was yelling at him in the dark.

Brian's former lover.

A former lover with a small but visible baby bump showing beneath her pink blouse.

Tracey stood stock still, both arms wrapped around Brianna to keep her from slipping. What else could she do when she'd already prayed to God to put an end to this nightmare?

The noise of Brian pleading with Lisette, the sound of snoring Brianna, and the rush-rush sounds of cars passing by on the highway overpass near the church blended together into one big blur. Darkness settled over the area like a wool blanket.

"Brian," Tracey said, announcing her presence.

Brian turned around.

He looked lost.

Tracey's eyes swelled with water. No! Absolutely no crying. She tried to remember her promise to herself. She willed herself to keep the tears off her face but knew that was a lost cause once she tasted wet saltiness mixed with the creamy lipstick inside her bottom lip. When Lisette finally turned the slight swell of her pregnant belly toward Tracey, the woman moved so quickly that at once she was right beneath Tracey's face. The air smelled sour. But the air was the least of her worries. Lisette sniffled, her small hand resting on the slight swell of her abdomen.

"Yes, this is exactly what it looks like," Lisette taunted.

Tracey spoke slowly, but deliberately, keeping her eyes riveted to the face of her enemy. "Go. Right now. Go." Tracey's words were cold and measured.

Lisette's small eyes narrowed even more. Brian's eyes scanned both of them as a look of fear crossed his face. He finally sprang into action. He pulled Lisette's arm, marched her across the parking lot and pushed her into the passenger side of a red Mustang, closing the door firmly behind her. Whoever had driven Lisette to Rise obviously did not want to be involved; the mysterious driver remained in the car.

After the car sped away, Brian and Tracey stared at each other. Brianna, snoring on Tracey's shoulder, didn't make one sound acknowledging she'd heard what had happened.

Sick to her stomach, her head throbbing so bad she had to blink away the pain, Tracey carefully stepped to the Lexus, opened the door, laid Brianna in the back seat, and shut the door. Then she walked back and snatched her purse up off the dusty asphalt where she'd dropped it and tucked it under her arm as she stood in front of Brian.

When she slapped his face the first time, her white-gold and diamond wedding ring scraped across the bridge of his nose, pulling off a bit of skin. With the second slap, she felt muscle strain in her right shoulder, the force of the blow making her fingers bounce up off of his sweaty face. A third slap and he grabbed her arm and forced it high over her head. Her fingers stung from the physical contact. He pushed her away. She stumbled twice before righting herself and walking back to the car again.

No words. Tracey stumbled into the car, but before she closed the door, she looked over at him. He stood with his arms by his side and his head down.

She called out to him, breaking the silence. "Let's go."

"Tracey . . . I . . . we should . . ."

She swallowed, and then repeated herself. "Let's go."

She closed the door, watching from the window as Brian pulled his head up then looked over at her with empty eyes. She faced forward and pulled down the vanity mirror to look at herself. Streaked makeup. Brown smears decorated the lapels of her suit. Crinkles around her eyes and between her eyebrows—proof that stress had gotten the best of her. Wet lipstick. Melted mascara. Brown-black streaks on eyes sodden with sadness.

She'd experienced too much of everything, and now her head, shoulders and fingers throbbed to the beat of her racing heart.

Brian slid into the driver's seat. He swiveled around and managed to look back at Brianna without looking over at Tracey at all.

Tracey sat with her arms around herself, purse resting by her feet, looking straight ahead. Anger and confusion pulsed through her veins. Brian drove them towards home, but the truth was, Tracey didn't know where they were going.

CHAPTER
Twenty~One

TRACEY COULDN'T REMEMBER EVER NEEDING Tyler in the house as much as when she returned home from church that Sunday night. As if not unsettled enough from the parking lot drama, as soon as she entered the back door, the house bugged her. They'd been gone all weekend and the rooms were shadowy and noiseless. No one in the house for two days meant the rooms smelled annoyingly clean, like too much Pine-Sol and Murphy's wood oil soap.

Upstairs, she undressed sleeping Brianna, pulled a pink cotton nightshirt on her, and slid her into the bed. Tracey pulled a comforter over her body, cushioned it carefully around her ears, then crept out of the room, shutting the door tight behind her.

She put a hand to her chest and felt her heart pumping. Lungs still moving oxygen in and out of her body. Heartbroken but alive. She dragged herself into her bedroom, peeled off her suit, and pulled on a red t-shirt, cotton shorts and flip-flops. Then she stood still for a moment to get her bearings.

Where was Brian?

She found him sitting in the darkened living room. She clicked on a lamp and he still didn't budge. He sat there stone-faced. His shoes, shirt, and tie scattered across the floor. She guessed he'd run out of energy for taking off anything else because he'd slumped over the end of the leather couch like he was trying to melt into the furniture.

"Say something!" Tracey stalked toward the couch.

He shook his head and waved her away. "I'm not ready to talk yet."

Tracey's eyes convinced themselves they didn't need to blink as her half-dressed husband pushed himself up off the couch and walked down to the kitchen. She followed. He grabbed a plate from the cabinet and warmed up some leftovers from the refrigerator. No talking, but dinner was okay?

God. Help. Me. This. Is. It. Tracey's hot lava feeling rose up and she transformed into Mount St. Helens. When the microwave dinged, she ran over to it, grabbed the plate out of it and winged it like a Frisbee at Brian, who had stepped over to the kitchen island. The plate hit him in his side, then bounced off and clattered to the floor. Pieces of sea bass and asparagus stuck to his t-shirt.

"Ow! Tracey!"

"You better talk! And I mean *now!*"

He held his hands up in front of him. A peace gesture? "We need to calm down. Please. We're too upset to talk now."

Totally reasonable and rational statement. Trouble was, Tracey was too hot to be reasonable and rational. She'd been rational for months. Now she stood in the middle of the kitchen floor steaming mad. Arms crossed. Eyes narrowed.

"You. Tell. Me. The. Truth!" Tracey ordered, anger welling up in her throat.

"She's pregnant."

"Oh I could see that!" Tracey cocked her head to the side. "And it's yours?"

"No."

"Really?"

"I told you before, we weren't together that many times and when we were I used condoms," Brian insisted.

"Why should I believe you?"

"I don't care what you believe anymore! It's the truth!" He rubbed his side and shook food particles off his t-shirt and pants. "Since you're so bent on hearing the truth, if you'd been loving me like you've been doing since May, there wouldn't have been a Lisette in my life to begin with!"

Tracey stared at him, unblinking. Her mouth hung open.

Brian kept going, fire in his voice. "I messed up! I get it, Tracey! I get it! If you wanted to leave me, you would have been gone! But where would you go, Ms. Perfect? All the money and support you have? From me! You have a better life than anyone else in your family has ever had and my slip-up that happened all of three times didn't take one thing away from you. You didn't lose my love, our home, or anything, so get over it already! There's truth for you!"

The noise she heard in her head right then sounded like the muted electronic tone she heard whenever she turned off a hot television set.

Click. Pffttt.

No more questions.

Tracey kicked off her flip-flops, sprinted out of the kitchen barefoot, and scrambled over to the dining room. She snatched open the china cabinet doors and grabbed their monogrammed Waterford crystal wedding heirloom flutes from the middle shelf. Yep. The right weight and size.

"Come back! Listen, I didn't mean that and we need to . . . hey wait . . . no . . . those are our . . ." Brian started after her and made it as far as the dining room doorway before he opened his eyes wide and ran straight back to the kitchen.

With her brain unplugged, Tracey transformed into an Olympic shot put athlete. She lobbed a flute right at his head as he cowered by the oven.

Zoom! The monogrammed glass whizzed past his ducked

head and smashed against the wooden cabinet door above his head, exploding before falling in glittery shards to the floor.

He shook glass off his arms which he'd used to shield his head and stumble-stepped away from the mess.

Zing! Tracey threw the second glass at him. He swerved again. It hit the oven behind him, shattered glass raining all over the kitchen floor.

"Stop! You're gonna kill me!" Brian yelled.

Tracey stopped.

There were more glasses, plates, goblets, and bowls in the china cabinet, but she'd made her point. Besides, if Tracey went back in the dining room she might grab the Waterford crystal serving bowl. If that shattered over his head she actually might kill him and she did not want to take a trip to jail. She stood still and met Brian's gaze. He blinked at her. It looked like he wanted to come at her again but the broken glass on the floor trapped him.

She sniffed. "You really need to learn how to clean up your messes. I guess you can practice with the one you're standing in."

Sweat appeared on Brian's forehead and blood came to the surface of the scratches on his hands and arms as he ran his hands over his face and brushed away particles and tears. "Why are you doing this?" Brian asked.

"You know why!" Tracey choked out.

He remained in place. "I've known about the baby for weeks now. It's not mine."

"Mmmm." The sound came out more like a moan. She shook inside so much her teeth vibrated.

"Look, there are miracles in life, but biology doesn't lie and I know how condoms work. I've repeated that to Lisette about a hundred times, but she won't listen to me. She's trying to run game on me!"

"Really?" Tracey shot him a *go on* look.

"Someone else is the father of her baby, probably someone she hooked up with for a minute, but she wants to name me."

Sweat ran down Tracey's temples. Her neck and shoulders throbbed as Brian kept talking.

"I told her she can't name me as the father just because we had sex. She got mad. First she started showing up here, then she tried to threaten sexual harassment. I blocked her calls. She mailed me a letter telling me she'd keep popping up where I least expected it. Once I saw her at the gym. Another time I saw her in the balcony at church, but I hustled you all out before you could see her. And this last time was in the parking lot."

"Why does she want you to be her baby daddy so bad?"

Brian grimaced. "My only guess is whoever the father is, he can't provide for the child or for her as well as I could. I offered her some money to help her out. She could have started a college savings account for her child with it. I hoped she'd take it and move on, but she refused."

Tracey shook her head and snorted. Young women these days and their idea of family. No. More like a sinful situation Brian dug himself into and resulting in more than he bargained for. Money?

"So that's how you found out I'd withdrawn cash from our account?" Tracey asked.

Brian nodded and bowed his head.

One sneaky person had managed to catch another being sneaky. Sad.

"How come you didn't tell me all this before?" Tracey said.

Brian shrugged and sneezed. He kept his eyes away from hers and looked at the scratches on his hands. "You'd been walking around hurt since February. You had a right to be upset, I know. But when things started getting better between us I didn't want to see our relationship turn sour again. Can we start again? Please?"

"What?" Tracey blinked, confused about what he was asking.

"We can start over again," Brian begged, stretched his hand

out to her. "We've been working so hard to get past it. And you know everything. If Lisette shows up again in our lives, I'll file a restraining order against her. If she names me on the birth certificate, I will demand a DNA test. This is all over now."

With a possible baby on the way by another woman? Was he serious? So what if there was very little chance the baby was his. Brian had fed her so many lies by now Tracey wouldn't believe him if he told her water was wet. She wiped at her wet eyes and runny nose with the edge of her t-shirt. Sniffled. Put her head down and sighed. She stayed silent as she tiptoed around the edge of kitchen and out into the main hallway. Her feet dragged wetness onto the wooden hallway floor. She glanced down. Both feet were cut and bleeding.

Lessons from God pepper all experiences, and Tracey had just learned a big one.

You can't throw glass without being cut by the shards.

CHAPTER
Twenty-Two

TRACEY WAS ten when she first heard of a child born from an affair.

She'd been out with her mother shopping at Macy's for new clothes. She was pulling on a pair of black jeans with silver zippers close to the ankle in the dressing room of the girl's department when she overheard Alice talking to a woman with a gravelly voice. Eavesdropping didn't give Tracey much information, though. She heard the words *boy* and *two years old* and *left town last week* and *doesn't have his last name*. The remainder of the conversation was whispered and Tracey couldn't make out the rest. She'd ended up choosing the pants and a pair of acid washed blue ones. When she walked out she took one glance at the look on her mother's face and knew something was off. A tall, smooth-skinned, mocha-colored lady Tracey had never seen before flashed a tight smile at her, then nodded at her mother and strolled down to the end of the dressing area.

"Who was that?" Tracey had asked.

"You remember Mr. Jack?" Alice took the jeans from her daughter's arms and headed toward the cashier desk.

"Sure. Daddy's friend. He fixed my bike chain the last time he came by."

"Yeah. That's him. Well, that was his sister. She was telling me about his son."

"Ma, Mr. Jack has daughters."

Alice stopped and made Tracey halt beside her. She turned and leaned down so close to Tracey's face she could smell the tuna macaroni salad Alice had eaten for lunch. "Marcella and Bridget are his girls with his wife Jackie. The boy—is a child from another lady."

Tracey paused. "What?" she asked, confused.

"A child that man created with another woman who wasn't his wife." Then Alice straightened up and looked down at Tracey again, as if she realized she was telling a child grown folk's business. "Never mind. Are these the pants you want, girl?"

Tracey nodded. She didn't think any more about it after that.

But she sure was thinking about it now.

A baby? What if it really was Brian's? What if Lisette had messed with those condoms he'd supposedly used? Wait. That's way too much to consider after showering Brian's scalp with glass shrapnel.

In the upstairs bathroom, Tracey's hands trembled as she pulled down tweezers and a box of bandages from the medicine cabinet. She placed the box on the sink then moved over to sit on the edge of the tub to examine her feet. Two cuts on her left foot and one on the right. She tweezed out two small pieces of glass, then scrubbed her feet clean in the tub and dried them on a guest towel. Bleary-eyed, she turned and glanced at the bandages on the sink and couldn't find the energy to move from the tub and grab them. She perched on the edge of the tub shaking. So busted up inside she yearned to howl long and hard, but she bit her lip and swallowed the sound. Salt water and mucus ran down her face, soaking her t-shirt. Better to let the tears flow. Each time she tried to stop crying her chest thumped like she was suffocating.

"Tracey," Brian called, as he knocked on the door. She heard the door handle jiggle.

"Go away!" she snapped, wiping her face with the front of her t-shirt.

"No fighting, I promise."

"There's two other bathrooms in the house." Tracey tugged her slimy shirt off and tossed it into the wicker hamper.

"Look, I'm bleeding, okay? I'll go to our bathroom but I wanted to check on you first."

"Check your own self out if you want to check on somebody!"

"Unlock this door, Tracey. Right now!"

Listen to him talking to her like she was a child. Like she was the one who couldn't control her impulses. So her anger escalated and she finally let loose. Any wife would have done the same thing.

The door handle jiggled again. "Tracey!"

"All right!" she acquiesced, lunging up and taking three paces to unlock the doorknob. Thank goodness Brianna was still sleeping like a hibernating bear.

She plopped down on the toilet seat and looked up at him as he walked in. They matched each other. Identical weary looks. Half-dressed. Ruddy skin. Wet faces.

Brian jerked his thumb toward the hall. "You left some blood on the floor out there. Your feet are cut?"

She pointed, still trembling. "I'm . . . I um . . . bandages."

When he turned to reach for the box off the sink, she saw several tiny cuts up and down his shoulders and on his forearms from where he'd shielded his head from the glass. He put the box back in the medicine cabinet, then reached into the other side and grabbed antibacterial spray, gauze, and a roll bandage. He bent down in front of her and sat down hard on the floor. There was a long cut on the back of his neck going down towards his back. Red and oozing.

She'd hurt him.

"Your neck," Tracey said.

"I know. I felt back there. It doesn't feel too deep." Brian guided her foot to rest on his leg. He looked at her cuts, and sprayed antibacterial ointment on them. "Let me take care of you first, all right?"

"Are your feet cut too?" Tracey asked, her heart softening toward her husband.

"A little. I'll be alright." He said.

She stopped shaking as he used a light touch and bandaged her wounds. When he was done, he cradled both her feet in his lap, his hands covering her toes.

Tracey had always loved Brian for the tenderness he showed during the smallest moments in their lives. But how could he show a soft side right after having their worst fight ever? Should she say "thank you"? Maybe. But she couldn't form the words. Her mind had transformed into an empty, dust-filled room. Particles floating everywhere in stillness.

"Tracey."

"No, not right now."

"Now you sound like me."

She shrugged as she wiped away tears. "Maybe I should have listened to you."

Brian rubbed her feet again and looked like he was going to say something else. She guessed he thought better of it because he put her feet down and left the bathroom. She listened as he moved around. Fifteen minutes passed and he walked past the bathroom in a t-shirt, shorts and sneakers. She kept listening as his footsteps headed down the stairs, through the hall and kitchen, then out the back door. Only then did she get up, walk into their bedroom and fall on the bed.

Tracey guessed he was on his way to the emergency room to have someone look at the back of his neck. Gotta give him credit for having the sense to let things go for the moment.

💔

HOURS LATER, Tracey shut the basement door behind her. She clutched her cell phone in her other hand. She stood barefoot on the wooden stairs wearing one of Brian's t-shirts and sweat-pants she'd changed into after she heard him come back in the house at four that morning.

Tracey started talking as soon as she heard her best friend answer. "I'm leaving Brian."

Monica's groggy voice croaked, "Tracey?"

"It's me."

"And what're ya telling me?"

"I'm leaving Brian."

That last sentence must have jolted Monica into a state of complete wakefulness because she yelled, "What the heck happened?"

"What didn't happen, ask me that!"

"Tracey, I just talked to you Friday afternoon. You said you packed some lingerie to wear in Atlantic City. You told me you were going to dance for him and everything was all good and God had everything under control. You did everything except sing the chorus from 'You Brought the Sunshine'."

Tracey clutched the phone tighter to her ear. "We had a fight and I cut him."

"A fight? When?"

Tracey closed her eyes and blurted everything out. "We were at church. Evening service. Service let out, I went to the parking lot and found Lisette in the back of the church with a baby bump, yelling at him. It was a mess. Then we came back home . . ."

". . . and you're telling me all this at . . . *four in the morning*? Why didn't you call me before?"

"I came in the house all I could see was red. As soon as Brianna was in her room, we had the fight and that's when I threw our crystal glasses and cut him. He went to the emergency room and I went to sleep. I heard him come back and then I got up to clean up all that glass before Brianna wakes up. So, yes, I'm calling you now."

"I don't know what to say," Monica confessed, disbelief in her voice.

Tracey rubbed her sore eyes. "Just tell me, what kind of idiot am I?"

Monica's voice was soothing. "Maybe the baby's his, maybe it isn't."

"You know what's scary? I don't even care. I'm so tired of all the stupid lies. I'm not even thinking straight anymore. I cut him! What if he decides to press charges against me for assault? I could get arrested!"

Once she'd snapped, all the verses she'd memorized about self-control slid right down the drain. Even after the fight, hours later while she stood in their bedroom changing clothes, she'd thought about what transpired in the kitchen and had the urge to hurt him again. Sure, he'd bandaged the wounds on her feet. Yeah, he'd tried to stay close to her and talk to her. And some part of her wanted to dive back into that moment and let him nurse her—let him rub away her pain. What a sick mix of love and disgust. This couldn't be normal.

"You were angry, okay? You had an angry moment and it's over now. You need to come over here and chill for a bit. Use your emergency key. Come on," Monica insisted.

"Mon, you've got a life. You don't need to be involved in all this."

"I'm your BFF; consider me involved since day one. What about staying with your Mom and Jamal for a little while?"

"Maybe." Tracey closed her eyes. Goose bumps covered her skin as she stood on the cold basement steps. Her feet throbbed. She envisioned shattered crystal and the long cut on her husband's neck.

"Are you there?" Monica asked.

"I'm here," Tracey whispered.

"What are you going to do, sweetie?"

"I'm not sure."

"Think about this a little longer then," Monica pleaded. "Leaving is a big deal."

True. But so was everything else she'd wondered about in the past few hours. Would they get divorced? Reconcile? How would they tell Brianna? Did Tracey even have the right to be upset about Brian having a child since she was a single mother when they married?

Tracey winced as she shifted her weight from one foot to another. Pain. Undeniable. "I need a little space to breathe, then maybe I can start thinking again," she said.

CHAPTER
Twenty-Three

PANCAKES. Scrambled eggs. Turkey bacon. Coffee. Orange juice.

Delicious smells wafted through the kitchen that morning. Shame Tracey wasn't going to eat any of it. Her stomach had shut down for good after the fight, but cooking busied her hands. It also made things seem normal for Brianna who sat at the kitchen island drawing a picture as she waited for breakfast.

"Hi."

Tracey turned around, an oily spatula in her hands. Brian stood in the middle of the kitchen, cleaned up and newly shaved. The white shirt and crisp gray pants he wore looked like he'd pulled them straight out from under the dry cleaner's plastic bag. A small clear plastic bandage adorned the bridge of his nose and puffiness resided around his eyes. His long sleeved shirt managed to cover the bandages that protected the cuts on his arms and shoulders. She couldn't see the back of his neck from where she stood, but she assumed that cut had been bandaged as well.

"Hi," She turned back to the stove. "Breakfast is done. I can make you a plate, unless you only want coffee."

"I uh . . . yeah, I'll take some coffee and eggs and bacon.

Thanks." He dropped his bag on the floor and slid on the stool next to Brianna. "Hey babygirl."

"Daddy, what's that thing on your nose?" Brianna asked.

"It's just a bandage. I had an accident. Your braids look great, I forgot to tell you last night," he said.

Perfect answer. He'd managed to activate the chatterbox button in Brianna's head. At least Tracey could count on him not to bring up the fight from the night before. As Tracey served their food and drink, Brianna babbled about how long she'd sat and how her scalp hurt a little bit but not much and how Auntie Char wanted to put in pink hair extensions but she knew mommy would get mad so she told her *no*.

As her family chatted and chewed, Tracey scrubbed hard to remove cooked egg residue from the bottom of the frying pan.

Tracey and Brian. Doing the impossible—making it seem like a typical day. The right smells. The routine sounds. Her husband was going to work. Her daughter talking more than eating. Hurry up Tracey. Get the dishes in the washer and the pots and pans cleaned up before taking Brianna to camp. Water. Soap. Scrub hard. Rinse.

She suddenly stopped and focused her gaze on the stainless steel pan in her hands. What was the point? Why should she care about some dumb dishes? Seriously. The script had flipped overnight.

"Trace, you all right?" Brian asked.

She dropped the pan in the sudsy water. "I'm good—" *Liar.*

"Listen, uh, I'll take Brianna to day camp this morning on my way out," he offered. "Then you can go back and rest a bit."

Tracey twisted around to look at Brianna. Pretty braids cascaded about her small brown head. Missing-front-tooth grin. She bounced up and down on the stool.

"Can Daddy take me, please?" she pleaded. "I never get to ride with him!"

That would make things so much easier. If Tracey could stay in the house she'd get some more sleep. After she woke up she could take a long bath and pray. Okay. All right. Maybe eighty-six the whole idea of leaving. Stay in the house. Pray. Rest. Don't even consider getting in the Volvo.

Tracey nodded. "Yes."

"Yay!" Brianna cheered, swinging her legs around the side of her stool.

"Finish those eggs first," Tracey said.

Brianna turned back to her plate and picked up her fork. Tracey glanced at Brian. He stared back.

"We . . . should uh," he paused and started again, "meet up to talk later."

Oh, they'd talk. That was a given. She leaned back against the sink and wrapped her arms around herself. Baby bump. Crashing glass. Smeared blood.

"Yeah," she said. That was all she could manage.

Tracey took Brianna's bear hug and kissed her on the forehead before watching her take her dad's hand and walk out the back door. Tracey stood and watched them walk down the stairs and into the perfectly paved driveway. Despite the clear bandage on his nose and the one on the back of his neck, Brian looked fine in the sunshine. Brianna flashed her grin one last time before Brian buckled her into her seat. Brian waved as he slid into the Lexus. Then he backed out of the driveway. Tracey waggled her fingers in a weak goodbye before she shut the door.

Back in the kitchen, she loaded dishes in the machine. Their crumpled paper napkins were wadded in her hand. She stepped on the lever to open the stainless steel trash can, threw the napkins in, then stared inside. Discarded slimy eggshells sat atop blood-streaked paper towels resting under a nest of broken crystal.

Tracey had just cooked and served breakfast to a man who, only hours before, angered her to the point of attempting to shred him with their wedding crystal. The definition of crazy—eggshells and coffee grounds mixed in with broken glass and bloody paper towels.

She backed away and let the trash can lid slam shut.

Sick. She'd been wounded on the battlefield and now she was officially sick.

She could either lay on the battlefield and keep getting hit, or she could take the other option.

Retreat.

FATHER, *you see me. I know you see me. I know. But. Still . . .*

Tracey should have been on her knees, or prone with her face to the floor, pleading for wisdom and guidance. She could have gone to the family room to sit in her favorite chair with her Bible open to Psalm 23. But no. Where was she instead? In her bedroom closet murmuring broken prayers as she stood atop a step stool. Rummaging through her purses and bags trying to grab one big enough to hold a few vital things.

Wallet. Checkbook. Bible. Cell phone and charger. Journal. Sunglasses. Underwear. Jeans. T-shirt. Sandals. A makeup bag. Other personal items just in case. She didn't need her pilot's case or suitcase. A suitcase wouldn't do because then she'd be packing for real. And she wasn't packing, right? So her big cinnamon-colored Coach bag would do.

Normal women don't walk out on their families. But sick people go to the hospital or rehab or somewhere.

Sneakers on her feet and bag on her shoulder, Tracey walked out of the bedroom and down the hallway. She paused in front of Brianna's bedroom and peered in. Pale peach-colored walls, multi-colored floor rugs, dolls, and games scattered all over the bookshelves. She stood still and breathed in the scent of powder, Vaseline lotion and hair oil— Brianna's smell. Without thinking she went in and grabbed a half-dressed, homemade Mohawk-wearing Barbie doll from the group resting beside Brianna's pillow, and shoved it inside her bag.

"PICK UP BRIANNA TODAY PLEASE," Tracey instructed Brian as she drove toward the expressway.

"Wait," Brian paused a moment. "Okay. I can do that. My schedule's clear."

"You need to get her by six at the latest."

"I know."

"I'm not cooking today, so grab some food for her before you bring her home."

"Where are you going to be?"

She guided the car steadily and chose her words carefully. "I don't feel good."

It took him a long time to answer back. She guessed he was rewinding the tape in his head. Perhaps he saw the same thing she kept seeing. *Baby bump. Broken glass. Smeared blood. Tears.*

"I understand. Listen, I have to go now. I'll make sure Brianna is taken care of, all right?"

"I know you will." She clicked off the call and tossed the phone in the back seat.

For most of the morning she drove around, stopping at unplanned places to let her mind wander or to eat or use the rest room. She considered driving by Brianna's camp, but turned around instead. All the while she hoped God would provide some sort of sign or emergency that would make her stay.

Tracey returned home for a nap where she lay down for two hours. She woke up hot, thirsty, confused, and still seeing unwanted images.

She left again.

"MONICA?" Tracey breathed.

"What did you decide? Where are you?" Monica said.

"Driving." Tracey gripped the steering wheel. "I'm on my way to your condo. I can't stay here anymore."

"Where's Brianna?"

"Day camp. I asked Brian to pick her up this evening. I gotta stop thinking about him for a while. I'm going nuts."

"All right, do you remember the security code? And you have your key?" Monica asked.

Tracey sniffed. "Yes . . . I uh . . . yeah."

"Well get over there and take a hot bath or something and calm down because you don't sound good. You know where everything is. I love you. You'll get through this."

"Thank you," Tracey whispered, her voice breaking on the last word.

"Now don't get me all teary. I have one more meeting today. I'll see you tonight."

"Okay."

The drive into Center City should have been simple. Routine. Tracey had driven to Monica's condo a million times. But this time when she drove the expressway she grew confused. The glaring sunshine increased her headache. She stayed in the wrong lane a few seconds too long and ended up missing Exit 344. She kept driving. No thoughts. Just driving, until she saw signs where she finally needed to make a choice.

I-95 North or I-95 South?

CHAPTER
Twenty-Four

THIS IS PSYCHOTIC. *You are a fool. Turn back now.*

Tracey made her way down I-95 South. Why south? In her delirium it seemed like the car was guiding itself. By the time she'd cruised into the Delmarva area, her head throbbed like someone had hit it with a hammer. Water began to fall from the dark gray sky in fat drops—a sign of the heat wave finally breaking. Intermittent streaks of lightning flashed across the sky. She clicked on the windshield wipers and drove on. The swish-thud sound of the blades seemed to mirror her heart.

You will lose everything. Nothing good can come from this.

Tracey looked straight ahead, keeping the air conditioner on full blast and the radio silent. *Don't replay last night's scene behind the church. Don't think about the fight. Don't keep track of how far you're driving or even think about where you'll end up.*

There's nothing righteous about this. What happened to your faith?

That last thought almost made Tracey pull onto an exit ramp and turn the car around to head back up I-95 North. Almost. Where was her faith in God right now? Quick review of the last few months. God hadn't shown up to keep Brian from sexing his nurse. God maybe allowed him to create a child with some mean-tempered woman. Dad was probably a few cold pizzas away from a heart attack or stroke. Ma and Jamal could lose their house if they didn't find a way to keep up the mortgage payments. Tyler flat out announced he'd rather live with Kyle than with her. The sun still shined through Brianna's smile, but that was probably because she was spoiled to death.

The cold air made Tracey's teeth chatter, but she continued gripping the steering wheel rather than turn off the air conditioning. She shook her head and blinked. Where was she going again? Her brain had stopped normal processing. All it did was ache.

She rubbed her temple and talked out loud. "Lord, why do you keep letting people hurt me like this? What did I do so wrong? I loved Kyle to death and he left me with a newborn son and a broken heart. Then you gave me Brian— I love Brian, but he messed around on me and lied about the whole thing. Why?"

Thunder rolled in with the rain and flashes of lighting. Tracey gazed ahead on the road and saw the sign for the Delaware Welcome Center coming up off an exit. It would be best to stop there, go to the bathroom, and grab something to eat and drink. Her stomach growled loudly after riding around for hours fueled by pure adrenaline.

In the restroom, as she exited the toilet stall and headed to the sink to wash her hands, the phone buzzed inside of her purse. She ignored it, finished washing, and walked back outside to the vending area. By the time she'd dropped some coins and bought a soda and a bottled water, her phone buzzed again. She fished it out of her bag as she leaned on the front of the machine.

"Hello." Tracey said.

"Where are you?" Brian demanded.

Tracey balanced the two cold bottles of liquid in her hands. "Out. Why?"

"I'm in the house now. I gave Brianna her dinner to eat and came upstairs to change. Why are your purses all over the floor and the bed?"

"I needed one of my bigger bags."

"Tracey." Long pause. "Where are you?" Brian insisted, sounding concerned.

"I left."

Another long pause. "Say that again?"

"I left." Tracey repeated, putting the sweaty bottles down by her feet. She glanced out the window and watched the rain pelting down from the dark gray sky. "I don't want to see a paternity suit, harassment or another fight. Keep your house! Keep your money! Keep your life. Go get your new woman if you want. But understand this, I have a Savior. It is *Not You!*"

"Look, you're hurt and tired. I know. I'm sorry about the fight, what I said—the whole night. I could apologize a million times for, but you're talking crazy now! What about Brianna?" Brian asked.

She moved to a corner of the room where people weren't milling around. "I'll settle somewhere and make arrangements for her."

"What are you saying?"

"I need space! After seeing Lisette . . . then what you said to me about it! I wanted to kill you. I'm not—I can't stay in that house with you!"

"I don't care where you are. Come back! If you don't want me here, I'll stay with Ricky and Charla until we work things out or even in an extended stay hotel. You can't do this!"

"Yes. I can!"

"You're my wife! This is our family! We can work this thing out. But we can't do anything if you're gone!"

"Brian, did you hear yourself last night? If I stay there, I'm changing the locks and calling a lawyer."

"Running away is supposed to stop that?"

"I don't know," she sniffed. "But it is keeping me from doing anything I'll regret right away."

"The world does not revolve around you! Can't you forget about how you feel for a minute and think about your daughter?"

"I *am* thinking of her! She's never seen me like this. All torn up and half-crazy."

She blinked and blinked at the vending machines. *Brave the storm. Have a meal. Find a hotel.* If she ate and slept for a while in peace, maybe that would be enough to change her mind and send her traveling back up the highway to Philly.

"At least let me know where you are. Why the mystery? You know, if I check transaction records on the bank cards I can see where you are headed."

What was the point of keeping him in the dark? "I'm on I-95 South. Traveling. I'll end up somewhere. Don't start worrying about me now when you weren't worried about me this past winter," she said. Then she hung up. Taking her compact umbrella from her bag, she put it up and rushed through the rain to her car.

Another thirty minutes down the road and sweating and dizziness, made her pull to the side of the highway. An uncontrollable cough seized her. She had trouble breathing. Frantic, she unscrewed the blue cap of her water bottle and took long sips. The first one cooled her down. The second settled her coughing fit. She would not faint if she kept breathing. She let her eyelids slide shut. Listened to rain. Willed herself to relax. She could push past an anxiety attack. Her marriage though? Probably over.

Prayers ceased to arrive in her mind. Only thoughts directed to God in a haphazard fashion. Nonsensical mental murmurings. Her phone buzzed again, jolting her. She pulled it out of her bag, flipped it over and looked at the caller ID. Monica.

Tracey talked first. "I'm supposed to be at your place. I kept driving."

"Brian called me," Monica said. "I'm still in my office. I thought you were crashed out sleeping at my place, then I get this crazy call . . ."

"Monica?"

"What you do is your business, but wherever you go and whatever you do, call me and let me know you are safe."

"I will," Tracey said, and ended the call.

Another minute passed and Tracey's cell rang again. Tyler?

"Mom, where are you?" Tyler demanded.

Leaning her back on the headrest, Tracey squeezed her eyes closed tighter. "I'm in my car on I-95."

"Brian just called me sounding upset. He asked me if I'd heard from you and if I knew where you were. What's going on?"

She choked up and started sobbing.

"Mom, what's wrong? Why are you crying?"

Tracey tried to get hold of herself but kept weeping with the phone pressed to her chest. When she put the phone back to her ear, there were voices and noises in the background. Tyler talked fast to someone.

A deep voice came over the phone. "Tracey? What's the matter?"

Kyle.

"Brian and I had a big fight. A bad one. We both got hurt. I left. Today I got in my car and I just started driving." Tears streamed down her face.

Tyler's voice floated around in the background. "She's still crying? Let me speak to my mom. I wanna speak to my mom!"

"In a minute, sit down," Kyle said firmly. His deep voice came through muffled. "Listen, your mom had a fight with Brian. She left the house and she's upset right now."

Tyler's voice escalated. "A fight? I knew I shouldn't have left her! He better not have hit her. He hit her didn't he? Nah-uh. No! Did he hit her? Where's the car keys? I'm going down there!"

"Hold on." Kyle's voice was still muffled. "Sit down boy, I'm handling this." Then Kyle said, "Tracey, wherever you are, drive to my house. You can't be out there alone like that."

"I'm not coming there," she sobbed as she wiped her wet face with a crumpled tissue.

"You don't have a choice. If Tyler doesn't see you by tomorrow I'll have to tie him to his bed because he'd actually go out there after you. I've got business to attend to and my father to be concerned about. Now come on. You'll be safe here," Kyle said.

"No. Put Ty on the phone and I'll talk to him. He'll settle down," Tracey said.

"I don't take no for an answer. I'm a busy man. Put my address in your GPS and get here."

What could she do? Brianna would be a mess when her dad told her that her mother was gone, but Brian wouldn't tell her about the fight. Now Tyler? A different story altogether. He actually knew about his stepfather's affair with Lisette, and now he knew about the fight last night. If she didn't go back to Philly or drive to New York, Tyler would go out on his own and walk if he had to until he found her.

She put the car back on the road and started looking for exit signs.

I-95 North.

Headed to New York.

CHAPTER
Twenty-Five

IT WAS ALMOST eleven when Tracey parked in Kyle's driveway. Her eyes were bone dry and her eyelids drooped. Her fingers had cramped into a curve from grasping the steering wheel for hours. She stretched out her fingers and wiggled them. Her jeans and shirt stayed glued to her skin, and her hips and legs had kinks in them, making her wobble as she dragged her body out of the car. All she wanted was to drop down on a bed and pass out.

"Whoa." She shut the car door and stood in the driveway looking up at Kyle's house. Her mouth gaped open when she realized pictures had not prepared her for its beauty. It was a gorgeous, stone-faced, mini mansion surrounded by a deep carpet of lawn edged by trees and woods. Green shutters decorated each window and a wide brick walkway wound from the front door to the long driveway. Rounded, landscaped flower beds added living colors to the front of the house.

Tyler yanked open the heavy red front door the moment Tracey leaned forward to ring the bell. As she stumbled into the foyer, he stood in place and stared, rubbing his jaw and nodding at her. She dropped her bag to the floor, wrapping her arms around his waist and squeezing him.

He whispered. "Mom, don't do anything like that again." She must have been hugging him a little too tight because he squirmed away after a minute, then looked down at her with sadness in his eyes. "I'm serious."

Stepping back, Tracey grabbed his hands and gazed in his eyes. They were bloodshot and a bit swollen. More words weren't needed. She'd been constant in his life since birth. There had never been a time when he didn't know where she was.

"Never again, okay," she promised.

He picked up her bag and guided her out of the foyer and down the tiled hallway. She loved Tyler so much. He'd been brought up right.

"Me and Dad, we have the back room down here ready for you. It's next to the laundry room. It's not much, but there's a bed in it and a closet and dresser. Dad wants to turn it into a better looking guest room, but he never found the time. Come on."

"Where is he?"

"He stayed up for a while, but he's got meetings and stuff tomorrow. Remember when I talked to you and you were passing by Newark?"

"Yes."

"Dad went to bed after that. He told me to wait up for you." Tyler pushed opened a door at the end of the hallway. "This is it."

The room was small and sparse but it looked like heaven to Tracey. Clean and quiet. She kicked her shoes off on the beige carpet and stretched out on the bed. Laying on her side with a pillow under her head, she closed her eyes.

Tyler's voice drifted above her head. "If you need anything, I'm right upstairs."

"Okay."

"What happened to your feet? You got bandages all over them. Did you jump out of a window?"

She kept her eyes closed. "No, nothing close to that. I'll let you know everything—it's a long story. We have to talk about it later."

"Yeah, all right. But when you wake up . . ." Tyler said.

"I know. Love you."

"Love you, too."

Tyler shut the door. Tracey fished her phone from her back and sent out a quick text to Monica.

I'm safe. Drove to New York. Here with Tyler, Kyle and the Addisons. Tyler is at peace and I'm resting in the guest room. We'll talk later.

Should she call Brian? Definitely. Did she want to? No. Tracey turned her phone off, slipped it back into her purse, and turned the bedroom light off. In the dark silence, Tracey slept hard and long. When she woke hours later, she climbed out of bed and staggered out to the hallway, found a bathroom to relieve herself, and made her way back to the room where she sunk into deep slumber once again.

She drifted in and out of sleep the rest of the next day. No nightmares. No images. Quiet and still.

NOISE COMING from outside the house woke Tracey. Alternating deep voices. She sat up and rubbed the sleep from her eyes.

"Tell her to come out now!"

Brian?

Tracey bolted up off the bed, lunged over to the window and carefully peeked around the curtain. Sure enough, Brian stood in the driveway having what looked like a face-to-face argument with Kyle. She squinted. No way. First, who told him she was here? Second, what time was it? Third, *who in the world had told him she was here*? Silent questions. No answers. Tracey kept listening. Brian's back was to the window so she couldn't see his face, but she could make out some of Kyle's facial expressions in the sunlight.

"Send her out here!" Brian demanded.

"I can't do that," Kyle answered, shaking his head.

Brian's jaw tightened. "Then we have a problem because she shouldn't have driven here, and no way is she staying."

Kyle stood firm. "Man, look. The woman is exhausted. She was a mess when we talked to her on the road. Right now I think she's sleeping. If she's awake, I'll ask her if she wants to talk to you, but that's her decision."

"I'm coming inside. I'll go and talk to her," Brian insisted.

Again with the head shaking from Kyle. "I'm telling you, no. My parents are in the house. I just got home myself. Go home. Brianna needs you. Tracey will call you when she feels better. You know how she is."

Brian's voice grew louder. "You don't need to tell me how she is! *She's my wife.* Why is she here of all places? She has friends and family where we live. What kind of game are you all playing?"

"Game? Man, think about it, why would I call you if something shady was happening. I wanted you to know she was here. When we called her on the road she was crying. Sounding crazy. Tyler lost it. He wanted his mother where he could see her. So I asked her to come here. She said you two were fighting? What's up with that?"

Tracey frowned. Kyle called Brian? No wonder he showed up in Long Island. He should have let her talk to him first. She wasn't ready to see him again yet.

"I'm not discussing our personal business with you. I'm here to help my wife." Brian said.

"You want to help her?"

"That's what I said."

"Then give her some space!"

Tracey kept the curtains clutched tight in her palm and watched, her lips pressed together hard. Neither man said anything for a moment. She wasn't sure but it looked as if Brian's fist was balled up. Holding her breath, she waited to see what would happen next.

"You don't want to do this. Come on, let me talk to you," Kyle offered, turning and gesturing for Brian to walk along with him.

They walked off. Out of Tracey's view and completely out of earshot.

Now what?

CHAPTER

Twenty-Six

SHOCKED AND TIRED? Yes. Stomach crunched in knots from hunger? Yes. Unsure of the condition of her marriage? Big neon green glittering sign flashing *yes*.

Still. Tracey didn't need Kyle to fight her battle.

She made a beeline out of the house and paced back and forth in the driveway waiting for Brian and Kyle to return from wherever they'd walked off to in the neighborhood. She rubbed her eyes and looked down the street. Nobody walking along the sidewalks in either direction.

So Brian drove to New York. Tracey knew she should've called him when she reached Long Island, but she was exhausted, still angry, and partially delirious. Staying in the house behind the window instead of coming out right out to talk with her husband? Ugh. Jellyfish move right there. She didn't have anything or anyone to hide from. If Brian wanted to see her, he could see her.

She gazed down the street until she saw the two men walking down the sidewalk toward the house. When they reached the driveway, Brian stopped in front of Tracey. Kyle gave a nod, but kept on moving, not saying a word to either of them as he went into the house and shut the front door.

Brian raised his hands. "I'm not here to fight with you."

"Good. Because I don't want to fight," Se raised an eyebrow. "Where's Brianna?"

He put his hands down. "With Ma and Jamal. I took her there this afternoon then I drove up here."

"Does she . . . uh? Where does she—"

"I told her you took a break to visit old friends. That's enough of the truth for her to handle." Brian said.

"Thanks," Tracey stammered. "You didn't have to come here. I mean . . . I'm okay. Ty's here."

"Are you serious? I called Ma. I called Monica. I didn't hear a thing from you all night and I was worried sick. Then Kyle calls this morning and tells me you're at his house! Do you know how that made me feel?"

Tracey wrapped her arms around herself and looked down at the asphalt beneath her bare feet. Memories of her delirium on I-95 passed through her mind. She'd thought nothing good would come from this. She'd was right.

Tracey raised her head up to stare in Brian's eyes. "Tyler is here and his father offered me a place to lay my head."

Brian's nostrils flared. "Fine. You rested. Now get your stuff. You can follow me back home right now."

Tracey didn't blink. "No," she answered, firmly.

"No?"

She stepped backwards as he leaned in toward her. "So help me God, if you lay one hand on me—"

"Stop it! You know I'm not that kind of guy!"

If Tracey could have raised her eyebrows until they touched her hairline she would have. "Really? I *knew* you weren't a cheater until you cheated. And I *knew* you weren't a liar until you lied to me."

"This isn't getting us anywhere!" Brian wiped away sweat from his forehead. "Shouldn't it be enough to know I drove like a bat out of hell to come up here for you?"

Tracey crossed her arms and stood her ground. Sure, Brian

had probably broken all major driving laws to arrive in Long Island before sunset. And he'd dropped his pride enough to ask Ma and Jamal to care for Brianna when he zipped off. Tracey meant a lot to him, no doubt about that. But why couldn't he have realized that at the beginning of the year?

"I'm staying put until I figure out what I want to do," Tracey said.

"You have a family!"

"You do too. That didn't stop you."

Brian placed a hand on the side of his jaw and rubbed. "So you want to keep making this hard?"

Water came into Tracey's eyes, but she willed herself not to cry. No more tears. Tears could not help the situation. Her insides throbbed with hurt. "Brian, I'm tired. When I go home, I have to deal with . . ." She looked so deep into his eyes she could see his pupils dilating. "I might be better off here for a minute."

"I'm not happy about you staying here. Not by a long shot. This isn't . . ." Brian looked away.

Tracey looked away too, staring down the quiet, tree-lined street. Why couldn't Kyle's house be on a busy road? Everyone in his house had likely heard their conversation, including Tyler.

"Our year has been one big mess. Now, I'm a mess. Nothing makes any sense to me." Tracey sighed.

"You've got a husband and a young daughter, Tracey. A daughter," Brian's voice caught. "You're hurting everyone."

No more words. Tracey stood still, holding everything inside as she watched Brian walk back to his car, climb in, and drive away.

TRACEY'S STOMACH ached and low blood sugar made her feel sick. After Brian drove away she entered the house and went straight to the kitchen to find something to eat before she passed out from starvation. Tyler wandered in while she served herself a dish of peach cobbler.

"Mom?"

"Ty, please don't ask."

"He didn't hurt you, did he? Cause if he did—"

Tracey spun around on the kitchen stool. "He went home, honey. Home. I didn't touch him. He didn't touch me. He's still your stepfather, and the man that helped raise you. Has he ever hurt you?"

"No," Tyler shook his head and frowned, a confused look in his eyes. "But what went on last weekend? Dad told me you and Brian had a fight. What happened to your feet?"

If she didn't tell him he'd keep asking. "On Sunday night we got into an argument. He said some things . . . anyway, I got mad and threw some glasses at him. They shattered all over the kitchen floor, and I managed to step on some and got cut."

"What glasses?"

Good grief, why did it matter? "Our wedding crystal."

Tyler paused for a second. "So he didn't hit you at all?"

"No. And we need to stop talking about this right now because the fight's over, and I'm not in the mood to relive it." She chewed and swallowed. "Where are your grandparents?"

"Oh, they have in-law quarters on the other side of the house. They have their own living room and everything. Dad hooked their area up nice. You gotta walk over and see it. Plus, they're in and out a lot. They do a lot with their church, and you know everywhere Granny goes, Grandpop goes with her. I think they're at a fellowship tonight."

"Always a duo?"

"Always." Tyler moved in closer. "What made you so angry that you threw your crystal at him? Things were better in the house last month."

"Ty?"

"I should leave you alone about it, huh?"

She nodded.

He stood over her, bent down, and kissed her on the fore-head. "All right then."

She watched him leave the kitchen. A minute later she heard the sound of a PlayStation being turned on in the living room.

Tracey dished out more peach cobbler and gulped it down along with a tall glass of iced tea. Ms. Celeste was a remarkable baker. Tracey loved to cook but she had nowhere near the skills Tyler's grandmother possessed with baking ingredients and a hot oven. The breakfast bar held a clear glass cookie jar filled with oatmeal raisin cookies, a cake stand holding up a sinfully rich-looking red velvet cake, and the baking dish that held the peach cobbler. To confirm Ms. Celeste had indeed made Tyler all his favorites, Tracey peeked in the bottom of the refrigerator. Sure enough, a round, green plastic container was filled with banana pudding. No wonder Kyle was a bachelor—unless he married one of the female chefs from the *Food Network*, he was hard pressed to find anyone who could cook from scratch like this nowadays.

But this was Kyle's home. Since he'd offered Tracey asylum, the least she could do was make an appearance and thank him. She needed to shower and dress, and then go find Kyle some-where around his cavern of a house.

TRACEY ROAMED around the house a bit after cleaning up and finally spied Kyle out on the wide backyard deck. She slid the patio doors open and stepped out onto the red-brown wood. Kyle was reclining on an outdoor chaise lounge, a burning cigar in one hand and brown liquid on ice in a glass on a small table next to him. It had been a couple years since she'd been around Kyle physically—not since Tyler graduated from middle school. He looked the same. Handsome. Short, curly black hair. Gray hair sprinkled at his temples showed his advancing age—that and the luggage hanging beneath his eyes. He wore black pants and a white shirt with the patterned tie loosened about his neck. He had his legs stretched out in front of him and he'd removed his shoes and socks, putting his bare feet on display.

"Mrs. Jones," Kyle gestured toward the empty chair next to him.

"Mr. Addison," Tracey stepped over to the chair and sat down. "You called my husband?"

"Yes, I did. I didn't think he'd actually jump in the car and come up here but I guess he had to do what he had to do." Kyle tapped ash off his cigar into a small glass ashtray on the table next to him.

"Out front . . . what did you say to him?" Tracey asked.

"I said, 'If you love her at all you'll give her what she needs right now, because if she leaves, seriously she is gone for good'. We said a few things after, but basically that was it."

She raised both eyebrows. "I didn't think you'd take up for me. I'm shocked."

Kyle shrugged, then reached for his glass.

"Jack Daniels?" Tracey said.

"It's what I like."

She settled back in her chair. "I'm not judging."

He sipped his drink. "You *are* judging, but it's cool. I won't kick you out."

"Gee thanks."

"You're welcome." Kyle took another sip then cocked his head to the side. "Now why are you here?"

"You asked me to come here."

"That's not what I mean." He turned toward her. "I mean, why'd you leave your house in the first place?"

"It's a long story."

"Well, I've got my drink and my chair and my smoke. I'm good. Go on and let it out."

Tracey sighed. "Do I have a choice?"

"You're staying in my house," He said, sipping from the glass again. "So, no."

"Brian had an affair."

"I already knew that, remember? And he's not the first dude to do so. Go on. Something must have happened after that."

Tracey studied the expression on his face. No shock there. No judgment either. His eyes riveted to her, and he'd stopped sipping his drink. She kept going. "We were on a rocky path for a few months. Just going through the motions with each other. I kept a lot of anger inside because I wanted to keep the peace in the house. Our relationship was different, you know, even after we tried to patch things up." She hunched her shoulders. "Then I acted out a bit, spending money without talking to him about it, but we got past that too. Our relationship got better and I honestly thought everything would work out in time."

"I hear you," Kyle said.

This was the hard part. "Now . . . he's having a baby."

"I'm confused." A puzzled look crossed Kyle's face. "With you?"

"With her."

"Oh."

Tracey kept her face downward. "Sunday . . . the woman . . . her name is Lisette . . . comes to my church and confronts my husband right there in the parking lot with her little round belly showing."

Kyle slumped back in his chair. "Whoa. Brian? Something like this? I would have never thought."

"Kyle, I lost it. Yelling. Throwing stuff. And since I don't want my kids sending me care packages addressed to Muncy Prison, I decided to go to Monica's for a bit. But then I got on the road and started driving. You know that show *Snapped*, where women lose it and drive their mates over with trucks or poison them with cyanide?"

Kyle nodded.

"It was like that."

He tsked. "I hate to hear stories like this. I like to believe I can have something like my Mom and Pops have, but I don't know. Look at you two—and you all are in the church."

Tracey winced. A violent fighting couple. Great. She and Brian made one heck of an impression on an unsaved person, didn't they? Out of her house, away from Brian and Brianna, and there she sat pouring out her married sorrows to Kyle, of all people. She tipped back her head and stared up at the darkening sky.

Lord. Please tell me.

What will it take to fix this train wreck?

CHAPTER
Twenty~Seven

BRIANNA.

Visions of the girl floated through Tracey's mind. The child's sunshine smile. Her plucky spirit. The ever present naked, tangled-hair Barbie dolls laying on tabletops and sometimes abandoned on floors. Her warm, toasty brown skin and constant hugs. Tracey's heart thumped hard inside her chest, and she put her hand over it as she turned over in bed and stared at the white ceiling of a strange room. She swallowed hard and blinked back water in her eyes. Being away from her small daughter made her soul ache. How could she drive away like that? Marriage broken. Family splintered. At first it seemed easy to point the finger at Brian as the catalyst, but now heavy guilt tugged at her as she considered her own actions from the last two days.

Tracey slid out of bed, grabbed her purse from the dresser, fished out her phone, and called home without thinking about it.

Brian answered on the first ring. "Tracey."

"I uh." Tracey cleared her throat, and started again. "I need to talk to Brianna."

"Are you on your way home? You should be on your way home."

"Brian . . . please . . . I'm asking you . . . don't give me a hard time."

A pause. "Hold on. She's in her room."

Tracey dropped back down on the bed and waited. A minute seemed like a lifetime before she heard Brianna's sunny voice.

"Mommy?"

"Hi baby. How are you?"

"Fine. I miss you. Can I come see you? Where are you?"

A five-year-old could only take the simple truth. Tracey could provide that at least.

"I needed a break. Kind of like a vacation."

"You didn't say goodbye to me."

"I know honey."

"I drew you a picture yesterday. Sailboats. You me and daddy were on a boat. We were on the water. I made the water blue."

Tracey swallowed hard at the lump in her throat. "The three of us on a sailboat, huh?"

"And a big sunshine. And the sunshine was smiling. Can you come see my picture today?"

"No honey, not today. But very soon."

"Soon?"

"Soon."

"When you get back can we go to the sprayground with all the water jets? And can I get ice cream from the Mister Softee truck?" Brianna asked.

"We sure will. I'll call you again sugar. Can you give the phone back to daddy?"

"Okay, bye."

Another pause, then Brian's voice again. "She misses you."

"I know." Tracey couldn't think of anything else to say. "I'll be in touch."

"Yeah. Right."

Their connection ended with silence.

TRACEY HAD EXPECTED her bestie to support her, so she was shocked when she called Monica later in the morning and received an earful of discontent in return.

"You . . . self-centered . . . unbelievable!" Monica yelled.

"Will you at least hear me out?"

"No! I was here for you! I'm always here for you. You could have followed through and stayed at my apartment! But this? Kyle? Don't you have enough trouble?"

"My staying in New York is so not about Kyle. I'm here because Tyler is here."

"Keep telling yourself that. Keep on! You can't tell *me* that because I was the one with you seventeen years ago when he broke your heart and you were about to lose your mind over him. I dragged your butt out of bed when you were determined to stay there until you starved to death. Now you think *his* house is safer for you than mine? Girl . . . " Monica whistled. "At least create a story better than the tale you're telling!"

"You think I'm running from a disaster with Brian straight into some mess with Kyle?"

"I don't think. I know! And I'm not going to sit here in the supportive sister-friend role while you jump from one crisis to another. I didn't trust Kyle when we were at Syracuse. I don't trust him now, even if he is my godson's father. I'm not on Team Brian either but using Kyle to make Brian jealous is low."

"Jealous?"

"Yeah jealous! Sleeping over at your son's father's house sounds like some hot ghetto mess to me and that's NOT you."

"Right, so somehow I forced Kyle and Tyler to ask me to stay here?"

"I don't know how you sounded or what you said, I wasn't on the phone with you, but I'm talking to you now telling you you're wrong for this!"

Tracey's chest felt like a wide rubber band stretched around her lungs, keeping them from fully expanding. "Well, I'm here. I guess there's not much else I can say."

"No, you can't. You've been my sister since we pledged and you always will be, but I'm not behind you. Not for this."

Then Monica was gone.

Tracey turned her phone off and buried it in the bottom of her purse. She'd wanted to call her Mom and Charla, but what was the point? It was plain crazy for her to think her loved ones would understand. How could they? No one stood with her behind the church on Sunday night. No one except Brian, in the kitchen surrounded by broken glass and smeared blood on the floor.

Kyle had offered her an option. She took it. Funny. Back in February Lisette had offered Brian an option. He took it. Later on he had to face the repercussions of his choice.

Tracey guessed it was her turn now.

TRACEY FINALLY RAN into Kyle's mother, Celeste, in the kitchen at lunchtime, and Celeste gracefully managed to co-opt Tracey into being her afternoon travel companion. In the course of four hours, Celeste had taken Tracey on a whirlwind tour to her favorite hair salon, a grocery store, and a quick visit to Home Depot. Celeste didn't ask or say one word about Tracey staying at the house. Big-mouthed Kyle probably told her everything, and for once, Tracey felt grateful for his talkativeness. It saved her an explanation.

Once they arrived back in the house, Tracey thought she'd be able to slip out of the woman's grasp and hide in the guest room, but she didn't move fast enough. Before Tracey had a chance to retreat, Celeste had managed to zip over to her wing of the house. She'd changed into jeans, gardening clogs and a long sleeved shirt, and come back to the kitchen with more plans for Tracey which included pulling weeds and tending plants. With no way to escape politely, Tracey found herself trekking to the backyard to work in the garden.

"Here, take this," Celeste said, pushing a potted green plant into Tracey's arms.

Tracey dropped the wooden rake she'd been using to clear away the weeds they'd pulled from a flower bed. "What is this? What do you want me to do with it?"

"This plant? Basil. There's an area over in the side yard where I need you to take it out of the pot and transplant it in the herb garden."

"Ms. Celeste . . . um . . . I don't know how to transplant anything." Tracey grasped the pot awkwardly, running her fingers over the nubby texture.

"I'll have to show you then. Come on."

Celeste led the way over to the side yard. More beautiful rows of colorful flowers next to a large rectangular patch with lots of green sprouting up. Tracey guessed that was the herb garden when Celeste stopped in front of the dark earth and knelt down on the grass.

"I started all of these herbs indoors and they've been doing great since I transplanted them here. Fennel. Chives. Dill. Rosemary. Oregano. Parsley. Now I'm ready to put the basil in here." She looked up at Tracey, sunlight bouncing off the gold rims of her glasses. "Come on. Kneel down here. Put your hands in this dirt."

"My hands?"

"Yes."

"In the dirt?"

"Yes. Get down here."

Tracey placed the pot on the grass beside her and kneeled next to Celeste, placing her fingers in the cool earth.

"We need to transplant this basil in the ground where it can continue to grow. Now here's the spade and I'm going to show you how to dig out the earth and make a hole for the plant." Celeste moved swiftly, her hands moving the crumbled black dirt to the side. "Take this and keep digging. Keep your hands with the earth as you move it."

"And why am I doing this?"

Celeste stopped moving the dirt. She stared into Tracey's eyes. "Because no one can stay angry with their hands in the earth. No one. Try it. You'll see what I mean. Put your hands in here."

Tracey wiggled her fingers in the earth and waited for some magical feeling to take over.

Nothing came.

Celeste moved further over to the left and gestured for Tracey to lean closer to the earth. "Dig your spade in and make the hole deep and wide enough to hold the plant's roots well."

Tracey shrugged. Make the right-sized hole in the earth. Take the plant from the pot and put it in the hole. No biggie. She grabbed the pot and turned it upside down.

Celeste grabbed Tracey's arm. "Stop!"

"Why?"

"You can't just dump a plant onto the ground. You have to move the plant carefully. Here, let me show you."

Celeste pulled the plant from Tracey's arms and set it back down on the earth. Then she started working with her hands in the earth again. "See, planting looks easy . . . but it requires a lot of care and consideration. Take this basil here. Weeks ago I planted the seeds in a small pot on my windowsill. Then they sprouted and I put the new plant in this pot here. I watered it and it grew more. But I needed to get it ready to live in the ground outdoors, so four days ago I started prepping this plant with fertilizer. Yesterday I mixed garden soil and fertilizer in this patch of earth we are right now kneeling in front of. I did all of that in order to grow a crop of fresh basil that will end up in a dish of lasagna."

Tracey glanced at Celeste. The older lady returned a warm smile and started talking again.

"Planting can teach you a lot about life you know. You've read your Bible. You know about sowing seeds. You know about harvest. But when you get out in your garden every day, you gain experience about preparation and nurturing. If your seeds won't grow, you'll start to look at the soil and the plants around the area. If weeds appear and keep your plants from thriving, you know you need to get in there and dig those suckers out."

Tracey snorted. "Even without a garden, I've definitely learned a lot about getting rid of weeds."

Celeste pulled back from the herb patch and sat down on the grass. She took off her glasses and wiped them with a handkerchief. "You had some weeds this year. I've heard."

"Yeah," Tracey conceded.

"You know . . . I called them weeds years ago . . ."

Tracey took her hands out of the earth and turned toward Celeste. "What are you saying?"

Celeste nodded her head toward the house. "With that man in there? You think I haven't had to pull a few weeds out of our garden?"

Tracey shook her head. "Every woman I know," she muttered under her breath.

"Pardon?"

"Seems like every married woman I've talked to has the same story. Well, not *every* woman. My sister-in-law—no weeds in her garden ever."

"She keeps her husband close to her then."

"Beyond close."

"That's why."

"Oh," Tracey sighed.

"Your marriage is a lot like a garden."

"I'm getting that now."

"Good. Now shut up and listen," Celeste said.

"Sorry."

"You're no slave. If you feel like a potted plant, a garden, or even your marriage isn't worth the effort to attend to it, get rid of it. You're an adult. Get rid of a pot of basil and there's no need to fertilize anything, but forget about enjoying fresh herbs. Let the weeds grow like crazy in your garden and forget about smelling flowers later on. Walk out on your marriage and you'll get your freedom, but you'll also never know if . . . "

Tracey interrupted, "I understand."

Gardens and weeds. Metaphors and wisdom. Tracey's garden? In shambles for sure. Should she try to save it? Get on in there with some fertilizer and daily watering and tend to the soil and transplant some seeds and God knew what else? Or chuck the whole thing, find a tractor and demolish it? Have it paved and make it a parking lot?

"Celeste?" a male voice beckoned. Tracey stopped and looked up to see who the voice belonged to. Judge Addison was walking slowly into the side yard.

"Excuse me for a moment," Celeste said, quickly rising to her feet.

Tracey watched as Celeste slowed her movements to match Judge Addison's, linking her arm with his as they walked across the lawn toward the herb patch together. His slightly stooped gait made him appear a few inches shorter than his wife, though Tracey could remember when he stood taller than her. As they walked, Tracey noticed Celeste effortlessly helped him to keep his balance. He seemed to walk faster and with more confidence with her by his side. They reached the herb patch as one unit. Tracey stood to greet him.

"Hello, Judge Addison. Nice to see you."

He nodded to her and offered a smile, though it seemed to strain his facial muscles. "Tracey. It's been awhile."

"That it has." Tracey leaned up on tiptoe and wrapped her arms around his shoulders for a quick hug. His frame felt rigid.

"Keeping my wife company today?" His voice wavered.

Celeste beamed as she wrapped an arm around her husband's waist. "She's been a big help to me today. And now I'm trying to show her some of the finer points of putting in an herb garden."

"I've been getting tired and learning a lot today following your wife around. She's kept me moving."

Judge Addison chuckled. It was good to see the twinkle in his eye hadn't been taken away by the effects of Parkinson's. "Well, don't let me stop you. I came out to see my darling here." He grasped Celeste's arm tighter.

Tracey moved back down on her hands and knees, becoming intimate with the loam again. When she turned to pick up the basil, she saw Celeste helping Judge Addison ease himself down on the black wrought iron garden bench. She continued watching them as they talked, their heads close together. There was something special about their relationship. Solid. Where he had visible tremors, she provided stability. The two completed each other, his slow deliberateness to her caring swiftness.

Tracey faced the dirt again, placing her fingers in the earth and moving piles to the side. Maybe there was something to all this. Digging through dirt. Transplanting from an area that was confining and small.

Moving a living thing to a place where it could grow bigger, stronger, and more fruitful.

CHAPTER
Twenty-Eight

LATE THAT EVENING Tracey walked past the patio doors and spotted Kyle sitting alone on the deck. He held a glass loosely in his hands. His head hung down and his legs stretched open on the edge of his chair.

"Kyle?" Tracey called as she stepped out on deck. "You okay?"

He brought the glass to his lips and sipped slowly before answering. "No."

"Want to talk?"

"No."

"Fine." She turned and slid the patio door open to go back inside, then she heard his voice.

"Wait, come here. Have a drink with me."

"You know better—but I'll sit with you." She made her way out onto the deck and eased into the chair next to him.

He reached over to the table with unsteady hands, poured more brown liquid into his glass then set the bottle down on the table so hard the wood rattled. He drank that down, poured another, then reclined back on the chair and sat with the glass in his hands.

Neither of them spoke. Tracey stared out over the pool. Twinkling lights surrounded its perimeter and tiny waves rippled atop the water. She shifted in her chair and looked over at Kyle, whose chest moved up and down with deep breaths.

"My pop . . . he didn't play sports. He loved to read. Loved to talk about law and current events. But he was right there at all my Little League games. Put me in Pee Wee football. When I told him I wanted to play basketball in junior high, he bought me three pairs of new sneakers. And he never missed a game."

Kyle squeezed his eyes closed tight then. It didn't seem like he needed Tracey to talk back him. He kept the conversation going as though she were some anonymous person on a bar stool. But this was no smoky bar. This was the deck leading out to Kyle's stunning pool in the middle of his ultra-landscaped backyard which included a vegetable and herb garden his mother cultivated daily. And Tracey? Far from being a stranger.

"I hated school. But I had to keep my grades up. Didn't want to disappoint my Pops, you know. He was a county judge. And my mom taught school and she loved reading. Me? I couldn't read a sentence without getting bored and wanting to jump out of my seat and find out what the next kid was doing two rows down from me. Mom thought I needed help. Pop took the pressure off. Told me to do the best I could to get through. He stayed up on the phone all night with me when I thought about dropping out of Syracuse my sophomore year. Remember that?"

She nodded.

"Mom and Pop . . . two peas in a pod, you know. When he got out of the Navy and went to college, my mom was the first girl he saw. He never had eyes for another woman after they met. Did you know that?"

Tracey stayed silent. She remembered Ms. Celeste alluding to the contrary, but now was not the time to mention that very private conversation.

"Yeah. When I was growing up, they had this big map in the

basement of the old house—map of the world. My Pop hung it up on the wall—put red tacks in it, you know, showing all the places where they were going to travel to once he retired. Rome. France. Peru. Even Australia and New Zealand. He wanted to take her everywhere."

He sipped his drink, and rubbed a hand over his sweaty forehead. "And this is what it comes down to for him? A man who has given nothing but his best to his family and his community, imprisoned in his own body for the rest of his life?"

"Kyle."

"This disease. It didn't take him but it took him, you know? His walk, talk, writing, all his movements, everything is different. We thought the medication would help, but he's getting worse each year. I have to watch old family videos just to remind myself how he took charge of everything, and all the corny jokes he made, and how much he used to grab my mom and hold her close to him . . ." Kyle's voice trailed off.

"Kyle, he's still here."

"And trapped."

Tracey reached over, grabbed Kyle's sweaty hand, and grasped it tight. "And still your father. Hug him. Talk to him. Use your motor mouth to tell him corny jokes. He's still here for you to make him proud, which you do every day, and you'll keep doing that."

Kyle pulled his head up and looked in Tracey's eyes, gazing for a moment before he spoke. "You remember what he used to be like, right?"

Maybe she should let go of his hand? No. Not now. "Remember? I can't forget. I was in the hospital room with Tyler sleeping in my arms. My face was a mess. My hair was a mess. All by myself looking at *The Price Is Right* trying to figure out what in the world I was going to do with a newborn baby, no home of my own, an unfinished degree, and no man to help with the load. I looked up and your father walks into the room and he takes the baby from me and sits down on the bed and kisses his grandson's face. Then he grabbed my hand and told me it was going to be all right. Told me you were stuck on stupid for the moment, but he and Ms. Celeste would always be there for Tyler. He wrote me a check and I used the money to get that apartment in Abington. I even had enough for nursery furniture. Your dad was my miracle."

"Miracle?"

"He came through for me. In a big way."

"Great man."

"Absolutely a great man."

"Did he actually say 'stuck on stupid'?"

"Oh, yeah. No way would I forget that."

Kyle's squeezed Tracey's fingers. She squeezed back. He squeezed again, tighter this time. She grasped his hand tighter, letting herself stare back in his eyes. His eyes held wonder and surprise. Something like an electrical current jolted her and she jerked upright. She dropped his hand and moved her own back into the zone called *that was then and this is now and don't even think about it*.

He picked up his drink again. "I talked to his doctor . . . the news about his condition . . ."

"Not good?"

"Terrible."

"I know you probably don't want to hear this but God does have a plan for his life."

Kyle grunted before taking a sip from his glass. "Whatever. It's dumb to believe in a God who allows this."

Tracey looked away. Small ripples on the pool water. A backyard oasis.

He reached out and tapped her on the shoulder. "What's the matter?"

"Nothing."

"You're mad?"

"Listen, you're entitled to your opinion, but I would think

you'd have more faith considering how your parents raised you."

"All right then, you tell me—why didn't you have faith God would work everything out for you?"

Tracey pressed her lips together until her face no longer felt warm. "We are not talking about me right now."

"You messed up your own marriage."

"I what?"

"I'm not buying for one minute you didn't figure out you had something to do with your husband stepping out there like he did."

"Whatever." She shivered. Not from the wind, but from the last comment.

He stared her up and down. "Have you looked at yourself lately?"

"Of course."

"You're okay with the fact that you're so thin you look like you've taken up crack smoking as a hobby?"

"I'm going through a rough time right now," Tracey justified, biting her bottom lip.

"You looked better before?"

She shrugged. Kyle was drunk and liable to say anything. Fighting with him wouldn't help. She doubted he'd remember anything in the morning. After four glasses of brown liquor he'd most likely forget he even came out to the pool.

Kyle pushed himself all the way back into his chair until he was reclining again. "Now that's why I'm not married. Probably never will be. No man wants a wife that forgets she needs to look good for him regularly. Running around taking care of the kids and the house and forgetting all about the person who put the diamond ring on her finger. When was the last time you sent the kids to a babysitter then showed up in heels and a teddy and surprised your man with dinner and dessert in the bedroom?"

"You don't know what my husband likes."

"Forget about what he does or doesn't like for a second. How much do you know about him?"

"More than anyone else."

"Okay, so when dude shaves, what side of his face does he start with? The right or the left?"

Tracey's face burned. She should leave Kyle right there with his liquor until he passed out. But she couldn't find the strength to get up out of the chair.

"What jeans does he wear most when he's not working?" Kyle asked.

"Those are small things."

He sat up and leaned in. "You don't know, do you?"

Tracey's stomach twisted. "You don't know anything about living day in and day out with a spouse. You have a lot of nerve to sitting there telling me I caused my own husband to cheat."

"Not the cause." Kyle said as he wiped sweat away from his brow. "But you played a part."

"Why do you care?"

"Because of Tyler. He'd call me on the phone late at night and we'd talk. He let me know how strained things were in your house."

Tracey stood up. The conversation was over. No point in trying to console a drunk male chauvinist. "I don't care what the two of you have been chatting about, there's no point in you going off on me about my life." She narrowed her eyes and frowned. "I came out here to make sure you were okay. I'm going inside. Sober up. Come talk to me about marriage *after* you get hitched."

Kyle stood up, shaking, but he made it onto his feet. "One of my business partners has been battling his wife in divorce proceedings for two years now. His wife had twin girls five years ago and she gained more than a hundred pounds. He can't stand to look at her, let alone touch her. Find a wife? No thanks. Unless I can have what my parents have, marriage isn't in the cards for me."

"Then how come Tyler told me he met two different women last summer, coming over here, cooking dinner with you?"

Kyle fished his phone out of his pocket. "I've got needs." His phone lit up as he speed-dialed someone. "Every man has them."

"Apparently," Tracey muttered.

CHAPTER
Twenty~Nine

"MOMMY!"

"How's my girl?"

"Where are you? Are you coming home today?"

Tracey swallowed hard. "Honey, how was camp this week?"

"When are you coming home?"

"Soon."

"Can you pick me up from camp today? Can we watch Doc McStuffins? I can help you make pizza."

How would Tracey handle this? She didn't possess the words to tell Brianna everything going on inside her head. "I'm not sure how much longer I'll be away, so we'll have to save TV and pizza for another time."

"Did I do something wrong?" Brianna's voice squeaked.

That did it. Tears welled up in Tracey's eyes. Her throat swelled tight making it hard to talk. She squinted against the morning sunlight streaming through the kitchen windows as she leaned against the breakfast bar. "No, not at all."

"Did Daddy do something wrong?"

Oh boy, he sure did. "Sweetie, I promise Mommy will be home soon. Where did your dad go?"

"He's here."

"Can you give him the phone back?"

Brian's baritone voice came on the line. "Yes."

"Brianna doesn't sound too good."

"She's been crying all night. She needed to hear your voice to calm down."

Tracey closed her eyes. "All right, what are we going to do now?"

"Hold on a minute," Brian said. The phone went mute for a moment. "I'm back. I sent her to go get her sneakers and her backpack. Tracey, pack up and drive home today. Make pizza and watch Doc McStuffins with Brianna this afternoon. Give her a bubble bath and put her to bed. We can talk about our situation tonight . . . all night long if you need."

Brian made it sound so simple. Like she'd been on a mystical healing vacation and all her emotional wounds had disappeared and she could resume her duties like the good little unappreciated wife she'd been before.

"You and me? We are a train wreck. I could come back today, but what are we doing? Have you figured that out yet?" Tracey turned toward the French doors, watching sun rays burn through the morning clouds and fog.

"Brianna's coming back down now. I gave you a plan. If you want to complicate things . . ." He trailed off, then said, "I'm taking her to camp now."

Tracey opened her mouth to come back with a quick remark but words escaped her. This cooling off time, although it had diffused some of her pain and anger, was fast becoming more trouble than it was worth.

IT WAS STILL early and quiet enough for Tracey to sit out on the deck and have uninterrupted devotions along with prayer time. She read from Proverbs and prayed for guidance. By the time she finished she'd made a half-hearted decision to go back home that afternoon. No matter what Brian's attitude, with Brianna upset and Kyle talking and acting like more a of a sinner than a saint last night, it seemed best to return to Philly.

She walked back into the house and straight to the kitchen where she busied herself frying bacon, scrambling eggs, cutting up fruit for a fruit salad, and making fresh waffles. Celeste had cooked all week and this was a good time for Tracey to return the favor. The morning news played on the small kitchen television set while she worked. The weather forecast predicted a clear sunny day but possible thunderstorms in the late evening hours.

Kyle appeared out of nowhere. "Making breakfast for me? You shouldn't have, but thank you!" He wore a royal blue polo shirt and white shorts, smelled like a bar of Irish Spring, and looked just as fresh. He could be a walking advertisement in *GQ* if he'd do something about those bags under his eyes.

"No. This is for the whole family. But I guess you have to eat too," she responded as she flipped bacon over in the cast iron skillet.

He stepped over to the counter by the stove, peering at the pile of waffles. "These are from scratch? Nice."

"Of course. What kind of a cook do you think I am? I don't do boxed anything." She tapped him on the shoulder and pointed for him to hand her a plate from the counter. She placed a paper towel on it and used it to drain the bacon.

"Smells delicious," Kyle said.

"It's your food. I just cooked it." She stopped and turned toward him. "Wait. Why are you here? Aren't you supposed to be working?"

"I'm taking the day off." His eyes opened wide. "You don't remember what today is?"

She shrugged. "Friday?" she guessed.

"Tracey!" Kyle gibed.

She scanned his face for clues. "No really, I have no idea."

Kyle walked over by the refrigerator, opened a cabinet door, and pulled out a glass. He shook his head. "I didn't think you'd forget my birthday."

So that was it. "Happy birthday?"

He turned back to her. "That was weak."

"That's as good as you're going to get after last night."

"Holding a grudge?"

"What do you think?"

Tyler interrupted their conversation. "Hey, it's Mom and Dad! Together! In the same room. What? Hold on, let me grab my phone. I can post this historic meeting on my Facebook and Instagram." Tyler had a huge grin plastered across his face as he joined them.

Tracey glared at him. "If you so much as snap one picture of us together you'll wish you hadn't. Put a t-shirt on and stop walking around bare chested in the kitchen. And how come you're up so early?"

Kyle smiled. "And wait son, she said all that without taking another breath."

"Not even selfie with all of us? Come on, now!" Tyler teased.

"No! Now go!" Tracey said.

"All right," Tyler said, laughing as he backed out of the kitchen.

Kyle filled a plate with food. "You've got him trained."

"Yeah, well, I'm his mama."

"He's up early because we're spending the day together. We'll play some ball. I'll take him out on the golf course with me. Grab some lunch and go out and shop."

Kyle and Tyler. The boy loved his dad and dad loved his boy. A good thing. Still. It jarred Tracey to see how happy and content Tyler seemed when he walked into the kitchen. Like he wasn't the least bit concerned about Brian or Brianna. Tracey shook off the thought and concentrated on scrambling more eggs. Tyler and Kyle would probably eat the first platter full themselves. As she heated up the skillet again, she felt a warm hand rest on her shoulder and linger for a moment.

"You're a great mom to him," Kyle said, hugging her around the shoulders. "I mean it. I give you a hard time sometimes, but I couldn't have asked for a better mother for my son."

"Thanks," Tracey responded. A half-smile creased her face.

He let her go then and moved back to his stool by the breakfast bar. She turned her focus back to cooking.

"So, tell me Mrs. Jones, you bring anything to wear out on the town?"

She snorted. "Of course not."

"Well then you need to buy something. My friends and I are going out tonight and you're coming."

No way. Out of the question. "I'm not going out with you."

"You're right. You're not going out with me because it's a group outing. It's my birthday, and I go out with my friends and have dinner and champagne. I invited you to stay in my house. That qualifies you as one of my friends, and you're coming along."

"No. I am not!" she restated.

"Tracey, you can't sit around here one more night, moping and watching TV like an old widow."

"No, I can't. Actually, it's time for me to make my way back to Philly."

Kyle kept talking. "Everyone's meeting me here at eight. You've got all day to go to the mall for something to wear and be ready."

Tracey whipped around. "What part of *no* do you not understand? I don't party and I definitely don't drink."

"Cool. So have dinner, sip some ginger ale, and listen to the music. Do this for me."

"For you?"

He munched bacon with a sheepish look on his face. "I feel bad about last night. I shouldn't have said . . . anyway, this is my chance make it up to you. Come on out tonight and have some appetizers, a good steak, and great company."

"You're not accepting *no* as my final answer?"

"Get a dress and some heels and get made up. Push your troubles out of your mind for a few hours. My friends will make you laugh—plus they'll treat you like family."

She turned back to the stove. The smell of cooked eggs wafted beneath her nose. She cut off the heat under the skillet. A bead of sweat formed on her brow. She wiped it away fast.

Tyler breezed back in. He took all of ten seconds to pile his plate full of food and sit at the bar next to his father.

"So what do you say?" Kyle asked.

Tracey had to shut the conversation down. "I'll think about it, okay? There are some things I have to consider, like when I'm going to go back home."

"Fair enough."

"What are we talking about?" Tyler asked.

Kyle winked. "I told your mom she's a good mother, and she needs to get out and relax."

Silent, faced the hot stove again.

Tracey do this. Tracey do that.

Why did her life seem so easy when other people tried to manage it?

AT NOON, Tracey paced the carpet in the guest bedroom, gathering together what little she'd brought with her that week. Forget about going to a birthday party. Brianna needed her. She could have packed up sooner, but she needed to wash some underwear, jeans and a t-shirt in order to get dressed for the day. While those items tumble dried in the laundry room, Tracey put everything else in her bag and plopped down on the bed. She snatched up her phone. She needed to call Tyler and let him know her plan to leave the Motel Addison.

The phone buzzed in her hands before she could call. Brian's ID lit up the screen. "Hi."

Brian's voice came through tense and angry. "You should be back home by now. What's the hold up?"

"Well, I . . ."

"I can't believe this! What does it take for you? Does your daughter have to have a nervous breakdown for you to get home here?"

"Excuse me?"

"You heard me. We are not playing this game anymore, Tracey!"

And this is the man who said they could talk all night after she returned? "I think you need to calm down," Tracey admonished.

"I am calm. But I don't think you heard me right this morning, otherwise you would have been at home when I called the house."

Tracey's eyes darted about the room. "I heard you loud and clear."

"Then you know I gave you a plan. I expected you to follow it."

"I was getting everything together to drive back home as soon as I talked to Tyler."

"Good. You're cooperating then. That's a start."

A nerve in Tracey's temple twitched. She clutched the corner of a pillow in her clenched fist. Screaming at Brian was out—Ms. Celeste and Judge Addison were right outside in the side yard.

"Brian, I'm getting off the phone now."

"I'll see you in a few hours?"

"I'm getting off the phone."

Tracey shut her phone off and tossed it to the other side of the bed. It could stay there. The nerve of Brian! Something must have ticked him off before he called. Whatever. Where was her bath towel? She snatched off her bra and panties, wrapped a towel around her torso and stalked out of the room. He must have lost his mind. He didn't have to keep pushing like this. Like she was the one who started them down this road.

She race-walked down the hallway, made a pit stop in the laundry room to pull her warm clothes out of the dryer then closed herself up in the bathroom. She took a quick shower, dried-off, and pulled on her clean clothes in a record ten minutes. In the guest room she pulled her wallet and car keys out of her bag, left her phone on the bed, shoved her feet into her sandals and headed out of the house.

"Ms. Celeste," she called out as she jogged into the side yard. "Ms. Celeste!"

"I'm here. What is it?"

"Where's the nearest mall around here? I need to buy some clothes."

Brian needed to cool off. No way could she go back home tonight. They'd be at each other's throats by the time Brianna went to bed.

Tracey had a standing invitation for dinner and a chance to distract herself from everything. She would have food, listen to the live music at the lounge, thank Kyle for letting her stay in his home, and head out the next day.

What harm could it do?

CHAPTER
Thirty

THE BLACK SILK halter dress skimmed over Tracey's head, caressing her skin as she pulled it over and down to cover her hips. She crossed the room to the full-length mirror and peered at herself. Uh-oh. A little too sexy. The dress had looked like a simple shift when she'd pulled it off the rack a few hours earlier. Who would have thought it would cling to the little bit of curves on her thin frame? She had no choice but to wear it. Either that or put on jeans and a t-shirt. Forget it. Time to strap on the heels and keep it moving.

Smooth jazz music coming from the living room floated to her ears as Tracey applied her make-up. When she finished, she stepped back and surveyed her reflection. Her flat ironed hair hung sleek and straight to her shoulders—no more messy pony-tail. Not bad! Not as good as she had looked in Atlantic City with Brian, but still, not bad. Too much drama since then. She shook her head and sighed. *Just get through dinner tonight, Tracey.*

She glanced at the wall clock. Eight-thirty. Brian was prob-ably sitting up with Brianna, watching the Doc McStuffins DVD for the third time and seething. Why had he called her with such a bad attitude, making her go off half-cocked and not caring? Now, instead of cuddling her daughter, she stood alone in Kyle's guest room wearing an "I'm too sexy" dress, missing her daughter and infuriated at her husband.

Someone tapped on the door. "Are you ready? Everyone's here. Let's go!"

Tracey adjusted the dress around her hips once more, and opened the bedroom door. "I'm ready."

Kyle staggered back two steps. "You look . . . *nice*." He dragged the last word out three syllables.

She smiled and said, "Thanks. You do too." And he did. He wore a tan suit with a crisp white shirt and a patterned silk tie.

"Ah. This is nothing." He brushed away the compliment with a wave from his hand.

Tracey walked ahead of him a few paces, then stopped and turned around. "Where did Tyler go tonight? I haven't passed him or heard him walking around for a while."

"He has friends here, two brothers who live down the street. He went by there to hang out tonight. Yesterday they told him their cousin from Miami came to visit. They said she's supposedly is a dead ringer for Zendaya, so you know Ty had to go meet her."

"Zendaya? Who's that?"

Kyle shook his head. "You really need to get out more. Seriously."

"Whatever."

They reached the living room and Tracey looked around as Kyle did a fast round of introductions. "Everybody, this is Tracey Jones. Mother of my son."

Everyone smiled and said hello.

With his arm around her shoulder, Kyle gestured to the men and women sitting about the room. "Tracey, over there on the couch is Lawson Evers and Zenobia Taylor. Lawson's my accountant and Zenobia is his fiance."

Lawson was a bald man with rimless glasses and a warm smile. Zenobia, a dark brown-skinned woman with shoulder-length brown dreadlocks.

"Congratulations," Tracey smiled.

"Thanks!" they said in tandem.

Kyle gestured over to the love seat. "Now, blondie over here —Danny Marshall—plays the best one-on-one hoops game ever. Don't sit next to him at the lounge, or he'll talk your ear off about classic jazz."

The tanned man with twinkling blue eyes smiled at Tracey. "Nice to meet you."

"Likewise," Tracey answered, smiling.

Kyle turned once more to point out a lady with long dark hair and medium-toned skin who looked like she might be Asian and black. "You've heard Sonia's voice on the phone before, but this is the first time you've gotten the chance to meet."

Tracey said. "That's right, Sonia Harris—you're his office manager. You used to go to high school with Kyle."

Sonia extended her hand to shake. "Yes. Nice to finally meet you. I've heard so much about you."

There was no telling what Sonia might know about Tracey since Kyle didn't know how or when to shut up.

Kyle gestured to a large man with a friendly face. "And this is James St. Louis. He's a school superintendent. I won't tell you about his skills on the court because he doesn't have any," Kyle kidded as he slapped James on the shoulder.

"Nice to meet you Tracey. I'm ignoring him right now because there are ladies present and I've got some champagne here we need to open."

"Let's start the celebration!" Lawson stood, walked into the kitchen for glasses, and poured everyone champagne. When he brought her a glass, Tracey shook her head and put up her hand. "Nothing for me, thanks."

"No?" Lawson raised an eyebrow.

"Yeah man, she doesn't drink." Kyle gestured toward the kitchen. "Can you get her some sparkling water out of the fridge?"

"No problem." Lawson headed back toward the kitchen.

Tracey whispered to Kyle. "I know you have a date for the evening. Where is she?"

"We had . . . some words on the phone this morning but we worked it out later," he whispered back. "She said she'd meet us at the restaurant."

Glasses filled and passed out, Sonia led the toast. "To Kyle Addison, the best business manager and entrepreneur I've had the pleasure of working with. My old friend and the fantastic founder of NY Sports Management, who now has the pleasure of representing Ronnie Wesley of the New York Giants, among others. To our friend, brother, and life of the party. Happy birthday! Cheers!"

"Cheers!" Everyone echoed, taking sips from their glasses.

Kyle downed his drink then looked around the room. "Thank you, everybody. And I just want to say, I'm happy everyone could come out tonight. I had to convince a few folks to join us and have a good time . . ." He flashed Tracey a mocking look. "But I couldn't start my year off right without getting together with some of my favorite people. Let's go!"

The women retrieved their purses. The men waited for the women to exit the front door following. Kyle, Danny, Sonia, and Tracey all climbed into Kyle's Escalade. Lawson, Zenobia, and James followed in a silver Range Rover.

"What's the name of this place we're going to?" Tracey placed her purse by her feet.

"Crimson," Kyle said. "You'll like it. Trust me."

A HALF-HOUR DRIVE from Kyle's house, Crimson turned out to be a rather upscale restaurant and lounge with a door that was like its name—crimson, from the red brick walkway winding up to the huge wooden doors, to the curtains in the dining area, to the red wooden floor. Tracey had to squint because of the low lighting. The host ushered them to a large table. Praise the Lord for the abundance of candles on the table, at least she could see the faces of her dinner companions.

When the appetizers arrived, Kyle left the table to take a phone call. He'd returned by the time she'd finished a bottle of sparkling water and started eating her crab cake salad. She'd been chatting with Sonia when she spied him leaving his seat a second time, this time for much longer. When he came back, he had to ask the waiter to reheat his filet mignon. Tracey excused herself from the conversation, stood up, and walked around to where Kyle sat at the head of the table.

She leaned down to his ear. "Everything all right?"

"Oh yeah, everything's good," he nodded.

"Is your dad okay? Tyler?"

"Yep, they're fine."

She leaned down further. "So why do you keep bouncing out on your own birthday dinner?"

"My lady, Essence, won't make it out tonight. She's . . ." Shaking his head, he reached for his drink. "Anyway, I'm staying, and I'm going to enjoy my steak."

Tracey shrugged. "All right," she said, sauntering back to her seat, taking care not to slip on the over-polished wooden floor.

The crowd at the table had emptied two more bottles of champagne by the time the waiter wheeled out a cake with glowing candles. Tracey peered at her watch. Nearly eleven. Time had flown by. Dinner had been great. Now, how could she ditch hanging out upstairs at the lounge and get a ride back to the house? She stared over at Kyle as he blew out his candles. When the smoke cleared, she rubbed her eyes. A pang of guilt pierced her soul as she considered Brianna's tears and the anger and frustration in Brian's voice earlier. Tracey had no business lounging at a lovely dinner table, eating gourmet food, dressed up all sexy like she didn't have a care in the world.

After dessert, as they stood to leave the table, Tracey tapped Kyle's shoulder again. "Dinner was fantastic. Happy birthday. Now I have to leave. I'll have the host call a cab for me."

He shook his head and took her arm. "No way, you can't leave before you hear the music upstairs. Come on."

She peered at Kyle's face as they walked toward the carpeted staircase. A slight sheen of sweat coated his face. Glazed eyes. Yep. No chance of getting him to drive her home. Someone else must be the designated driver in the group. She'd have to find that person.

Once they reached the lounge, Lawson led Zenobia away to dance. Danny looked like he wanted to dance, so Sonia grabbed his hand and they walked over to the dance floor. Kyle made a beeline for the back of the room. Tracey sat alone for a minute, trying to figure out when would be a good time to give Brian a call.

A voice interrupted her thoughts. "Here, take this," James said, sitting down on the couch next to Tracey and passing her a glass. "Looks like you need some company and conversation."

Tracey stopped rummaging for the cell phone in her purse. "Thanks. But I don't . . ."

He insisted. "I know. But just try it. It's a Continental #2. It's got a little Hennessy in it, but it's mostly pineapple and cranberry juice."

She glanced around the room. If the drink only had an ounce or so of alcohol in it, maybe it wouldn't even register in her system. She took the glass and tasted the amber liquid. Sweet. She took another sip. "Are you single like everyone else here?"

James laughed. "No, I'm married, but Kyle and I have been buddies since junior high. I didn't want to miss coming out. My wife didn't want to come out tonight because she's exhausted. We have a one-year-old daughter who runs her ragged."

"Whew. I've been there," Tracey breathed out. "Am I glad to talk to someone who's married."

"Me too, actually."

"How long have you been with her?"

"Sixteen years total. We've been married for ten. She's a teacher."

"And you're a superintendent, right?"

"Yes. I started out as a teacher, though. By the way, I talked to Tyler several times last summer. What a wonderful young man you've brought up. Kind and polite."

"Thanks," Tracey said, blushing. "He's a great son. I love him to death."

James smiled. "I can tell. He'll do just fine here at our high school. I heard his grades are excellent."

She must have heard wrong. "Excuse me?"

"In September, when Tyler starts school here? You know Kyle wants nothing but the best for him."

Sweat beads formed across the top of Tracey's forehead. "I'm sorry, but would you excuse me for a second. I'll be back in a few moments."

"Certainly." James swung his legs to the side so she could pass.

Tracey clutched the side of the couch. "You might want to start praying for Kyle now," she told James.

"Huh?"

"Nothing," she muttered, straightening up. "I'll be right back."

One mixed drink? Dumb idea. The alcohol hit her stomach, making her queasy. She scanned the room. Where was Kyle? The standing room only dance floor obscured her view. She budged and pushed her way past the dancing couples.

Tracey managed to spot Lawson and Zenobia grooving. She tapped Zenobia's shoulder.

"Have you seen Kyle?"

Zenobia shouted over the music. "Over at the far end of the bar."

"Thanks."

Tracey pushed her way through the crowd once more, made her way to the far end of the bar and practically tripped over Kyle when she stopped.

"Whoa. Take it easy!" He grabbed her to keep her from falling. His heavy hands lingered on her shoulders for a moment, then he reached down and grabbed her hand as he stepped back from the bar. "Come on lady, dance with me," he drawled.

"I don't think—"

Forget it. Kyle might as well have had cotton in his ears. In less than fifteen seconds Tracey found herself doing a stiff two-step in the middle of the crowded dance floor.

Kyle leaned down and spoke in her ear. "You know what the problem was, right?"

Tracey shrugged, confused. "No."

"Essence didn't want *you* to come to Crimson tonight. She's been a bit upset since you got here."

"You didn't have to invite me."

"I'm my own man. My house. My life. My decision. She wanted me to propose to her tonight. Actually asked me about it on the phone an hour ago. I told her that wasn't going to happen."

Should Tracey console him? Congratulate him? What?

"I'm not ready," he leaned down further, slurring in her ear.

"Okay. I heard you."

He moved closer. "I like her a lot, but she isn't what my Mom is to my Pops."

Oh no, not this story again. "Right. Got it. Get married when you want to, or don't."

"What's the problem?" Kyle asked.

Tracey halted her two left feet. "Have you been telling your friends Tyler's going to be living with you and going to school here?"

He nodded. "I let a few people know. What about it?"

She raised an angry eyebrow. "That's not true."

Kyle stopped dancing. "You and I both know Tyler's not happy about going back to Philly with you and Brian, even if it means missing his friends and his church. If you want him to stay with you . . . then hey . . . you talk to him."

"I'll do that!" Tracey turned and looked for space to escape.

He clamped a hand down on her shoulder. "Wait, stay, the music is changing. One more dance. I love this song!"

She peered up at him. He put his hands up, giving her a playful *I'll be on my best behavior* look.

Kyle placed one hand on the small of her back. She put a hand on his shoulder and the other in his hand and they danced in rhythm to a slow and jazzy version of "What You Won't Do for Love." He even managed to shut his mouth long enough for her to enjoy swaying to the music. Nice and gentle. Easy.

He leaned down and whispered. "Hey. You remember the fall season after Ty turned six? You know, when I came down to see him play his first Tiny Mite football games? Back when you both lived in Abington?"

A wave rippled in her stomach. "I remember."

"We were real good together," Kyle said, pulling her a little closer to him.

That season seemed like a lifetime ago to Tracey. Years after they broke up, she let her guard down and invited Kyle back into her life so he could build a relationship with Tyler. She even let him stay in their apartment during blustery fall weekends when their little boy played his first sports games. Bad move. Tracey and Kyle ended up growing close. Closer than close. Intimate.

It had happened the month *after* she'd started dating Brian. She'd always been bothered by the timing, but she'd push off the bothersome thoughts by reminding herself she and Brian had only recently met at the time. They had gone to the movies once, and out to a concert once. By the time things looked serious with Brian, Tracey had told Kyle about the new man in her life and her plans to move on with him. Kyle didn't say anything about it except to wish her well.

Tracey felt warm as she looked up at Kyle. "I thought I could be friends with you back then," she said, softly.

Kyle gazed back at her with a mischievous glint in his eyes. "Oh, you were more than friendly as I recall," Kyle mused.

"Don't talk to me like that. I'm a married lady—"

"So why are you up here in the mix with the single folk? You tell me."

"You invited me and I needed a break!" she reminded him.

"Take a break with your husband."

"He cheated on me, lied about it, made a baby, tried to hide it, tried to bribe his former mistress, and then tried to hide *that*," she hissed, trying to push away from him.

He kept her tight in his grasp. "And you had a fit and left him. Are you both even now?"

Even. Was there such a thing in marriage land? And was it Tracey's imagination or was Kyle's body pressed against her even more?

"Or are you trying to get even in a different way?" Kyle said.

Still the same unpredictable Kyle! His words made her uncomfortable, but the strength of his arms imprisoned her. He looked in her eyes as his hands slowly stroked her back and shoulders. A shock like the one she'd felt a few nights earlier passed through her belly. Then another.

"Scared to answer?" Kyle's hands crept down the sides of Tracey's body.

She could feel the curve of his muscles and smell his skin. He felt amazing and smelled so good she wanted to get closer. And she used to love him. Maybe a little too much. Tracey's forehead grew moist and a deeper shock kept her pressed against him. Was this how easy it was? The right mood? The right heat?

"Ever tell him about that time?" Kyle questioned, his lips brushing her ear. "Or do you like to keep secrets?"

Tracey turned her face to the side and pushed against his chest with so much force they stopped dancing. "I'm going to forget about this moment as soon as I walk out of here," she snarled before stumbling backwards. "You're drunk, but try to remember, what's in the past will stay there."

She stalked away. "Don't you dare look back," she whispered to herself as she wiped away sweat from the side of her face.

Off the dance floor, she spied James on a couch talking with Danny and Sonia. She tapped him on the shoulder. "Are you staying much longer?"

He looked down at his watch. "No. I've got to get back home soon."

"Would you mind dropping me off at Kyle's house?"

He glanced around the room quickly, his eyes scanning over the heads of the crowd. "Let me tell Kyle we're heading out."

"He's over there."

Tracey stayed silent on the drive back. She thanked James for the ride, let herself in, went straight to the guest room and lay down on the bed, still in her black dress. Two beats later she searched for and found her abandoned phone.

Brian answered on the second ring. "Tracey?"

"I'm coming home."

"When?"

"Tomorrow morning. Early."

CHAPTER
Thirty-One

LORD, *don't let me come back here a fool. I'm lost. I have no control. Please lead me through this. Help me. Help my husband. Forgive us. Heal us.*

Tracey ended the prayer and opened her eyes. Her bag slung over her shoulder as she rested her hand on the back door. She hesitated before putting her key in the lock, staring at the round gray metal, trying to summon the power to move forward.

The knob slid out of her hand when the door swung open. Brian stood inside the doorway gazing at her.

He gave a slight nod. "Hi."

"Hi," she whispered, lowering her arm slowly, keys still clutched in her palm.

He rubbed his chin, his eyes still fixed on hers. "Have you eaten yet?"

She shook her head. "No."

He stepped aside for her to enter. "I heated up some muffins. Brianna and I had eggs. I can get you a plate of food and pour you some coffee."

She shook her head. The rich hazelnut fragrance smelled delicious, but she couldn't swallow a thing. "You fed her early for a Saturday," she commented.

"I have to go to the practice. I thought I was going to have to take her to Ma and Jamal's house."

Tracey looked him up and down. His trim body dressed neat. Black pants and a crisp white button down shirt. "But I'm here now."

He shrugged before walking over and switching off the coffeemaker.

She got the message. He'd made plans in case she didn't show up. Whether she disappointed him or not, life had to go on.

"Where's Brianna?" Tracey put her bag down on a stool.

His head nodded toward the stairs. "Hanging out in her room playing."

"With the naked Barbies?"

Brian scratched his head, a half-smile on his lips. "What else?"

Tracey walked around the kitchen, peeked down the hallway, walked through to the living room, family area, and dining room, and circled back around to the kitchen again. The house smelled clean, like lemon-scented cleanser. The floors gleamed. Nothing in the kitchen looked out of place. Red coffee mugs hung on their hook above the coffeemaker. No dirty dishes in the stainless steel sinks. The kitchen island was bare except for the wooden fruit bowl filled with apples, bananas and pears.

Everything was spotless. *Hmm.* The Clean Team came only once a week which meant for things to be this immaculate Brian must have gone out of his way to clean up after himself and Brianna every day. Tracey almost wished there were brown splashes on the countertop where Brian mixed his coffee each morning, or Brianna's coloring books and crayons were scattered across the kitchen island. It would have been comforting to see the house trashed. The way it looked now, she knew he'd gotten along well without her.

"Were you standing outside praying?" He asked as stepped closer to her. "I saw you out there before I opened the door."

"Yes."

"For something good to happen I hope?"

She nodded. "And direction. I mean, what do we do now?"

He shrugged. "Whatever is the opposite of what we did to get here."

She cleared her throat and started again. "The secrets . . . the fight . . . you hurt me. You did."

"I'm so sorry, Tracey." Brian reached out for her, dropping his hand when she moved a step away. "I'm hurt too," he said.

He'd be more hurt if Tracey told him what nearly happened the night before between her and Kyle, but why add insult to injury. What would be the benefit? She picked her bag up, took a few steps toward the hallway, then turned around. "What happened yesterday?"

"Yesterday?" he asked.

"Right before you called me. In the afternoon. You know."

He stared at the floor. "I don't know if we should get into that so soon."

"No, go ahead. I can handle it," Tracey said, still gripping her bag.

Brian sighed. "News about Lisette's pregnancy and rumors about my involvement have been circulating around the practice. Dan, Doug, and I had a talk. Dan asked me if you heard about it. He took one look at my face and I think he knew you'd left."

Tracey bit her lower lip. Flames leapt inside of her but she kept silent. No one knew if the baby belonged to Brian but since people love scandal, gossip would spread like wildfire. Among the nurses. With his colleagues. In his professional circles. Around their church.

One day at a time, Tracey. Start with this one.

No throwing up, snapping out, crying, losing it, or running away.

"All right," she said. "We're going to talk later, right?"

"Yes. We will."

"I think it's important to be professional. Get over there and do what you do best." She gazed down the hallway. "Right now there's a little girl upstairs who needs her mom."

BRIANNA BECAME A KOALA BEAR. A crying one. She left a trail of tears on Tracey's shoulders. The only thing missing was a bamboo shoot sticking out of her mouth.

All morning and into the afternoon, Brianna attached herself to Tracey's body and refused to move unless she had to go to the bathroom. Even then, she'd leave the room with a warning glance that telegraphed to Tracey *if you exit this room before I get back you'll be paying for my time on the therapy couch as an adult.*

Brianna insisted Tracey stay with her in her room while they endure a movie marathon. Tracey obliged, and they spent hours together eating snack bowls of buttered popcorn, pretzel M&Ms, and Hershey kisses while they sat on fluffy pillows watching Brianna's collection of DVDs.

They were in the middle of *Frozen* when the house phone rang. Tracey looked down at Brianna's face, content and dreamy, and decided to ignore it. Two minutes later, the house phone rang again. She disregarded it that time as well. Five minutes later, her cell phone buzzed. Tracey pulled it from her pocket and looked at the caller ID.

Her mother. Tracey called her back.

Alice answered on the first ring. "Tracey?"

"Ma, what's going on?"

"Glad you managed to call me back. Brian called this morning and told me you were home. When were you gonna contact me?"

"As soon as I got time away from Brianna—which isn't happening anytime soon. How are you?"

"You looked at your phone today?"

"Not until now."

"Jamal called you. Then he called me."

"How is he?"

"Working so much now I barely see him."

Ma's great. Jamal's good. Terrific. "Why so many calls?"

"Well Cinderella, you picked a good time to come back from the ball," Alice said, her voice sounding heavy.

"Huh?"

"It's your daddy."

Tracey's heart felt like it skipped a beat. "He needs me to come with him to the doctor?" she asked, hoping that's all it was.

"No, he had a stroke."

"Another mini-stroke?"

"No," Alice said quietly, like she either exhaled hard or blew out smoke. "A full one."

AT TEMPLE HOSPITAL with Brianna plastered to her hip, Tracey listened—gathering bits and pieces of her father's story from Alice, Jamal, Uncle Ray, and Pernell's neighbor, Miss Lottie.

Pernell had been sitting in his car after driving home that morning from the Rite Aid. But after opening the car door, instead of getting out, he sat there in the driver's seat and threw up. His neighbor, Miss Lottie, who'd been sweeping her front porch, saw him. She called for her son and both of them helped him out of his car and up to the house where they gave him some water and called Uncle Ray. Uncle Ray came home from the bar and when he tried to talk to Pernell, Pernell's speech had come out garbled and confused. Uncle Ray called for an ambulance. Pernell's blood pressure? Through the roof. When he reached the hospital the doctors diagnosed a cerebral hemorrhage.

In a daze, Tracey exited the hospital room where Pernell lay sleeping. She paced the hallway, grateful for her daughter's chattering company.

"Is Pop-pop gonna be okay?" Brianna asked, clutching her stuffed Hello Kitty doll to her chest.

Tracey picked at her cuticles. "Pray for Pop-pop, honey. Just pray for him."

Brianna nodded. "I prayed already. He'll be fine."

Tracey offered a weak smile. "Keep on praying, sweetie. Keep on."

Uncle Ray and Jamal had gone for something to eat, and Alice and Miss Lottie had gone outside to smoke by the time Dr. Srinivasa came to talk to Tracey.

"His CT scan indicated intracranial pressure. A hemorrhage caused his brain to swell. We must relieve the pressure," Dr. Srinivasa said.

Tracey wrapped her arms around Brianna's body. The warmth soothed her. "What happens now?"

"We prepare him for surgery."

"Surgery?"

"A decompressive craniectomy to relieve the brain swelling," Dr. Srinivasa explained.

Tracey lost her balance when two muscular arms reached around and pried clingy Brianna out of her arms. She turned around and looked up.

Brian settled a hand on her shoulder. "The surgeon will cut a hole in your father's skull and insert a drain tube to alleviate the swelling. Correct?"

Dr. Srinivasa nodded at him. "Yes, that is correct. The team will insert tubes to allow for fluid drainage," he continued. Then he turned to Brian. "Hello, and you are?"

"Dr. Brian Jones, the patient's son-in-law. Tracey's husband."

"Good to meet you," he said. "Now, time is important," he told everyone. "We need to get started right away."

Tracey nodded, saying, "Certainly. Thank you." She watched

Dr. Srinivasa walk down the corridor to speak with two other doctors. She turned back to Brian. "You got my message?"

He squeezed her shoulder. "Yes. As soon as I saw it, I rushed over here."

"Thanks," she sniffed. "I should have checked on him more. I should've gone over there more. For months, all I've been thinking about is you and me. I knew my dad wasn't eating right. I knew he wasn't following his doctor's instructions to the letter. I knew all of that and I still ran off to New York."

"Stop, Tracey. The only person responsible for your dad's life is your dad. We love him. We'll take care of him."

"We need to pray for him."

Brian grasped Tracey's hand and pulled her closer to his side. "Let's pray. Father, you are our Lord and our God. We honor your name and your presence in our lives. Heavenly Father, we lift up Pernell Watson to you. He needs the power of your healing touch right now. We ask you, Lord, to guide the wisdom and actions of the doctors who will operate. We pray that you heal Pernell completely, minimizing all potential brain damage, and restoring him to full capacity so his healing will serve as a testimony to your greatness. We ask this in the name of Jesus Christ, our Savior. Amen."

"Amen," Tracey echoed. She kept her fingers intertwined with husband's. "Thank you."

"Daddy, I told Mommy Pop-pop would be fine," Brianna announced, clinging to her father's shoulders.

"That's good. Keep praying for him." Brian squeezed her small body against his.

Tracey looked at Brianna. "Baby, pray for your Mommy and Daddy too, okay?"

"Are you sick?"

Tracey squeezed Brian's hand. "No, but we could sure could use God's help in other ways."

CHAPTER
Thirty-Two

PERNELL SURVIVED SURGERY.

Brian and Tracey? At home. No fights and zero shattered glass.

The minute she'd exited the hospital with her family, she'd wanted to grab her phone, dial Monica and tell her about coming home and about her father's stroke. But when she remembered her best friend's harsh words about staying in Kyle's house, Tracey changed her mind about calling. Eventually they would talk again, but at the moment she needed to keep breathing.

The family could have stayed at the hospital longer, but there was no need. Pernell was resting and the hospital professionals monitored his vitals. The full extent of the stroke damage? Dr. Srinivasa would tell them after reviewing the tests. But her father lived! And something about his survival made Tracey hopeful. Like Pastor Downes told her months ago, as long as everyone was still alive, everything else could be worked out.

"Trace?" Brian called out.

"Yeah . . ."

"What are you doing back here on the lawn? I was looking all over the house for you."

After she put Brianna in bed Tracey ran downstairs and over to the back of the house. She'd stood outside the back door, unhooked her sandals, pulled off her t-shirt, dropped everything on the back porch and walked straight to the middle of the yard. Barefoot, in a camisole and faded jeans, she'd crashed down to the earth, looked up at the night sky, and dug her fingertips as far into the grass and dirt as she could get them, taking as much oxygen into her lungs as possible.

"Come out here!" Tracey yelled back and closed her eyes.

Her body shook when he dropped down on the grass next to her. She opened her eyes long enough to see him sitting with his legs outstretched, a few inches from where she lay prone. "Thank you for being at the hospital today," she said.

"Pernell is family. No matter what we're going through, I'm going to show up for family."

"I appreciate it. But you know you aren't my favorite person anymore."

"No?"

"And I'm probably not yours either."

"You aren't."

"Yeah, well," Tracey pushed her fingers through blades of grass. "I don't have any more questions and I don't have any solutions. My dad is alive. Our house is still standing. Praise God . . ." she trailed off.

Wind whistled through the trees and replaced words for a while. Tracey felt the ground shake as Brian moved again. She opened her eyes to see him laying next her on the grass. "And I'm all cried out," she told him.

He sneezed, then replied, "Yeah? Me too."

"Really?"

"Every night this week I'd get up out of bed and sit in the bathroom, put a towel on my face and cry like a baby," he confessed.

"You wanted me to come back that bad?"

"Come on, you already knew that."

"Did you actually want me to come back? Or were you upset because I left?"

"That's the same thing."

"No it isn't. If you were like, "Wow . . . how dare she leave me!" that's pride, not longing. If you longed for me, then you missed me personally."

Quiet. Wind moving through the trees.

"Brian?"

"When you put it that way, I have to say both. Pride made me try to drag you out of Kyle's place. But being in our home without you? A whole part of me slipped away and I didn't know if I could get it back."

"And I'm not your favorite person?"

"Did you make love with him?" Brian said, "For revenge."

The *him* was Kyle. Tracey didn't have to ask.

"No," she said. "Is that all you care about?"

"You... think about it?"

"No."

"Did you touch him at all?"

"Brian?"

"Is that a yes? Because if it is I want details. If you didn't have sex, there's a lot more you could have done. Kissing . . . feeling each other . . . tasting—"

Tracey interrupted, "I get the point."

"Go on then."

Oh, the temptation! She pushed her fingers deeper in the earth and fought off a wicked urge to fill her husband's mind with an elaborate tale of hot, sticky, passion-filled nights with her ex-man. Moments that brought her near the point of no return. Specifics that would keep Brian wide awake at night and troubled during the day wondering how much his wife liked it or loved it or couldn't get enough of it and whether or not she was plotting to go back and finish what she'd started. Enough sweaty fine points to make him understand what he'd put her through by sexing Lisette.

Brian and Lisette. Their affair had taught Tracey a great deal. Mostly that there were no winners. Only losers. And spinning a fake story to her husband, no matter how much she thought he deserved it, was unwise.

Tracey sighed. "After Kyle's birthday dinner last night, the one his friends threw for him at this fancy red restaurant, we all went upstairs to the lounge to listen to a jazz funk group. I needed to talk to him for a minute about Tyler, and I ended up dancing with him and . . . it turned into a slow dance with him. So I was in his arms and I felt . . ."

"You felt *what*?"

She paused. What term could she use? Not desire. Familiarity? "I remembered what it was like to be with him."

"And what is that supposed to mean?"

"It just...it felt good to hold him. He's a man and he's funny and strong and sexy and he smells like TOM FORD cologne."

"Maybe I don't need to hear this. Since you like his cologne so much . . ."

Tracey sat up. "You wanted *details* so you hear me out. We danced. We talked. He was drunk and ticked off 'cause his lady stood him up for the night and I was ticked off at you *and* him and that wasn't a good mix—though some women would have used the moment to do some dirt or whatever. Me? I left the dude on the dance floor, packed my bag and came home." She lay back down on the ground and closed her eyes. Her heart thumped hard.

Brian's hand cover hers. She flipped her palm over and grasped his fingers.

"Thank you for telling me," he said.

"You're welcome."

"I need you to believe me. Lisette's baby is not my baby. That's the truth."

Tracey winced and snatched her hand away. She ached to trust him. To grab him by the arm and dash upstairs with him and forget about everyone and everything else in the world. But she couldn't. Too much had happened. Sure, right now they were together. On the lawn. Trying to talk things out. But pain still loomed over

"DNA testing," she said. "I need to know for sure."

"Of course."

"Please stay calm," Brian said.

"What makes you think I'm not calm?" she countered.

"You're grinding your teeth."

Tracey relaxed her jaw. "Why'd you do it, Brian. Why?"

"Which 'it' are you—"

"Sex with Lisette. I danced with Kyle and I felt something for him, I admit it. But now I know there's a moment when you can either walk away in the middle of something like that, or you can go for broke. Me? I exited the dance floor. You? You went for broke. Why?"

"She invited me up to her apartment. I went and you know the rest." Brian said.

"Uh-uh. You're telling me what happened. I asked you *why* it happened."

He cleared his throat. "You sure you want to talk about this now?"

"Why not? What else can happen to us at this point?" The words rushing out of Tracey's mouth made her sound cool and brave. Like she could walk stark naked into a tsunami and come out unscathed. Inside? She shook like the ground underneath her was a volcano about to erupt.

"Lisette and I, we developed a camaraderie. She was my main buddy every day. We talked all the time and she made me laugh I gave her a goofy nickname and she smiled every time I said it. She did silly stuff to make me laugh like texting me memes with pictures she'd taken of me with captions on them like, "Lighten Up Cliff Huxtable." And she was kind. Once a week she brought Starbucks for the whole office and no one was allowed to pay her back. When we weren't talking about her future med school plans, we joked around about music and books and movies and food. So when we had sex, at first it felt like I wasn't doing anything wrong because I wasn't deliberately trying to hurt anyone, especially you."

Tracey swallowed hard. She yanked her fingers from the ground and brought her hands up above her body, rubbing her fingertips together and letting the dirt rain down. "Sounds like you were having a great time, really," she said.

"Sweetie, I'm sorry. That's all over and . . ."

"I'm not being sarcastic. This conversation was long overdue. I'm glad you told me while my hands were in the dirt though."

"What?"

"Something Ms. Celeste taught me this past week. No one can stay mad for long when their fingers are in dirt. Maybe it helped. Who knows? I'm not angry. And you can rest assured no amount of joking or Starbucks or fun conversations would make me want to jump in bed with Kyle. And since we are all into truth right now, I need you to know a few things."

"Okay."

"First, it is not okay for you to cheat on me. I won't tolerate it. If we go through this again, I'm filing papers. Second, we don't know everything. I don't care who we talk to about our marriage, but we need to talk to someone. Let's be wise going forward."

Brian reached out and pulled her hand to his again. "Okay."

"And one more thing."

"What's that?"

She let go of his hand, rolled her body over and climbed on top of him. "My name is Tracey and I'm your main buddy now and forever."

CHAPTER
Thirty-Three

"SHARE THE FULL STORY, not the CliffsNotes version," Pastor Downes said.

Two weeks after Tracey returned home, she and Brian sat side by side in Pastor Downes office at Rise. Brian had made the call to their pastor himself, asking for a listening ear and guidance.

Brian talked first. The lies. The affair. More lies. Bribery. Coercion from Lisette. The pregnancy. The fight with Tracey. Trying to drag Tracey back home.

Then Tracey spoke. Threatening to run over Lisette with the Volvo. Taking thousands of dollars out of their joint savings. Paying her mother's bills and going on a shopping spree. Cutting Brian with their wedding crystal. Leaving her own home and family and ending up in New York with her son's father's family.

Pastor Downes sat and listened as the sun rays of the late afternoon faded, bathing the office in a soft orange glow. He nodded from time to time, but otherwise, let them talk for a full hour. When they finished, he wiped his face with a handkerchief, took a long sip of water, and leaned back in his chair.

"I will not counsel you two," he finally said, frowning. "I'm disappointed. I've seen both of you mature here at Rise and frankly I'm shocked at your behavior. You know better. Both of you . . . you know better!"

"Pastor—" Brian said.

Pastor Downes held up a hand. "No, hear me out. Brian, you betrayed your wife in the worst possible way. That's not who you are. When we first met, you confided in me. You told me you were exhausted and depressed going through your residency. I told you God would keep you if you focused on Him and took it one day at a time. I also advised you to get your dreadlocks groomed properly and trim your mustache so you would stop scaring the women you passed in the church hallway."

Tracey stifled a giggle but couldn't keep a small smile from her lips.

Pastor Downes shifted his weight and turned toward her. "I also remember when you didn't laugh so much. You were a workaholic single mother when you came to me and Sister Downes in tears because Tyler's father wouldn't spend any time with him and you were lonely caring for him by yourself day after day. We prayed with you and told you the Lord would provide for you." He turned his eyes skyward, then looked back over to them and sighed. "Both of you tell me, did those situations end?"

Tracey and Brian nodded.

"Did either of you consider your unique life situations worked out for the better because God guided you to be together? Brian, you've become distinguished and confident and able to run a medical practice well because your wife is in your corner one hundred percent. Tracey, your husband is an outstanding provider and I don't know what happened this year, but prior to this you both seemed happy with one another," Pastor Downes said with a stern look. "God didn't bring you this far for you to act like fools!"

Tracey focused her gaze on a piece of black lint on the grey carpet. The truth hurt. Like a quick kick to the backside.

"Mrs. Jones, what did you do with the book I gave you? The one by Dr. Dockens?"

She kept staring at the floor. Gee that lint looked really interesting. Nice form and contrast.

"Never mind," Pastor Downes said, picking up his desk phone receiver and pressing a button. "Mrs. Gunning? Yes . . . just making sure you hadn't left the office yet . . . yes . . . can you please pull up and print out Dr. Zhang's contact information for me? Thank you."

He hung up, put his hands on his desk and leaned in again. "Relax," he said. "I'm done fussing."

"So you'll be counseling us?" Brian asked.

Pastor Downes shook his head. "No, I meant what I said. I am referring you to an excellent Christian marriage counselor and family therapist. He'll be completely neutral while you work out your issues. His name is Dr. Peter Zhang. Mrs. Gunning has the contact information at her desk up front."

"Fine," Tracey said, shrugging. What choice did they have?

Pastor Downes stood, motioning for them to join hands with him. "Now let's pray so you all can go home and I can go take an Advil. Both of you have given me a headache."

THE SOFT "NO ARGUMENT" zone they'd built around themselves cracked during the drive home. Tracey had hung up her phone after leaving a message at Dr. Zhang's office. Considering all they'd been through, seeing him sooner rather than later made sense.

She looked over at Brian as he drove. "Have you been in contact with Lisette?"

"No. Why?"

"To talk to her about scheduling DNA testing to establish paternity."

"Why would I do that?"

"Because you agreed to it."

"I don't need to stir that pot right now. We can wait until the baby is born."

"Why? Paternity can be established through CVS or amnio-centesis testing."

"I know all about those tests. They can only be done within a certain window of time, and both are invasive. Besides, calling Lisette wouldn't be good. She still talks to Janette and I need gossip to die down at the practice. I helped build our practice and I need the trust and cooperation of my co-workers."

Tracey turned her face toward the passenger side window. "Maybe I should be the one to ask her?" Tracey said.

"No."

"Brian, if she's going to be a part of our lives—"

He interrupted, "For the last time, she won't."

"Then we need to know where her head is. Instead of treating her like an enemy, maybe it would be best to see where she's coming from."

"I can tell you where she's coming from. She's coming from a place of trying to trap me." Brian said.

Tracey bit her lip to keep from responding.

Brian reached over and touched her shoulder. "You and I, we've been getting along. We're having great conversations. We're starting counseling soon. I feel like the Lord is leading us to still waters. Please, let's leave Lisette and her pregnancy alone for now. We'll find out the truth soon enough, okay?"

She gave a slight nod and turned away again, watching the scenery rush by. It was a cooler night than usual for July. More comfortable.

For the moment at least.

♥

IT TURNED out Tracey didn't have to tell Charla anything. Ricky had already told her about Brian's affair with Lisette, the trip to New York and back, and the opinions of their in-laws. God bless her sister-in-law's upbeat personality. When she picked her up later that week to go shopping, a dressed-to-the-nines Charla started blurting out family business and cracking jokes like only a sister-in-law could.

"Girl, you know you're our MIL's favorite topic of conversation right now. I need to thank you. At least you took the pressure off of me to have some grand babies for her," Charla said.

Tracey sighed and guided the car out of Charla's neighborhood. "Yeah, I know, I ran off and left her baby boy and his daughter then I came back and . . . can we talk about something better."

"Like grand babies?"

"Grand babies would be good," Tracey said.

"Well, me and Ricky are trying."

"For real?"

Charla nodded. "Its official! No more pills for me. We're gonna go for it."

"Congratulations! You'll enjoy your kids, and they'll be beautiful," Tracey said, then dropped her tone of voice. "Now listen to me, you keep being your fabulous self, keep your interests, grow your business, and love your babies but keep doing everything you do with Ricky right now."

"Wait, you're getting all serious on me. I don't have any news yet! It might take some time."

"Well sis, that's my first piece of advice for you. And I hope you remember it and sign me up as babysitter the first time you want to go out on date night." Tracey winked.

They stayed silent after that. But Tracey had some unfinished business and instead of directing the car toward King of Prussia, she pointed it toward Bala Cynwyd.

"Where are we going?" Charla swiveled her head around as

Tracey drove around to Presidential Blvd, then parked in a lot beside a tall modern-looking building.

"When's your first client coming in today?" Tracey asked.

Charla slid her big sunglasses off. "Not until three. What is this place?"

Tracey shut the car off and stared at the building. "It's a medical office building and on the third floor is Family Care One."

"And we're here because?"

Tracey looked sidelong at her sister-in-law. "This is where Lisette works now, or so Ruthie tells me. And this is where I'm going to talk to her about DNA testing."

Charla's eyes widened. "Hold on. On her job? You have more class than that."

Tracey gripped the bottom of the steering wheel and sighed. "Yes, because I have enough composure not to ambush her at night time, with her family standing around in a parking lot."

"Sis, I hear you, but . . . seriously? Once the baby's born, you might not ever have to see her again."

"You sound like Brian," Tracey scolded. She sat back and stared at the blue and white painted brick building. She blinked, turned her gaze to the dashboard then looked up again.

"Tracey, look, we're going shopping, remember? We can swing by the boutique where I got this dress and get you something to jazz up your wardrobe. Come on," Charla insisted.

Tracey extended her hand. "No. I have to go talk to her. Let me borrow your Hollywood shades."

"What for?"

"If she gets a good look at my face when I walk in the door she'll run off somewhere."

Charla hesitated for a moment, passed Tracey the glasses, and turned away. "Here. I can't stop you."

"Char, I might not do anything other than take a look and retreat."

Tracey donned the glasses and peeked at her image in the rearview mirror. Since the shades covered half of her face and her hair was pulled back tight, she doubted Lisette would recognize her right away. She left the air on for Charla, scrambled out, shut the car door, and marched to the front of the building.

Inside, the first floor looked much larger than the outside architecture made it seem. A huge waiting room sprawled out before her as she walked inside. The nurses station stood more than sixty feet away from where she stopped next to a long silver coat rack.

She had to sit down quickly. Her heart thumped as she rushed to an empty chair near the back of the room. All right. That worked fine. She snatched a *TIME* magazine from the table next to her elbow and shoved it in front of her face. When she peeked around the side of the magazine, she spied two nurses behind the front desk, but neither one was Lisette. Good. Now she had a moment to let the adrenaline die down. Kids of all ages milled about the place, their parents in chairs positioned around the perimeter. She'd picked the right time to visit. A side door swung open into the waiting area and a nurse stepped out. Tracey jumped, but managed to keep *TIME* in front of her face.

"Jordan Shields? Jared Shields?" a voice called out.

Tracey recognized the voice and peeked around the magazine. Lisette stood across the room. Light pink scrubs and white nursing clogs. Pretty. Gorgeous thick hair held back by a braided headband. Small bulge in the abdomen area. Red file folders in her hand.

Lisette.

Chubby twins toddled over to her, with a woman Tracey guessed was their mother trailing behind. Lisette kneeled down and smiled at them, showing them two stickers in her other hand. When she stood, she grinned at their mother, greeting the woman warmly, ushering them all inside the door before shutting it.

Tracey put the magazine down in her lap. Lisette seemed different. Smiling and gracious. Warm and friendly.

Still shocked, Tracey didn't even bother to pick up the magazine again when Lisette returned several minutes later. This time she greeted a red-haired teenage girl with braces.

"How are you? Come in. The doctor will see you in a minute. Now how old are you?"

The girl giggled. "Thirteen."

"Thirteen. My goodness, you're a head taller than me! Come in, let's see how much you've grown," Lisette kidded with the girl before closing the door behind them.

It didn't make any sense. How could a warm, gracious young woman turn into the vicious female she'd seen in the back lot at Rise? Did she turn on the charm at work and become a barracuda at night?

Tracey crossed her arms and legs tight. Maybe the woman she'd seen previously was hormonal, flustered, and unsure of what to do next. For someone to go from charming to hellish, well, something pretty devastating must have happened.

That something might have been Dr. Brian Jones.

Tracey knew all about being broken-hearted and pregnant, all her dreams shattered while carrying a member of the next generation inside her womb. Been there. Done that. Bought the souvenir t-shirt and the highlights DVD. She'd lived it the morning Kyle informed her he'd drive her to the local women's clinic and she flatly refused. When he broke up with her the next day, the future she'd dreamed of vanished.

She shut her eyes behind her sunglasses. A film played in her head. She envisioned twenty-one-year-old Tracey Renee Watson. The Tracey who couldn't stop Kyle from smashing her heart into smithereens. The bitter young lady who had no choice but to drop out of Syracuse and come back to Philly. She'd had nowhere to go with her mother and father practically homeless and divorcing. Had to stay in North Philly with Aunt Zee, who was just crazy enough to share Christ with her. A blessing she didn't recognize at the time.

She clicked the fast forward button in her head. Thirty-seven-year-old Tracey Jones. Christian. Confident. Classy. In control? No. She couldn't control Brian. She couldn't snap her fingers and fix her marriage. She couldn't even control Tyler's choice of living arrangements. What made her think she could control the outcome of Lisette and her baby?

It won't work.

So. Just. Stop.

Tracey sprang up, dropping the magazine on the floor. She stooped to pick it up, and when she stood again, she saw Lisette come through the door to call another patient. Tracey shuffled to the corner, beside a fake ficus tree. Thank goodness there were so many kids and teenagers moving around that Lisette didn't notice her.

From Tracey's view, Lisette's face looked kind of swollen. Tracey squinted at her belly from the side. Interesting. She appeared a lot smaller in the middle than Tracey thought she would be, if she became pregnant in January or February. From February to late July. Six months. Second trimester. Back when Tracey became pregnant with Brianna, her abdomen had pushed out pretty far by the end of six months. Lisette sported a belly that appeared more like three months.

Before Tracey could squint any more, Lisette left the room. Tracey turned and sprinted for the office door, making it to the side parking lot faster than Usain Bolt could.

"Did you ask her about DNA testing?" Charla asked as Tracey climbed in the car.

Tracey took a deep breath. Her hands shook as she placed them on the steering wheel. "No."

"So you went in and she . . ."

"Didn't do anything. She didn't even see me. I sat in the back and looked at her . . . and . . . I don't have any business being here. I can't keep . . . there's . . ." Tracey shook her head. "Forget it. Here's your glasses."

"Thanks." Charla slid the huge shades back on her face.

Tracey's breathing slowed. "We're out of here sis. What's the name of that boutique you wanted me to see?"

"Fancy Free. It's on the Main Line."

"All right, show me where to go," Tracey said.

No really, Lord, show me where to go.

CHAPTER
Thirty-Four

THE LAST HOT Saturday evening in July and Tracey sat with Brian on Alice's living room couch. Jamal had just arrived home from his job. Brianna sang to herself as she played in the kitchen making ice cream sundae replicas out of brightly colored Play-Doh.

"Dad's going to need a visiting nurse." Tracey said, as she fanned herself with a *Woman's Day* magazine. All of Alice's fans were on and her front window was open but it was still hot in the house.

Jamal swallowed a mouthful of purple Vitamin water before he spoke. "No, he doesn't. I've been with him four times this week and he's doing fine."

Brian unbuttoned the top of his polo shirt. "What does his care plan say?"

Tracey turned toward her husband and said, "He needs to continue his physical therapy and see his doctors regularly. Since he doesn't have lasting paralysis, I guess his care plan doesn't need much more than that."

"That's what I was saying," Jamal insisted.

Tracey wiped sweat from her forehead. "What happens when we get to a week where you can't check on Daddy, and I can't either? I don't trust he'll always take his medication, and you know Uncle Ray gets busy with his bar and store and he's—"

Brian finished her sentence. "Too busy to keep after his brother all the time."

"Exactly."

"Tracey, we can't force Dad to do the right thing, know what I'm saying?" Jamal placed his empty water bottle on the glass coffee table.

"I know. Please, I'm not about forcing him to do anything. Getting him some help isn't forcing."

Alice, who had been sitting across the room the whole time, blew out a billow of smoke. She smashed her cigarette butt into the lid of a jar. "Y'all going round and round about this isn't getting you anywhere."

Tracey glanced over at her mother. Cool as a cucumber. You could tell her the entire world was about to blow up in seven minutes and she'd still be sitting in her overstuffed La-Z-Boy with her feet up and a Virginia Slims in her hand.

She was right though.

Tracey kept fanning. *Stop controlling things*, she told herself. "We need to figure out an alternate way of checking on him when Jamal and I get busy."

Brian took her hand. "We can start going over as a family on Saturday nights. As long as there are no emergencies for me, I'm right there. I think it would lift his spirits if he had someone to watch ESPN with on the weekends."

"How come none of you thought about me?" Alice inquired.

"You?" Tracey asked, confused.

"Yes, daughter. I can go on over and see about the man when none of you can make it."

"You?" Jamal said, widening his eyes.

"Yes, me," Alice repeated, putting her feet down. "I take care of people all week long. I know something about taking blood pressure and checking medications." She winked at Brian. "You aren't the only person in the family that knows something about patient care."

Brian nodded and smiled. "True."

"You'd really do that for him?" Tracey shook her head in disbelief.

"Sure," Alice shrugged.

Jamal rubbed a hand over his scalp. His hair cut was so low now he appeared practically bald. Looked just like it did when he was in the Army. "We didn't think of you because you swore you'd never do another thing for him after your divorce."

Tracey peered at her mother. She *had* said that.

"Yeah, well, we're older now. Time heals if you let it. I did have some good years with the man. If he needs my help, he's got it." Alice eased onto her feet. "You all can keep talking. I'm going to turn the heat off under these greens. If the mac and cheese is done, we can set the table and eat."

Change. Guess a person's never too old for it.

Tracey pushed herself up from the sofa.

"Where are you going?" Brian tugged her hand. "We're going to eat in a minute."

"I gotta call Tyler." She had put off the call all week. She might as well get it over with.

WHILE SHE WAITED for Tyler to answer his phone, she counted the cracks in her mother's bedroom ceiling. Seven. Then the piles of *Women's Day* stacked on the sagging dresser. Four. She was about to count the tubes of hand lotion lined up on the nightstand when her son finally answered.

"Mom?"

"Hey Ty."

"How's Pop-pop? How are you and Brian?"

"First, Brian and I are doing better, thanks for asking. But your Pop-pop is weaker than you've seen him in the past."

"But he's going to be all right?"

"We think so. The stroke scared us all a lot, but it scared him, too. He's more serious about how he cares for himself. And he's home now. He's going to retire."

"He has to, huh?"

"It's what's best. He's got all his mental capacities, but his left side is weak—there's no telling how long it will be that way. So keep praying for him. Anyway . . . I wanted to talk about you."

"Me?"

"Yeah." She cleared her throat. "About where you're going to live and go to school before the end of the summer."

"You know, Dad's been thinking I'm going to stay up here."

Tracey sighed as she lay back on her mother's soft floral comforter. "What do *you* think?"

"Mom, I'm not sure. At first I thought I might. But, with you and Brian and your thing? And I'd miss being around Brianna. Now Pop-pop's doing bad. Man. I don't want to run out on you all."

"Well as long as Amtrak is still moving or you get your car, you aren't running out. You can always get to us."

"I know, but . . ."

Tracey listened closely as Tyler described how he felt on the matter. It turned out he was torn. Not a simple decision. If they factored in Kyle's view on the situation, it became more complicated.

"Where's your dad?" Tracey asked.

"Out by the pool. He's grilling steaks tonight."

"Can you put him on the phone, please?"

"Okay."

Tracey waited. Her mother's room still smelled like musk cologne and body powder. Just like when she'd lay on Alice's bed as a girl, enjoying the feel of her fluffy pillows and blankets before Alice would come upstairs and order her back to her own bedroom.

"Mrs. Jones." Kyle came on the line.

"Got a minute to talk?"

"I'm about to put food on the barbecue. What's up?"

"Can you step inside for a second? I have something to say."

Tracey gazed around the room while she waited for another minute. Why did Alice have all those magazines? Was she becoming a hoarder?

Kyle came back on the line. "I'm in the kitchen, now. What's going on?"

"I talked to Tyler about him staying in New York."

"Are you shipping his things or do you need me to rent a small U-Haul?" Kyle asked.

Tracey countered. "Put the brakes on. I'm still not in agreement about letting him stay."

"But this is where he wants to be."

"No, he still needs to sort it out and decide. And he has to decide fast, because he'll need school records and other items. It'll be August in a few days," Tracy said with a sigh. "If he tells me he can't make the decision, I'll have to make it for him."

"And . . ."

"He comes back to Philly."

"How do you figure?" Kyle's voice ratcheted up a notch.

Tracey didn't want to go there, but she had no choice. "I have full custody of him. You and I both know the only reason he started spending the summers with you was because you and Ms. Celeste asked me and I allowed it."

The custody card. She hadn't pulled it since Tyler was eight.

Kyle's voice turned cold. "You really think he wants to keep living with a prissy, over-controlling mother who can't even keep her own husband in line?"

Ah, Kyle. Always coming at her with the below-the-belt comment. She couldn't control that. He'd always been that way, but he was still her son's father. *God bless him and please help me to not cuss him out,* she prayed.

Tracey let her words ooze out. "Oh, I don't know. I guess he wouldn't have any more trouble staying with a prissy mother than he would living with a workaholic, whore-mongering, borderline drunk father."

Silence.

Tracey continued. "Kyle, I'm so sorry Ty is your only child. But it's not my fault I loved my kid enough to bring him into this world against your wishes. Now if you have any stories about other women you tried to force to have an abortion and you feel guilty and desire to confess, you can have your 'come to Jesus moment' right now." Tracey rubbed her temple with her fingertips. "Otherwise, put Ty back on the phone. Thank you."

She heard Tyler's voice half a minute later. "Mom?"

"Hi." Tracey shook off the tiny twinge of remorse she felt for saying what she said to Kyle. She spoke the truth. Nothing wrong with that.

"Mom, what'd you say to Dad? He just stomped back outside."

"He'll survive," she sighed. "Back to you. We love you. Your church, friends and school are here. And any weekend you want to go visit your dad and grandparents you know can."

"So that means?"

"Where you live? You decide. Make your choice and let me know."

"For real?"

She sniffed as she climbed off the too-soft bed and made a beeline to the bathroom for a tissue. "Do this for me, though. Pray for discernment and guidance. Get on your knees, and ask God to speak to you. If you feel like He's guiding you and New York is best, I'm not going to stop you."

"Okay," Tyler drawled.

She wiped her nose with a wad of tissue as she sat down on the toilet lid. "Listen, this is your first lesson in making a major life decision by finding God's will. Learn from this." She threw the tissue away. "Lord knows I will."

"Thanks, Mom."

"I gotta go. I hear your grandmom screaming, something

about Brianna needing to scrape that Play-Doh mess off the kitchen table. We're eating here tonight. Your grandmom made ribs."

"Sometimes Grandmom yells too much. She used to yell and swat me for leaving my Tonka trucks on the front steps," Tyler revealed.

"Yeah, she's a screamer. But we love her. Call me tomorrow."

"No problem."

"And give your Dad a hug and tell him to please stop sulking because I know he is."

She heard Tyler's rich laugh before she hung up.